THE SUNSTROMS

Thanks so much! – Gene

GENE E. WILLOUGHBY, II

ISBN: 978-1-4834-6809-9 (sc)
ISBN: 978-1-4834-6810-5 (e)

Lulu Publishing Services rev. date: 09/19/2018

This project is dedicated to

Tameshia (My Support, My Love, My Oasis),

Alaysia and Jalen,

Mom, Dad, and Stuart

Special Thanks

The Entire Dillard Tiger Family,

Michael Holley,

and

Anyone who has ever supported my hopes and dreams in any way.

Thank you.

PART 1

"I realize that as supportive, free-thinking parents we're supposed to encourage our children to follow their hearts, find their own pathways through life. But I think deep down inside – if a man is completely honest with himself – there is an admittedly selfish piece of every father that would love to see his children pick up his legacy from where he left it and carry it just a little bit farther down the road. So imagine the pride I felt when my first- born looked up from his toys this morning and said he wanted to be just like me. Sam wants to be an adventurer. And I can barely contain my excitement."

Taken from The Adventure Log Vol. 14
F. Douglas Sunstrom

CHAPTER 1

Sam's alarm clock sounded in his ears like a siren. He hated that piercing racket. And one day he would wake up and crush the blaring nuisance into tiny pieces with his fist, he assured himself. He opened one eye, sending his right hand fumbling over the nightstand next to his bed. He clumsily pressed the snooze button again. 5:34. "Already?" he grumbled. "Damn it."

He turned over in his bed and pushed himself up so that he was sitting on the edge and rubbed his face as if he was forcing life back into his skin. The TV he'd left on last night was the only light source in the small dim room. With an annoyed wrinkle in his brow, Sam looked up at the flat screen, which was showing a year old documentary on the Legacy Network.

He shook his head at the still photos of his parents and the not quite focused news videos of them flying across the screen in their burgundy and gray uniforms. Beside the TV in a framed photograph, a dark haired young woman smiled broadly while holding a polished kickboxing trophy over her head. A sticky note with the words 'Call Mom about dinner' scribbled on it was still attached to the nightstand.

"But in the Twenty-First Century, one thing is for certain," the television narrator continued. "The Sunstrom name and their adventures are recognized all over the globe. And the only thing more amazing than their powers is the level of their celebrity." Sam found the remote control in his rolled up, twisted bed sheets. "And when we return, I will show you my interview with Torrance and Janesha Sunstrom in which I ask the one question we'd all like to know the answer to: how does it feel to be the children of world famous superhe –"

Sam pointed the remote, and the TV went black. He stood and took off his gray t-shirt. "Or you could actually report something important, you know," he mumbled. "Like news or something."

After flipping a light switch, Sam walked over to his mahogany wood dresser where he stared at the well-carved three hundred and nineteen pound man in pajama pants reflected in the tall, wide mirror on the wall. Looking into his own brown eyes and forcing a smile onto face, he hunched over the dresser and ran his hand over his shaved head. That same hand then brushed over his rock solid chest and found the long, hardened scar that stretched diagonally across his abdomen. Sam turned his eyes away from the mirror, closed his fist, and made his way to the bathroom for a hot shower.

Soon, Amica Bay, Washington's shining skyscrapers and sleek bridges were passing blurs on both sides of Sam's sparkling red convertible. The jewel of a sports car his dad had once designed and built for his sixteenth birthday zoomed down the highway, its heavy-duty engines running as cool and silent as an industrial whisper. Sam looked directly into the early morning sunlight from behind his sunglasses and let the cool autumn air clear his mind as he imagined soaring through the sky.

Jovita Vargas' gloved fists pounded the shuddering punching bag hanging in front of her with steady, rhythmic aggression. Each hard pop and its accompanying grunts echoed throughout the small workout room as she bounced from side to side on her toes. Surrounded by weights, jump ropes, and pieces of dismantled exercise equipment, Jovita shot another strong right hand at the bag, followed by two sharp kicks. And then she stopped. Her toned, honeyed arms dropped to her sides.

Sweat stung both her eyes and the tiny, healing cut on her chin. She tugged at her black tank top and wiped her face with it while taking a few deep breaths. Jovita's sore forearm knocked brown hair away from her eyes as she visualized the wide, baldheaded woman with the tattoos and sledge hammer fists from last week's sparring session.

Her nostrils flared, and she punched the bag again. Two more punches. Another hard kick. "Coldblooded" by Rick James. Jovita turned around and jogged over to her smartphone which was vibrating on top of her gym bag while the song sounded all over the room. She kneeled beside the bag as it finally stopped and read the text on the screen.

Sam: Almost there. Can't wait. See you soon.

Jovita smiled and began ripping the tape from her wrists with her teeth. She walked over to a digital panel mounted on the near wall and entered a brief numerical sequence. "What's up, Dr. Vargas?" a voice sounded from the panel.

"Greg, I'm about to hit the shower and then we need to meet upstairs really quickly before we prep the Chamber," she said.

"But what about...?"

"Don't worry. Mr. Sunstrom is on his way."

Sam rolled into an expansive parking lot and stopped at checkpoint where a long red and white barrier arm blocked his car from moving any further. A short, overweight security guard in a black cap and matching uniform walked up to his vehicle. He shot Sam a sideways grin as he removed his sunglasses. "You know the deal, Sunstrom," he said with a gruff yet friendly voice. "Gotta make sure you check out. Even though I probably couldn't stop ya if you didn't."

"Everybody's got a job to do, Brad," Sam smirked. He allowed the guard to scan the laminated ID card that hung around his neck on a lanyard. "How's the family?"

"Pretty good, pretty good," Brad answered. "Lacey's starting college classes next week. Moved her into the dorm yesterday morning."

"That is so crazy. Where did the time go?"

"I know right? Hey, look. What the devil is goin' on, Sam? Place is definitely buzzing today. Musta been some helluva breakthrough last night."

Sam noticed the security gate opening in front of his car and put it in drive. "Let's hope so," he said. "I could use the exercise." He drove past several rows of cars and finally pulled into a parking space in front of a white ten-story building with black tinted windows. The white sign on the perfectly groomed lawn seemed to point towards the walkway that split into several concrete paths stretching all over the gigantic research and development campus. The stylized words on the sign matched the ones on Sam's ID card: Sapien Rex.

Rushing down a white, red-trimmed hallway, Sam began removing his blue and white button down shirt, stripping down to his black Sapien Rex t-shirt. A brisk walk turned into a jog after he checked his watch again. Twenty minutes late. He balled his shirt up in his hand just as Greg Lectchman popped out of the nearest office room. A blonde-haired man in a plaid shirt and jeans, he jogged alongside Sam with a clipboard in his hands. "You're late, man," Greg said. "Dr. Vargas is about to explode in there."

"I know, I know," Sam said hastily. "Suit ready?"

"Yep."

"Doughnuts?"

"You're really asking me about doughnuts right now."

"Didn't get breakfast."

"Just suit up, man. I'll tell the doc you're here."

The hallway ended in a gigantic silver door with a digital keypad on the wall beside it. Sam looked at Greg and smiled as he swiped his ID card on the keypad. The silver door parted down the center and opened. "See you out there."

Greg grabbed Sam's arm and stopped him before he could enter the dark chamber. "You're gonna love this one, man," he said. "I mean absolutely love it."

The doors closed behind Sam, and the once black room lit up accompanied by a low booming sound. "Let's rock," he said to himself. He got out of his clothes and stuffed them into one of a series of sterilized silver casings in the wall. As he held his breath, thin ivory robotic appendages entered the room through the ceiling and floor, spraying him with a cleansing mist that made his super dense skin feel like it was on fire. Once the citrus scented gas was gone, the metal arms secured Sam inside a white form fitting body suit that made him resemble an astronaut. A loud, teeth rattling drill locked glossy black chest, knee, and shoulder guards into place.

The wall behind him gently split apart and allowed him into a room called the Launch Station. It was a brightly lit eight-sided area covered in computers, consoles, view screens and wires. Tall spiral generators stretched from the polished orange floor to the ceiling in each of the room's corners. And in the room's center was a scarred oval platform made of cold gray metal.

This was where the 'magic' took place, as Dr. Jovita Vargas was so fond of saying. It was where the men and women of Sapien Rex's Launch Team created experimental technology to reach into the void and touch the universe's hidden places.

Ready for action, Sam pulled his environmental suit's zipper up until it stopped underneath his chin. Three young men and two women in black Sapien Rex shirts, khakis, and sneakers swarmed on him and began checking his vitals and sealing his suit. Greg slid away from his console in a swivel chair and made his way over to him carrying a box of doughnuts. A young brunette in jeans and glasses joined Greg and looked Sam over as he stretched out his arms and let the support staff work on his suit.

Then, a door on the far side of the room opened. Sam turned his head and watched Jovita walk in. The Puerto Rican woman with a short, neat trim strode across the room wearing a white lab coat over her Sapien Rex shirt and jeans. She was solidly built, long-legged and athletic. Confident and incredibly serious.

"Just drop by anytime, Sam," she deadpanned. "It's not like we're on a schedule or anything."

The young woman standing behind Sam stifled a snicker and held a half-eaten doughnut up to his mouth. He chewed and talked. "Slept late," he said. "Sorry. Won't happen again. And I asked for the powdered ones. With the blueberry cream."

"Whatever. Greg. Show it to him."

With childlike enthusiasm all over him, Greg ran over to the nearest computer console and typed until a three-dimensional model of a red, sweltering globe appeared in the center of the room. "This is what I was telling you about," he said. "We call it the Furnace."

The support team scattered, donned their headsets, and sat at their computers. One of them attached a thick white tether to a round connector at Sam's lower back.

"It's not a fully formed world from what we can tell," Jovita continued. "Hotter than hell, but as far as we can determine, it does have an oxygenated atmosphere."

Greg handed Sam a black helmet with a tinted faceplate. "Take this anyway," he said. "Just to be safe."

Sam finished chewing his doughnut and swallowed. "So what do you need from me?"

Jovita looked up from her clipboard. "Soil sample. Elemental scan. The usual."

Sam walked over and stood next to Jovita who stared at the digital model of the unknown world hanging in the air above them. "You be careful," Jovita said softly.

"Explain to me why I do this again, Vita," Sam said so only she could hear.

Jovita's lips curved as she looked towards the ceiling. "The more than substantial paycheck," she whispered. "The doughnuts. And...it turns me on a little."

She slid closer and squeezed his hand before he slid his helmet on and locked it in place. Smoke colored polymer plating hid his face. A tech assistant straightened the tube-like tether attached to Sam's back as he stepped up on the platform in the center of the room. With his shoulders squared, Sam licked his lips and rocked from side to side, shaking his fingers anxiously. "So what's taking so long?" he asked with a smug grin. "Let's see what's out there this time."

The platform underneath Sam's feet lit up and glowed with a piercing golden brilliance that made him turn his head and shut his eyes. At the same time, a white metal shell emerged from the floor around him and closed him up in an oblong structure resembling a high tech egg. Sam kneeled inside it, and the light flashed again.

Greg typed a series of commands into his keyboard. The white cocoon separated and collapsed back into the floor. Only the glowing platform remained, and the tether connected to Sam ran across the floor, disappearing into the cascading light bubbles in the center of the room.

Jovita stared at the platform and exhaled through worried, pursed lips with her hands resting on her hips. Then, she grabbed the nearest headset, sat down in a swivel chair, and checked a computer monitor for Sam's body temperature and blood pressure. "Ok, people, we have a job to do here," she said. "Mr. Sunstrom is going to retrieve some geomorphic analysis for us. Let's make sure he gets back here with it. And with his head still on his shoulders."

CHAPTER 2

One hundred and ninety-eight degrees. Sam looked at the temperature readings on his wrist and silently thanked God for the coolant coursing through every seam of his environmental suit. He removed a white rectangular shaped device from his waist and swiped his index finger across the touchscreen on its face. After pressing the box into the hard, scorched rock beneath him, he took a long look at the red skies, hazy atmosphere, and burning horizons. The glass shielding in front of his face flickered with digital cascading numbers, signaling that the box's scanning- tunneling laser beam had broken through this world's crust and initiated its search for exotic minerals and fossil fuels.

"Sam do you hear me?" Jovita's voice crackled in his earpiece.

"Yep. Clean connection," Sam said. "Minimal feedback. You guys weren't kidding when you named this place."

"I'm looking at the temps now. If it gets too hot in there let me know, and we'll reel you back in."

Sam looked behind him at the tether that uncoiled from his suit and disappeared into a glowing, rippling circle on the ground. "I'll be fine," he said. He turned back around and checked on the white box at his feet. Twenty-three percent complete. "Think I'll do some sight seeing."

"Don't go too far," Jovita shot back.

"Course not, "Sam said. With a smirk, he leaped in excess of two hundred feet to his right. The ground cracked when he landed in a crouching position. He stood and looked directly into the dull red sun. "Probably the end of somebody's world by the looks of it."

Before Sam could say another word, a crunching sound rumbled underneath the ground behind him. He spun around and watched the rocks grow and splinter until they had taken a humanoid shape that towered over him. The crimson sunlight twinkled in the shiny black volcanic ore that formed the being's skin; lava gushed through tiny canals in its stone hide like fiery blood rivers. Its glowing red eyes opened and focused on Sam who stared upwards and swallowed hard. "Um, Vita?" he said. "Were there any indigenous life forms you neglected to tell me about?"

Jovita's answer was lost in the rock creature's all-consuming roar, which knocked Sam off his feet and cracked his faceplate. In an instant, the beast pounced on him, knocked his helmet across the landscape, and pinned him to the ground with its massive three-fingered hand. A mountainside of a forearm scraped his face against the ground. "Ok," Sam said with his teeth clenched. "This is not what we discussed."

Jovita sat at her computer and glared at her monitor, her eyes carefully trained on the red blip that indicated Sam's location. It disappeared. She stood up and interlocked her fingers. "Sam!" she yelled into her headset. "Sam! What is your situation? Sam!"

Silence echoed throughout the Launchpad chamber until Greg rolled his chair over to Jovita's workstation. "Dr. Vargas," he said gently. "We need to..."

"Get back to your monitor, Letchman," she snapped. "Activate the platform. Bring him back. Sandra. I need sound back in my ears. Now."

Sam brought his fists down on the monster's wrist, shattering the stone hand to pieces. As he got to his feet, he noticed his suit was melting off him. The blistering air around him scorched even his damage resistant skin and scalded his lungs, but he pushed himself off the ground and dove boots first. The impact split the rock thing's chest in several directions, and as it bellowed into the blood red sky, Sam rammed his fist into its face, knocking its head from it shoulders. The thing's entire body broke apart and collapsed to the ground in a heap of misshapen, dusty boulders.

Sam's earpiece came to life. "Sam," said Jovita. "Can you hear me? What's happening?"

Sam pressed his fingers against his ear. "Just met the man inside the Furnace," he joked between breaths. "Not very friendly."

"Well, technically, we're invading his environment, so I can understand the hostility. But I'm not taking any chances. Activate your tether. We're bringing you back."

Sam examined his boiling, destroyed uniform. He could see his own skin through the charred holes. His right hand felt his lower back; there was nothing attached. After searching the baked ground for a moment, he found his frayed tether lying there like a spent water hose. "I think that's going to be a problem," he said. "Tether's shot."

"Ok. Then find your entry point and we'll do it manually."

Sam gazed a few hundred feet away and found the glowing hole from which he had emerged minutes earlier. "Got it. Look for my signal," he said.

Suddenly a pillar of pure rock erupted underneath him and sent him barreling across the ground. Arms and legs sprouted violently from the new formation, and fierce eyes beamed in Sam's direction. By the time he got to his feet, he was surrounded by at least twenty of the stone giants. Without hesitating, Sam leaped into the sky, planning to bypass them entirely. The nearest monster sprung into the air and slapped him back to the ground. Sam groaned as he slowly got to his feet inside the crater his body had just created in the rock.

"Alright," Sam grumbled. "The old fashioned way then."

Sam pushed off with his right foot and dashed directly at the closest leg he could find. His momentum sent his shoulder crashing into the rock figure and broke the monster's leg into shards. As that one fell, the others screamed and ran after him, their thundering footsteps vibrating deep within Sam's bones. With the glowing entry point just yards away from him, he dared not look behind him. He could just imagine smoldering, mountainous giants trailing behind him as far as he could see across the hazy desert plains.

"Sam, what's happening?" asked Jovita.

"Gonna have to give me a minute."

Two stony hands grabbed Sam and slammed him to the ground. He rolled away from an incoming stomp and punched a hole in the beast nearest to him. Another craggy fist hit the back of his head. Sam turned around and knocked off the beast's jaw. Rubble and pointed scraps of stone cracked and shattered; slabs of human shaped ore crumbled into gravel underneath Sam's fists. And still, more of the massive living sculptures grew out of the churning dust in their places.

Sam turned and ran for the entry point. With each long stride, he felt his pursuers' unbearable heat searing his back as they reached and clawed at him. "Almost there," he said. His peripheral vision picked up the white scanner planted in the ground on his left. "Wait. One more stop."

"Sam," Jovita argued. "Don't you worry about that damn box."

"Sorry." Racing towards the glowing hole in the ground, Sam leaned over to his left and scooped up the box. He slid onto the golden circle and turned towards the volcanic horde rushing at him. As they screamed alien curses at him, Sam kneeled, smiled, and saluted them. "Ok, Vita. Anytime you're ready. Actually right now would be pretty awesome." With that, Sam vanished from sight inside a column of luminescence, and all that remained were his hot, steaming boot prints.

Jovita ran across the Launchpad chamber, nearly tripping as she kneeled at Sam's side. The glow within the platform beneath him faded slowly as he lay flat against it and allowed himself a relieved smile. His exploratory suit was a bubbling, smoking pile of sloppy goop, and his exposed skin was visibly singed. Jovita yanked her hand away from his shoulder. "Ow! God, you're hot," she said. "And don't you ever scare me like that again."

While she massaged her fingers, Sam handed Greg the scanning-tunneling box. "Scare you?" Sam scoffed. "I was the one running from the lava men nobody seemed to know about until they tried to kill the superhuman probe. That would be me, by the way."

Jovita stood up and gave Sam a stern look. "You do this on purpose. You thoroughly enjoy torturing me don't you?"

"Highlight of my day," Sam said with a smile.

Since the day Sam was hired at Sapien Rex, Jovita and her Launch Team had discovered four extra-dimensional environments. The first of these, they named Eden for its lush, untouched forests and perfect blue lakes. Sometimes, when he was feeling particularly romantic, Sam would sneak into the Launchpad chamber and secretly bring Jovita to Eden for dinner.

Tonight, the two of them lay under a green leafy canopy beside one of Sapien's glowing cone-shaped exploration lights. A stack of pizza boxes sat between them. Their white environmental suits and tethers were in a wrinkled heap meters away. With the stars shining down on them, Jovita took another bite of her folded New York slice while Sam laughed and stared into the clear night sky.

"I'm serious," Jovita said after wiping her mouth. "That was amazing work today. We've encountered a brand new species because of you. The board is looking at expanding the program. Maybe even building as many as two more Launch models. And you're a big part of that."

"Yeah, I do alright I guess. With the right motivation."

"Ok. I didn't mean to swell your head any bigger than it already is. We really don't need a super ego to go along with the 'strength and durability' you're always throwing around the place."

Sam sat up a bit and flexed his bulging arms underneath the gray Sapien Rex shirt he was wearing. "You don't seem to mind the extra power any other time," he said with a sly grin.

"Oh, shut up," Jovita laughed. She slid the pizza boxes out of the way and cuddled with him, pulling his arms snugly around her. As he kissed her bandaged right hand and then her lips, she closed her eyes and listened to the light breeze that rustled the branches overhead.

"I have to ask," Jovita said.

"What is it?"

"When are you going to quit all this menial labor and get a uniform of your own? Like Messian or... or Alexandor."

"Like my parents you mean. And you do know Alexandor is an android."

"I think they prefer 'synthetic entity'. I mean you've obviously got the raw talent for it. Your parents would be so proud if they could've seen you out there today."

Sam was quiet.

"Ah, hell. I'm sorry," Jovita muttered. "If it's a sore subject, just..."

"No, no. It's alright. Made peace with it a long time ago. I just don't feel like I need a cape and a symbol or whatever to make a difference. And I don't have to follow in my parents' footsteps. What we do here matters. I'm just a normal guy with a slightly abnormal job, and that's enough for me, you know?"

"Makes sense, "Jovita said. " You get to do something important and use your gifts at the same time. I get it."

"My twelfth birthday. It was a Saturday, so no school work or anything. I blow out my candles at lunch and open my gifts. You know what I got? An adventure suit. Tailor made. Just for me."

"Wow."

"Mom and Dad took me on a mission with them. To find some elixir Dad had been studying. We ended up running up against a couple of Dad's enemies, blew up a submarine in the process. I thought it was completely awesome. I was so excited I couldn't even sleep that night."

"So what happened? What changed?"

"I did. Wanted control over my own life. Started thinking for myself. Grew up. Stuff like that."

"So...you're sure? As far as becoming a quote, unquote hero one day, that's a no?"

Sam smiled and brushed her cheek with his fingertips. "That's a never," he said, pulling Jovita closer to him. "I've already got everything I want." She kissed him deeply once more, inviting the soft, cool grass to slide between her fingers as Eden's triplet moons watched over them both.

CHAPTER 3

Amica Bay was a blue- green megacity on the Washington's southern coast. Each week, news reporters from around the world flocked to the technological marvel in an effort to score the exclusive stories and accompanying pictures that could only come from the city that Douglas and Zoa Sunstrom built. Smooth, needle shaped buildings shot up into the clouds, and gleaming monorail trains raced both through the city's heart and below its streets. The Sunstrom family's architecture and clean burning fuel cells kept everything running efficiently with virtually no cost to the taxpayers. And as people drove to work or played in the perfectly groomed parks, it was normal to see someone look into the clouds, checking the sky for their heroes.

At just over one hundred thousand square feet, the Sunstrom Estate was the pride of Amica Bay. Miles away from the office buildings and commercial sector, the main part of the house towered high among the tallest of the surrounding fir trees with its great sandy brick walls. The Olympic-sized swimming pool as well as the tennis and basketball courts were each adorned with the black and white family crest which was actually an 'S' surrounded by flowery gold-trimmed arcs. Near the bubbling fountain in front of the home, a winding cobblestone walkway led through laser-cut trees and bushes to the polished bronze statue of Christopher Sunstrom dressed in his Word War II era U.S. Army uniform.

The underground hangars and garages with their rounded brownstone walls and white stone columns housed Douglas Sunstrom's two crimson jets as well as his assortment of specially designed sports cars, trucks, and at least one tank. His collection was famous all over the globe thanks to the three-page foldout spread he and Zoa allowed to be published five years ago. Beneath Douglas' toys was the command level that served as the Sunstroms' headquarters. This was where Douglas and Zoa did the work of safeguarding Amica Bay and the planet. No one except family was allowed down there.

But on this particular afternoon, Zoa Sunstrom was standing in the kitchen trying to keep two irate college freshmen from killing one another. She had just returned home from a day at the hairdresser and set her leather handbag on the counter near the sink with the intention of showing her husband her new short, naturally curly haircut. Not to mention the beige pantsuit and matching pumps she was wearing fresh from the boutique. Instead, she found herself cleaning up yet another of her son's messes.

While the two young women threatened one another at the top of their lungs, Janesha Sunstrom pretended to ignore them as she sat at the kitchen table in her white shorts and t-shirt. She played with her long braided hair, trying not to laugh. But her dimples showed anyway when she cut her eyes away from the schoolwork in front of her. Sitting directly across the table from the slender seventeen-year-old, Maddie – heavyset and stoic - tapped her pencil on the table and stared at Janesha with a strict warning in her eyes. A housekeeper, nanny, and assistant, she was the Sunstrom family's closest friend. And she was also the children's teacher. "Back to work on those computations, young lady," Maddie said.

"Ok, ok," Janesha sighed as she began writing again.

The mechanical engineering student with the short bob hair cut and red sweater leaned over and glared past Zoa at the caramel skinned, pony-tailed journalism major in the v-neck and plaid skirt. "I don't know who you're supposed to be," said the engineer in the red sweater. "But Torrance is giving me a tour of the house this afternoon for my final project. He didn't say nothing about no other chicks being here."

"I'm not some other chick," said the journalist. "I'm his girlfriend. Mutt."

"For real? Excuse me?"

"Stop this!" Zoa interupted with controlled force. "Right now." The kitchen fell silent. Janesha looked up from her math paper. "Now, I take pride in being a gracious host, but don't make me throw your preposterous backsides out of my house. You two ladies are much too intelligent... much too beautiful to conduct yourselves in this manner. And over my son at that. Where is Torrance anyway?"

Janesha turned, looked towards the kitchen doorway and snickered as Torrance walked in mouthing the words to the song blasting in his overpriced earbuds. Baby faced with a meticulously trimmed beard and flowing dreadlocks, he filled out his clothes with his lean yet powerful build. It was no wonder the internet gossip sites referred to him as the 'Sunstrom supermodel'.

As he adjusted the collar on the white button up he was wearing, his soft, dark eyes recognized both girls and more importantly, his mother's stone serious face. He took a deep breath while his nervous hands glowed with a bright orange light and melted clean through the headphone cord he was holding. His smartphone hit the floor. "Oh damn," he said under his breath.

"What was that, young man?" Zoa asked sternly. "I don't care if you are nineteen. As long as you're under this roof, you will watch your mouth."

"Um, sorry, Mom. Sorry. Is...there some kind of problem?"

The perturbed young ladies crossed their arms and glowered at Torrance who took another deep breath and grit his teeth. "Fix this, Torrance," Zoa said. She walked away from the girls and pointed towards the adjacent living room. "All three of you. That way."

Janesha leaned back in her chair, watching Torrance and his visibly annoyed guests leave the kitchen. "Yep," she murmured. "They're gonna murder him. Badly."

"And you," Zoa said to Janesha.

"What did I do?"

"Care to explain why your Advanced Spatial Navigation grade has dropped to a 'C' this semester?" Zoa sat beside Janesha and looked her in the eye. "If I need to cut you off from your little social circle, let me know. I can get in touch with Cammi's mother right now. And you know I've been looking for the slightest reason to separate you from that obnoxious 'Lord Brash' character you find so intriguing."

"Mom, this stuff is hard."

"Are you to have me believe you don't understand the difference between light speed calculations inside a gravity well and those appropriate for traditional space?"

"No, but..."

"Then, anything less than an 'A' on that last exam is unacceptable." Zoa stood up and headed out of the kitchen. "If that grade doesn't improve, you'll be packing your bags and taking your classes at Protectorate Academy next semester. And use the textbook. I didn't write it for my health."

After watching her mother exit the room, Janesha looked at Maddie and blew out a frustrated puff of air. Her pupils flashed with a yellowish orange glow. The pencil she'd been using lifted off the table and hovered in the air beside her right ear. Maddie smiled at her and pointed to her paper with her own pencil. "You've got five more to do," she said.

Janesha snatched the floating pencil out of the air, shook her head, and got to work on the next problem.

Levitating just above the carpeted floor, Zoa glided into the spacious upstairs bathroom. She carried her shoes in one hand, and with the other she opened the white wooden cabinet on the wall. Her unsteady free hand grabbed a bottle of pills. Within moments, two red capsules were in her trembling palm. The brand new heels dropped to the floor, and Zoa took hold of her hand and stopped herself from shaking.

As she swallowed the pills, she sat on the rounded edge of the bathtub and covered her face with her hands. Pedicured toes curled themselves tightly on the bathroom tiles, and Zoa doubled over squeezing her fists while the sensation of a thousand fiery nails jabbed into the brain all at once flooded her senses. A lone tear dropped on her foot and faded along with the disappearing pain.

The Sunstroms' headquarters was a nerve center made up of stacked, interlocking hard drives, widescreen monitors, and rectangular holographic displays that lit the immediate area with a cool blue. It was a network of interlocking circular rooms in which chemical and bio labs led to a robotics workshop and a vehicular repair garage. Douglas sat in the center of the communications wing dressed in his burgundy adventure suit, leaning back in a cushioned swivel chair. A three-dimensional person made of light and pixels paced back and forth in front of him.

A gray haired, brawny man with a pronounced limp, Special Agent Marcus Covey had decided to give his old friend a holographic call. "So... have you had time to think about our conversation?" he asked in his usual chalky voice.

"Antarctica. Next week."

"I know it's a lot to ask on such short notice. But I figure with all we've been through, you kinda owe me one."

Douglas smiled and stroked his graying beard. "I owe you one? You must be forgetting the Pharaoh incident. And the Isaiah Stone thing. And the Mansekt invasion. Pretty sure I've saved your life more than once."

"Yeah. And who's kept every president since Ford off your back?" Marcus said dryly. "Some of these secret government agency types. They've got a whole lotta interesting toys they'd like to test on you and that pretty wife of yours."

"I'm sure. But they know better. Don't they?"

Marcus twisted his mouth thoughtfully, smiled and looked directly at Douglas. "We sure do."

Douglas stood up and turned his back to Marcus. "Zoa and I will meet you in Antarctica to help you with this... anomalous object you've discovered. Wouldn't want you to get in over your head, would we?"

"It'll be just like old times. I'll send you the specifics tomorrow morning. We appreciate this as always."

Douglas turned slightly and cut his eye at Marcus. "See you then. Douglas out."

With that, the hologram disappeared, and Douglas sat back in his seat. He pressed a button on the computer console in front of him. A picture of the entire family posing in front of the mansion appeared on the monitor. He zoomed in on the photo until Janesha's twin brother Julian was the only visible family member onscreen. His joyful smile took Douglas back to a more innocent time. Before the family legacy had decided to eat one of his children.

"What happened to Julian isn't your fault," said Zoa from behind him.

"I know. You've been telling me that for years. You don' t have to keep saying it."

"I'll say it until you stop punishing yourself for it."

Zoa walked up to Douglas, leaned over, and kissed him on the cheek. She grabbed his hand and crouched beside his chair. "You know I don't like it when you spend too much time down here," she said.

"How are the kids?"

"The usual. Janesha's trying to do just enough studying to get by. Torrance thinks he's some kind of player. David's tired himself out. He's taking a nap."

"At least he's not antagonizing the others."

"Oh. Sam called me today. I invited him over for dinner tomorrow. And he said yes."

Douglas' eyes lit up. "He said yes?"

Zoa smiled back at him. "He said yes. And he's dating someone now. A doctor of some kind. She seems nice."

Leaning his head back on his chair's headrest, Douglas rubbed his hands together. "Wow," he said. "I was beginning to think he didn't want anything to do with me anymore."

Zoa stood and placed her hand on Douglas' shoulder. "You should stop underestimating him. He may not want our particular lifestyle, but he's going to be great one day. In that respect, he's more like you than you may think. Promise me you won't start pressuring him as soon as he walks through the door."

"Promise. It'll be good to see him again, won't it?"

"Yes. I..."

A light boom resembling distant thunder sounded several floors above them. Douglas got to his feet. "That will be David, I suspect," he said.

The twelve-year-old appeared inside a flashing column of red energy directly behind Zoa. His sneakers squeaked on the floor as he frantically turned from side to side looking for his pursuer.

"David, what have we told you about teleporting in the house?" Douglas asked.

"Sorry, Dad. Sorry," David mumbled. "She's coming."

"What did you do?" Zoa demanded.

"I...I was just practicing my matter displacement powers. I only moved a couple of things. You know, ink pen, a spoon...." David licked his lips and let loose the broad smile he had been trying to hide. "And a bowl of milk and cereal."

The elevator's low, smooth hum announced Janesha's entrance, and she stomped into the room soaked in milk and covered in sugary animal shaped corn pops. When she found David standing confidently between their parents, Janesha pointed at him and forced her telekinetic power to lift her younger brother off his feet and carry him over to her until he was hovering in front of her at eye level.

"Hey!" David yelled. "Mom! I told you she's bullying me."

"Jan," Zoa said. "No fighting in the house."

"Oh, I'm not gonna do anything to him," Janesha answered. She pointed her index finger at the boy who now floated nearly upside down inches from her own nose. "Just remember, you little gremlin. Mom and Dad can't be everywhere. And I never forget."

David sneered back at her. "I'm not little," he said. "And put me down."

Zoa folded her arms and corrected Janesha with her eyes. "Nesha. Put him down."

As Janesha waved her index finger, David dropped slowly to the floor. He looked up at her with a 'gotcha' grin, and for a split second, Janesha could have sworn he stuck his tongue out at her.

With a short, angry huff, she pushed her entire body into the air and flew out of the lab towards the elevator. Douglas kneeled and looked David directly in the eye, giving him a look that could suck the light out of room. "David," he said. "Do. Not. Teleport. Anything. Yourself included. Inside the house. Understood?"

David gulped. "Yes, sir."

"Use the elevator."

"Yes, sir."

Douglas and Zoa watched David make his way to the elevator in the next room. "Those two," he exhaled. "They love each other so much."

Zoa turned towards Douglas and raised an eyebrow. "Obviously."

CHAPTER 4

Khartoum, Sudan was definitely not one of Commander Lisa North's favorite places. Not even in the top fifty. It was a dusty, burning oven of a city that made her feel utterly abandoned and thrown away. Broiling underneath its one hundred and twenty-seven degree heat, she told herself that Khartoum must be hell on Earth. Of course, that was perfectly logical since her bosses had sent her here to keep an eye on the devil.

She had been perched in an uncomfortable crouching position for hours on a hospital rooftop watching the city's pedestrians go about their daily business on the sidewalks, corners, and streets. North had made sure to cover herself in long earth- toned pants and free-flowing layers that covered her shoulders and arms. She'd even covered her head and face in white linen. It wasn't mandatory as it was in some of the other Muslim countries she'd visited, but she knew better than to flaunt her Daytona Beach tan when she was in this part of the world.

She hid herselfbehind the brick latticework that outlined the rooftop's edges and leveled her long sniper rifle at the building across the street. A short dirty van with a Pepsi logo from the 1970's cruised by the building's front doorway, and before she could lower the dull black long- range killing machine in her hands, she spotted three black Mercedes parallel parking in front of the entrance. North narrowed her eyes and tightened her jaw when she finally spotted him through her scope. Isaiah Stone was getting out of the lead car.

His white hair pulled back into a ball at the back of his head, he walked ahead of a group of Sudanese men in fatigues wearing a long-sleeved white robe-like shirt that fell down to his shoes. His dark sunglasses reflected the intense sunlight that smoldered overhead as he stopped and looked around at the tops of the buildings. A middle-aged blonde with short slicked back hair followed Stone and seemed to be watching everything and everyone in the immediate area. Even from underneath the loose fitting burka, her gargantuan frame gave away her identity. Damsel.

North rested her index finger on the trigger and exhaled softly as she focused her eye on Isaiah's face. The silencer would make it a hushed incident, and the specially engineered shells she used would keep it mostly bloodless. "It would be so easy," she said. "One tap. Maybe two. And no one would even know."

Her earpiece fizzled. "And what happens when Damsel steps in front of the bullet, eats it, and pulls your spine out through your chest?" Marcus Covey asked into her ear implant. "Or have you thought about what you would do if you fire only to find out that he's wearing that alien suit of his under those clothes? Are you ready to unleash a superhuman event on all those innocent people?"

"I'm just saying. One less uber criminal. You do realize this is the same person designing those amphibious killing machines we encountered in Japan last month."

"We let the heroes deal with the so-called villains. I just need you to keep tabs on him for now. Report his movements. Anything out the ordinary. You know the deal with Stone."

"Yeah, yeah. I know," North sighed. "Stone belongs to Douglas and Zoa." She watched Stone and his entourage file past curious onlookers into an alley and disappear into the shadows. She imagined them finding some half-hidden doorway on the backside of one of the brown non-descript buildings and loading onto a freight elevator that took them someplace deep underground.

She sucked her teeth and forced her finger off the trigger. "They're off the main road," she said.

"Good," Covey said. "Report on anyone who follows them."

Isaiah Stone stood face to face with Damsel as the dimly lit cargo elevator carried them countless levels into the city's belly. With his Arab garb folded across one of his bodyguards' arms, he held his chin up as Damsel straightened his plain black tie and the lapels of his matching suit. She took off her burka and adjusted the white sleeveless pantsuit that showed off her large, chiseled arms. And with an expression on her face that was all business, she kissed Stone on his rough cheek.

The old elevator doors creaked and split apart allowing Stone to lead Damsel and his followers down a series of dingy hallways with cracked floors. They walked briskly for minutes, stopping only when some well-dressed men appeared from one of the nearby rooms and whispered intensely into Stone's ears. Finally, they arrived at a faded red curtain. Stone grabbed Damsel's hand and led her through the curtain and onto a stage where he stopped behind a glass podium and put on a pair of wire rimmed glasses.

He took note of the white spherical symbol surrounded by curving bladed arcs that adorned the podium. The same symbol hung behind him on a black silken sash flowing from the ceiling to the floor. As Stone stared out at the packed auditorium, Damsel stood at the back of the stage with her hefty arms crossed and scanned the crowd full of rich looking criminals from all over the globe.

Stone cleared his throat and glanced over this audience made up of murderers, monsters, and psychopaths. He didn't recognize anyone, but there was a particular dark skinned woman in the front row. He'd seen her before. Once when they locked eyes at a French produce market and again at a secret speaking engagement in Malaysia.

Her eyes were a sparkling shade of reddish brown, and her long black dreadlocks hung around her shoulders with tiny seashells at their ends.

She crossed her long, smooth legs underneath her white floor length fur coat and stared at the Stone with her tongue sliding across her teeth.

Stone breathed and addressed his congregation with calm, measured words. "My name is Isaiah Stone," he said into the microphone. "Many of you are here because of what you have heard or read about me. They say I am a criminal. A sick and twisted individual. Or they say I am a planet- conquering madman. Or a world destroyer. That I am a heartless murderer. A demon. Honestly, at my core, I am none of those things. And yet, at various points in my life, I have been all of them. The truth is I have discovered the secret of our place in the universe. And I am prepared to do whatever is necessary to bring godhood back to humanity. Society's frail notions of morality are no longer relevant to me."

He smiled and again made eye contact with the intriguing young woman in the front row. "It is time to propel mankind forward into the next great age," he said. "Kindly allow me to explain."

Well after midnight, Isaiah Stone's wealthy hosts had moved him into the most expensive hotel in the city. Damsel stood inside their suite's spacious luxury bathroom in front of an oval mirror wearing a uniform that hadn't touched her skin in decades. The royal blue and gold swimsuit style top that was zipped down to her navel hugged her brutish yet shapely frame. A blue mask hung around her neck like a scarf and accented the short golden cape draped across her shoulders.

As she stared into her own face, she tried not to notice the lines at the corners or her eyes and mouth. They hinted at the dye she had begun using so that her hair was strawberry blonde instead of sprinkled with gray strands. They reminded her of how long it had been since the day she'd first met Isaiah Stone. They mocked her weakness, singing constantly about how she'd never be free of the monster deep inside her mind that had long since loosed itself from all restraints and refused to go back inside its prison.

"This hotel makes me think of our first vacation together," she called out. She put on a wet coat of red lip-gloss and pressed her lips together while leaning towards the mirror. "Remember the room service in Madrid? The food? You hear me, baby?" she called. "Isaiah?"

No one answered. She put the black tube down on the vanity, blew a kiss at herself, and turned towards the open bathroom door. "Master Stone?" she called again. With a smirk, she floated over to the door and landed like a gymnast in the bedroom. As she stood in the entrance with her hands resting on the white wooden double doors, she curled her lips into a snarling grin. "I wore my old uniform for you, baby," she cooed. "Well...parts of it anyway."

Her eyes scanned the off white room, taking in its golden lamps, hand carved furniture, and heavenly king-sized bed. No one. Then, she noticed the open patio doors and the white curtains blowing in the night breeze.

On the patio, Stone stood several stories above the city streets with a folder in his hand, watching the quiet lights around him. He breathed in the hot, sticky air and closed his eyes, wondering which government agency had him under surveillance tonight. Damsel hugged him close from behind, breathing heavily and kissing his neck. Wearing only a pair of white linen pants, he was a coarse, scarred callous of a man, and yet there was a beautiful nobility underneath the hardened, damaged flesh that drove Damsel crazy.

Stone flipped calmly through his folder, which held loose black and white photographs depicting gilled humanoid beasts from various angles. Some of them lay dead and bloodied on concrete floors while others swam freely in murky tanks of water. 'Splice Successful' was stamped in bold red type across several of them.

"I'm ready for you to enlighten me, darling," she whispered into his ear.

Stone closed the folder, pulled away from her, and leaned on the railing in front of him. "They don't understand," he said without looking at her. "Those idiots in that auditorium today have no idea what they're capable of. Pinnacle Tier intelligences every one, and all they can think to do is build death traps and steal things. They're as useless as the heroes and their obsession with preserving the status quo."

Damsel walked up behind him and massaged his shoulders. "That's why you're here, Isaiah," she said. "To teach them. Look at me. I was once as blind as they are. But you opened my eyes to the truth. Come on. I hate it when you're like this. Let me relax you."

Stone turned and looked Damsel up and down. Then, he sighed and walked back into the bedroom, leaving her on the patio with the arid evening winds tossing the ends of her cape. "Put some clothes on," he said. "I'm not in the mood."

The large bodyguard sitting in the suite's living room area scrolled through a webpage on his touchscreen phone as Stone entered and flopped down on the long couch in front of the ninety-inch flat screen television. He looked over at the bald, Sudanese member of his security team who had long since gotten out of his suit jacket and sat hunched over with the sleeves of his white dress shirt rolled up to his elbows. "I'm cutting the trip short," Stone said to the man. "We leave in the morning after breakfast. It's a tragedy really. I could show them how the universe really works, you know. How they could be true masters of humanity. Like the original humans. But all they want me to do is tell them how to be better 'supervillains'. Exceptional men and women content with irrelevance. And they call me sick."

"Yes, sir," said the bodyguard.

"Did you contact my Headhunters?'

"Yes. About an hour ago."

"And?"

"They're ready to move as soon as you give the word. And the Bull agreed to the two-year contract. He signed it electronically this morning. Via email."

"The one from Honduras?"

"Venezuela, sir."

"That should be interesting. His resume is quite extensive...and horrific."

Damsel walked in, yanking a long white bathrobe over herself. "I heard he likes to get his hands bloody," she said. "I suspect I will very much enjoy killing superheroes with him." She stopped next to Isaiah's empty suit of black metallic armor, which hung like some dismantled idol in the corner. Its leg casings and knee joints had been removed and taken apart on the coffee table while black and gray cables spilled from its guts onto the carpet. Damsel ran her hands across the chest plate's glossy enamel finish and outlined its red embossed sphere and arc insignia with her ring finger. She stared at the glyph and remembered the night Stone used a diamond- cutting laser to etch a similar one into the flesh between her shoulder blades.

Someone knocked hard on the door three times. The bodyguard looked up at Stone who in turn sent him over to the door with a sharp head gesture. The man opened the door and stared down at the slightly shorter black woman in front of him. Her dreadlocks hung well past her shoulders, and she wore a lavender blouse, white suit pants and heels. "Good evening, sir," she said cordially. "I apologize for this...intrusion, but it is of utmost importance that I speak with Isaiah Stone."

"You've got the wrong room, sweet thing," the bodyguard said. "Trust me."

Before his security officer could slam the door in the young woman's face, Stone looked past the man and instantly recognized her from the underground auditorium. Secretly, he'd thought about her all day, pondering her identity and why she was so interested in what he had to say. "Wait," he said. "Let her in."

"Are you sure?" Damsel asked. "We don't know this person at..."

"Quiet, woman."

The bodyguard stepped aside and the woman walked into the suite as the door closed quietly behind her. Stone rose from the couch seemingly mesmerized by the vision before him. Damsel sat down and crossed her legs, never taking her eyes off this elegantly morbid angel standing before them.

"My name is Osiria Makabray," the woman said with a British accent. "And I have committed many degenerate acts in order to be in the position to stand here. In this place. Right now. I am both student and weapon. Raw clay ready to be molded by your hands. My only desire is a simple one. To learn at your feet."

Damsel's eyes narrowed as Osiria reached out and touched Stone's hand. The bodyguard instantly grabbed her arm and pushed her into a wall. "You don't touch him," he said. "Understand? Yeah, I think you do." Damsel watched and smiled.

Osiria's free hand found the bodyguard's chest and flattened against it. He choked and dropped to his knees while black, shadowy tendrils coursed all over his skin and beneath his flesh. And as the burly, muscle bound man convulsed, wheezed, and came to an end on the floor, Osiria's arms straightened, her fingers curled, and she tilted her head back with pleasure in her eyes and quaking lips. With her left hand clutching a handful of her own hair, she forced her mouth shut to keep back the sharp scream in her throat.

Growling, Damsel stood up and moved to attack her, but Stone raised his arm and silently instructed her to sit. And then, it was over. Osiria breathed heavily, and the man who had just attacked her had stopped moving and lay dead with blood streaming from his eyes, nose, and ears. She looked Stone directly in the face. "I am a necrokinetic. A death dealer. If you and your misshapen thug whore over there wish to try and kill me now, I suppose we could probably bring this entire hotel crashing to the ground between the three of us. But I'm not here for a fight. I'm here for the instruction that only you are able to provide. Marx Manning would have wanted that."

"Marx," Stone said. "The Pharoah. So you...you are the wife he was always going on about. Jennifer."

"I took the name Jennifer years ago. It sounded more...mainstream. And widow is more accurate than wife nowadays. Marx suffered from an inoperable cancer. Spinal column. Passed away eight months ago."

"It grieves me to hear that. He co-wrote my original Pangaea manifesto with me. Brilliant man. Sinister... but brilliant. He understood what this is all really about."

"I want you to make me a Headhunter, Isaiah. And I want to know what you know. To see what you've seen. To become what you will become."

Damsel finally stepped forward, tossing a table into the far wall. Wine glasses and plates shattered off in the distance. "This is ridiculous," she barked. She stood over Osiria with her gigantic form and glared at her. "You can name drop all you want, but at the end of the day, you're just another groupie. You don't know anything about us, you insignificant speck."

Osiria didn't even blink. "Damsel the Manslayer," she said with a dash of arrogance. "I know that your real name is Karla Lockwood. That you were once married to a hero named Professor Helios. Solar powers if I remember correctly. You operated as his partner until you finally convinced him to marry you. Turns out you have an embarrassingly long history of psychotic behavior, and Dr. Lockwood thought he could 'fix' you. When he cheated on you with his assistant, you went and lost the rest of your damn mind, joined the Headhunter Association, and helped Stone kill the man. That good enough? I tend to be meticulous in my research."

Damsel's eyes bulged, and her hands shook terribly. Osiria walked away from her, picked up one of the broken dish fragments from the floor, and held it up to the light before dropping it. "I also know about your abduction by the Rakken, Isaiah. Those alien things that some people have come to call Stygians. I know what they did to you. How they changed you." She moved closer to Stone and placed her palm softly against the raised scars on his chest. "I've seen your maps of Pangaea. Not the digital copies. The ones you painted with your own hands. I know about the White Transition Chambers that lead to the Great Continuum and the beings that operate them. And I know that everyone must die in order for us to reach them."

Stone took Osiria's hand. His eyes never left her. "You've studied my work," he said.

"All of it. Even the transcripts of your earliest speeches in Cuba and Tokyo. You are a visionary in every sense of the word. Your adventures are legendary. Your final age theory is poetry that I recite to myself every night before dropping off to sleep. I have no doubt that you will achieve the next step in human transcendence. And my heart's desire is be at your side when you do, so I may taste it with you. You're Adam reborn. And you need your Eve, Isaiah."

Stone turned his head and stared at the walls for a moment. And suddenly he'd made his decision. "Damsel," he said finally. "I need the suite."

Startled, Damsel whipped her head around. "What? You couldn't possibly trust..."

"Damsel. Take a walk. We'll reconvene later and discuss Headhunter affairs."

"But..."

"Don't make me say it again, Karla."

Damsel closed her mouth abruptly, and with a frustrated grunt, she flew out of the room with a gust of wind sweeping through the suite behind her. As she soared out the window and into the cloudy night sky, her empty white robe dropped onto the balcony railing.

When Stone turned back towards Osiria, she was unbuttoning her blouse. "And what would you propose we do about the dead body you left on the floor behind you?" he asked with a subtle smile.

Osiria threw her head back and laughed as he pulled her close. "Leave it until we're done here," she said. "I have something of a corpse fetish. That's not overly weird is it?"

CHAPTER 5

The Sunstroms' family room was one of the most guarded areas in the mansion. This was where the entire family came together, relaxed, and spent precious moments together. So, for news reporter Susan McKenna, getting an interview with the Sunstrom family – and inside the hallowed family room – was a once in a lifetime opportunity that she didn't imagine would come her way again.

With her handpicked cameramen planted in various corners of the plush, beige carpeted den, Susan straightened her light brown, medium length hair and crossed her spray- tanned legs as she smiled into the camera directly across the room from her. From his position near the fireplace, her producer pointed at her, and she leaned in closer to Douglas and Zoa Sunstrom who were seated across from her in a soft white couch dressed in a black tuxedo and complementing evening gown.

In a long black strapless dress, Janesha sat up straight with her hands in her lap on Zoa's side. Torrance tried not to lounge too much in the seat next to his father as he didn't want to wrinkle the new white leisure suit he'd bought earlier today. And David sat with his legs crossed on the floor in front of them, pretending to be a perfectly behaved little gentleman in his short set and bowtie.

"So let's talk about Isaiah Stone for a moment," McKenna said bluntly. "This is a man that many would call your rival or 'arch-nemesis' for lack of a better term. He's been considered deceased several different times only to pop back up again and cause some kind of trouble. Take me back to May 6, 2004 when he and the Pharoah tried to, and I'm quoting now, 'unveil Earth's new race of world conquerors.' I don't think the country or the world for that matter will ever forget those test tube super thugs marching on Amica Bay in the middle of the afternoon. That seemed to be quite a tough day for you."

Douglas let a reserved smile come through. "Isaiah... can be a handful at times," he said. "He actually believes that he is destined to achieve some type of ultimate godhood, you know. A person who subscribes to that kind of deluded thinking has the potential to be extremely dangerous given the opportunity. But as I remember, that day ended with both Isaiah Stone and Marx Manning in containment and everyone else resting soundly in their beds. And I can't take all the credit either. Everything is a little easier when you're married to a woman like Zoa."

"Ah, the famous Sunstrom love story," McKenna sang. "Now, I do want to talk about the kids in a moment and why they haven't suited up yet. But you two have become America's model couple. The story of how Zoa accidentally travelled here from another world and how the two of you fell in love while trying to find her a way home. That's like right out of the movies, isn't it? Zoa, is this marriage everything that it looks like when we watch you guys on television?"

Zoa leaned against Douglas a bit and looked directly at McKenna. "I believe there's a place in our book where Douglas characterizes our failing to return me home as the most fulfilling failure of his career," she said. "I like to call it my favorite miscalculation. So, I'd have to say, it is that and more."

"Well, this family is certainly a blueprint for the entire world," McKenna said. "Superhuman or otherwise."

Then, McKenna leaned back in her chair and looked over at Janesha.

"Okay," she said with relaxed confidence. "I wanna know what it's like for a teenage girl with super hero parents..."

Zoa's head turned away from the interview as she looked over at Maddie who was standing patiently in the doorway wearing a black formal dress. "Hold on a minute," she told McKenna. "Maddie?"

"Mrs. Sunstrom," Maddie said. "I apologize for the interruption. But you asked me to let you know. Sam's here."

Zoa turned back towards McKenna with a delighted smile. "I'm sorry, Susan," she said. "But this interview is over. We'll continue at another time."

McKenna's face went pale, and she instantly gave her producer a silent, wide-eyed call for help. "But..."

The smile dropped from Zoa's face. "I said it's over."

Sam and Jovita walked together along the curving cobblestone path on their way to the mansion's front steps. And as Jovita tugged at her lime sweater, she noticed Susan McKenna and her production crew walking quickly in their direction. McKenna was visibly upset, huffing and puffing with each grinding step. "Is that...?" Jovita asked.

"Looks like her," Sam said, smiling. With his hands in his jean pockets, he waited for McKenna and her cameramen to pass him. "Mom strikes again," he said to Jovita. "She's not a big fan of the media. Never has been."

Jovita watched McKenna and company walk to their off-white news van, which was parked on the driveway next to Sam's freshly washed and waxed red sports car. She could have sworn she heard the highly perturbed woman mutter something along the lines of 'damn weirdoes'. "Your mother just kicked Susan McKenna out of her house," Jovita said in amused disbelief. "Five time daytime Emmy winner Susan McKenna."

Sam put his arm around her and began walking to the house again. "I know. She's been trying to get that interview for years. Wonder why Mom cut it short."

The two of them looked towards the huge door on the front of the house just as Zoa and Douglas opened it and stepped outside. "Now you of all people should know that nothing comes between my children and me," Zoa said. "It's good to see you, Sam. Seems like you've been gone forever."

Sam rushed up the steps and hugged his parents tightly as Torrance, Janesha, and David waited to greet their big brother. "I didn't mean to ruin a T.V. thing for you guys," Sam said.

"No harm done," Douglas chuckled. "You know how your mother is about these things."

"Um, Sam?" Jovita interjected.

"Oh, man. I'm sorry," Sam stumbled. "This is the...friend of mine I've been telling you guys about. Dr. Jovita Vargas, I want you to meet my parents. Zoa Sunstrom. Douglas Sunstrom."

"I'm honored," said Jovita.

"Welcome, Doctor," Zoa replied.

For the next few minutes- as brittle red and yellow leaves blew in the wind- Jovita became acquainted with the family of genetic miracles that once seemed so untouchable and unrelatable on her television. Janesha amused her, ignoring David's annoying questions and putting on the mature sounding voice she always used whenever she tried to sound older. At the same time, Torrance kept finding new ways to inquire as to whether or not Jovita had any sisters. And with Sam's ultra-solid frame standing inches behind her, she felt closer to him than ever while surrounded by his parents and siblings.

A family reunited, the Sunstroms sat at the long black dining room table in the separate area next to the kitchen. Torrance, Janesha, and David seemed more comfortable since they had changed out of their formal wear and into their t-shirts, jeans, sweatpants, and sneakers. The meal spread out in front of them was immaculate. Douglas had spent all day preparing the large browned six-legged bird that stewed in a mixture of piping hot juices, vegetables, and seasonings in the table's center. Salads, casseroles, bread, and dessert made up the rest of the meal, and everyone's plate was covered in chunks of uneaten food.

Douglas wiped his mouth in his cloth napkin and sipped his lemonade. "Dr. Vargas," he said. "I've always been interested in cross-dimensional travel. How's the lab at Sapien going? Any progress?"

"Oh, yes sir, Mr. Sunstrom," she answered. "We've opened four temporary holes so far and we're currently doing geological and atmospheric impressions. Preliminary tests look promising."

"Hmmm. Sounds like amazing work. I'm assuming that you've just about turned intercept theory into a new scientific law."

"Actually, no," Sam said. "It may actually turn out to be a little outdated."

Douglas leaned back in his chair with a smug look on his face. "Am I to understand that because of your work at Sapien Rex, dimensional intercept theory is now inapplicable?"

Zoa smiled and took a swallow from her glass while the other children shot each other quick, questioning glances.

"After what I've experienced in my probing missions, Jovita and I are in the process of coming up with something to replace it," said Sam.

Douglas leaned forward. "Go on."

"Tumors."

"Excuse me?"

"Tumors. Teratomas to be exact."

Sam gestured in Jovita's direction, and she gladly took over. "It's like this," she said. "Sometimes surgeons cut open teratomas and find teeth, hair, and even organs growing inside them. It's like the body's attempt at growing new parts for itself or the beginnings of some sort of asexual reproduction. Anyway, all four of the environments we've discovered-no matter how interesting- are unstable and unfinished."

"If I were to run far enough in one direction, I'd probably float away into some sort of void space," Sam added.

With a reserved, approving smile, Douglas folded his hands in front of his mouth and cut his eyes at Sam, Jovita, and Zoa. "So if the universe were an actual living organism instead of a construct," he said, "these extra-dimensional worlds would be its tumors."

Jovita grinned and leaned back in her chair. "That's it."

"Cool," Janesha said.

"So does that mean the universe is sick and dying?" Douglas asked.

"That's a tad bleak, Mr. Sunstrom," Jovita replied.

"Just teasing," Douglas said. "Always push your questioning as far as it will go. You will often find the answers amazing. You are quite an impressive young lady. Sam, you're a lucky man."

Sam nodded. "I keep telling him that," Jovita joked.

"They do need reminding sometimes, don't they," Zoa said with a light smirk.

"And of course, Sam does extraordinary work himself," Jovita explained. "We definitely wouldn't be able to complete the exploratory missions without him, and the Board of Directors are in the process of giving him more of a leadership role at the company."

"Promotion, hm?" Douglas asked.

"Yeah, I guess," Sam answered. "Looks like my powers are useful after all, huh?"

As soon as he'd said it, Sam realized his mistake. The silence and uneasy glances between family members made him flinch on the inside, and he instantly wished he could take it back.

Acting as if he hadn't heard Sam's comment, Douglas scooted his chair away from the table and stood up. "And speaking of scientific breakthroughs," he said. "Would you mind helping me with something, son?"

Sam stared up at Douglas with questioning eyes. Then, he stood up as well. "Sure, Dad," he replied. "I'll be back, Vita."

Sam walked side by side with his father out of the dining room. "Teratomas," Douglas said thoughtfully.

Jovita twisted her mouth playfully while Zoa's eyes followed her husband and son. "So does that happen a lot around here?" Jovita asked. "You know, the whole 'let's leave the women in the kitchen so we can pretend to go do important man stuff'? If so, I say the two of us grab Janesha and stage a revolt."

"We'd never get past their gargantuan egos," said Zoa with a wink.

Surrounded by mahogany wood-grained walls, Douglas and Sam stood shoulder to shoulder inside the home's elevator while bright orange circular lights flashed in succession in front of them. As the elevator car lowered them deep into the Earth, Sam turned, looked at his father, and looked back at the double doors. Douglas continued to look ahead with the tiny lights creating alternating patterns of brightness and shadow on his face.

"All this time and I never knew there was a basement level...below the basement, I mean," Sam said.

Douglas took on that prideful demeanor he often displayed whenever he'd built something amazing. "There wasn't one until about a year ago," he replied. "Look, a government friend of mine. Covey. He wants me to help him investigate some sort of vessel at the South Pole. Zoa's going, but I'd like you to be there too, honestly. No heroics, no villains or anything like that. Just some old fashioned discovery."

"Sounds like something that may have originated off- world," Sam said. "Discovery, huh? Sure. I've got a few vacation days to spare."

Douglas leaned his head back and crossed his arms in satisfaction. "Good. It'll be fun. And bring your friend. Seems like she'd love that sort of thing."

Sam's eyes darted all over the elevator car for a bit as he listened to its faint hum. "So...have you reached out to Julian lately?" he asked.

"No. I...keep meaning to. But...it's never the right time..."

"He's still a part of this family, you know. He's still a Sunstrom."

"I know."

Then, Douglas turned and looked at Sam. "I've missed you a great deal, son."

Sam was about to answer when the elevator doors slid open and light flooded the shadowy car. He stepped into the room, and the sight that lay before him grabbed his words and stuffed them back into his chest.

CHAPTER 6

Outside the Sunstrom Mansion, just in front of the basketball court, Jovita stood inches away from Zoa and stared into the sky, completely and utterly mesmerized. She smiled and used her hands to shield her eyes from the sun. "Wow, she said. She never took her attention away from the bright, golden spot that zipped back and forth over their heads. "How in the world is he doing that?"

Torrance rolled out of a dizzying tornado spin and hovered high in the sky with his sizzling aura pulsing quietly around him. He grinned proudly and looked down at Zoa and Jovita.

Zoa waved at Torrance and continued watching him fly while he took off again into the clouds. Jovita turned and looked at her. "I've heard of a few superhumans using the sun as a power source," Jovita said. "Is that what this is?"

"No, not at all," Zoa answered. "His heart generates its own power. Each beat is akin to a tiny controlled nuclear blast. It's what allows him to fly and radiate various types of energy. That organ beating in his chest creates so much power he doesn't need to eat…or even breathe our oxygen. He only does it, I suspect, to feel normal. To fit in."

"A human reactor," Jovita said under her breath. "Holy damn."

Just then, Janesha flew past them dressed in a gray sweat suit. She skimmed the ground, causing the grass to part like water underneath her. And as she dove upwards, she rolled twice before closing her eyes and climbing high into the sky with her round, joy-filled face turned towards the sun.

"Man, I'm so glad to be outta that itchy dress," Janesha yelled.

"That one's telekinetic," Zoa said with her lips stifling a smile. "And spoiled rotten."

They watched her chase Torrance in the clouds above the mansion for a moment and laughed as Janesha purposefully fell out of the sky like a dead woman, caught herself before she hit the ground, and levitated inches above the lawn with her arms stretched out.

"She needs to learn control, but she's becoming very powerful," Zoa said. "Very nice, Jan. If you ever stop clowning around…"

"I know, I know," Janesha said quickly. "I'll be dangerous one day."

In a burst of loose grass, twigs, and leaves, Janesha launched herself back into the air with her body straight as an arrow. And as fast as she left the ground, David appeared at Jovita's side in a flash of redness. When she looked down at the eleven-year-old who was only as tall as her shoulder, he pressed his index finger against his lips and shushed her. "Watch this," he whispered.

High above the mansion, Janesha tightened her fists and started to make a sharp turn when a large bright red ellipse made of pure light appeared directly in front of her. Unable to avoid it, she shut her eyes tight and crossed her arms in front of her face. "David, you better…" The energy field sucked her in and swallowed her whole just before it blinked out of sight with a muted pop.

David jumped and pumped his fist with excitement. "Yes!" he screamed. "I got you! I got you!"

And as quickly as David's energy field had zapped her away, Janesha reappeared and dropped out of the air. She hit the ground hard and rolled onto her back, staying perfectly still for a few seconds. Jovita and

Zoa turned and looked at one another barely masking their amusement. "Teleporter?" Jovita asked.

"To his own detriment," Zoa said.

Seething, Janesha sat up straight with her braids littered with dried leaf pieces. Her wild, angry eyes pointed straight at her giggling little brother. David stopped laughing, turned and ran. Torrance landed on the mansion's rooftop. The glowing aura left him as he rested his hands on his knees and laughed at them.

"That's it, you nasty little...you little imp!" Janesha yelled. She flew after David who ran at full speed across the yard all the while fading in an out of existence like a flashing red traffic light. Normally, David would have been able to teleport himself out of Janesha's reach, but to use his power, his mind needed to be focused, free of distraction. And at this particular moment, David feared for his very life.

"Mom!" he screamed. "I keep telling you your daughter's bipolar! Mom!"

As the two of them neared the mansion's nearest corner and carried the latest battle in their ongoing war out of sight, Zoa shook her head and turned back towards Jovita. "I apologize for this...display," she said. "I'm sure you haven't seen anything quite like this."

"Actually," Jovita replied over David's screams, "in a way, this all seems perfectly normal."

Sam had never been speechless a day in his life, but this was a moment for which there were absolutely no words. As Douglas stood behind him exuding that proud, fatherly essence he often had, Sam walked slowly across the pristine metallic floor and surveyed the enormous underground chamber that stretched the length of more than a few football fields in every direction. In the room's center, a gleaming burgundy and silver jet cast a long predatory shadow over both of them. Beside it, perched a smaller two-man plane, and as Sam looked around, he spotted four crimson ATVs and at least one golden mini-submarine with jet wings.

With black computer consoles, keyboards, and monitors surrounding them on every wall, Sam toured the area as sparkling light radiated from the high ceiling. Douglas followed him as, he passed through several smaller rooms. Each time Sam left one section, he ended up in a different laboratory or library. There was even a break room with couches and video games. Sam finally stood still, and his feet stopped on a section of floor covered in ancient artwork. Underneath his shoes, a black iconic human figure –the kind one would expect to find on the interior walls of a pyramid or an ancient vase – handed the sun to a group of similarly rendered figures with outstretched arms.

"What is all this?" Sam asked.

"This...is all yours, Sam," Douglas said. "We're a half-mile below my old headquarters. Frankly it makes mine look somewhat pathetic. Your mother doesn't even know about it. The access code is Helmsman Twelve. Remember that."

"Ok...what is this all about?"

"That man under your feet. Look at him."

Sam turned his attention to the jet black print embedded in the floor.

"That's our great ancestor, Atum Shamash," Douglas continued. "Translates roughly into 'Sun Lord'. It's widely believed that he and his queen ruled the Kushites from about 700 BC to 651 BC. They used their solar powers to create a veritable utopia with the Nile River as its center, effectively unifying Upper and Lower Egypt."

Sam sat in a nearby chair and listened with suspicion etched in his brow.

"Their legacy continued into the nineteenth and twentieth centuries through men like Joshua Sunstrom who served the Lincoln administration and even World War II heroes like Christopher Sunstrom. It lives on through me. And through you, son."

Sam stood up, his mind flooded with memories of how it felt to have a Sunstrom adventure suit against his own skin. He felt a nervous chill as he thought about how he once ran through his father's lab, screaming and laughing, pretending to be Douglas Sunstrom.

"This is a fully functional base of operations and a science lab," Douglas said. "Bio, physics, experimental. You name it, you can do it here. You'll be the next generation of Sunstrom heroes. Torrance, Janesha. Even David when he's old enough. And I want you to lead them."

Douglas walked over to a wall panel and pressed a series of buttons.

The panel slid away, revealing a small, narrow room full of color coded adventure suits. "Your uniforms are here," he said. "You've seen the vehicles. I wrote owner's manuals for each of you. The unabridged adventure logs are next to the particle chamber and ..."

"Arrogant. Pigheaded. Egotistical...you just don't stop do you?" Sam groaned.

Douglas looked Sam in the eye and held his tongue until he couldn't anymore. "Have to admit," he said, "I'd hoped you'd done some growing up by now. Look, son. I didn't bring you down here to argue with you. It's just time. It's time for you to accept who you are. There was a time during prehistory when all people were like us. Magnipotents. Superhuman. It's why every civilization ever known has created its own stories about people with extraordinary abilities. All available evidence indicates that human beings are on the verge of a return to that. But our current age... ours is that natural period of turmoil and cataclysm that precedes all great changes. Humanity will need you to get them through it. You see? This thing is bigger than you and your feelings."

"Really? Really?! But you know how I feel about this. And you do... you do all this anyway?"

"Son."

"We've discussed this!"

"Son."

"Like a hundred times already!"

"But you were a kid then, son. I probably shouldn't have, but I indulged your irrational fears and let you wallow in them. But that's gone on long enough. Do you honestly think these people at Sapien Rex actually give a damn about you beyond your powers? All you are to them is this... this super probe. An object they can use to clumsily explore their environments without getting their own hands dirty. A piece of equipment. Stop being such a child about this and..."

"No, you stop!" Sam screamed. The walls around them shuddered under the weight of his voice. The lights flickered. "I SAID NO!"

The entire estate trembled with those thundering words. A statue on the front lawn cracked, and birds scattered away from the trees in droves as the ground shook and buckled. Jovita got up off the ground and dusted herself off. Her wide eyes full of anxiety, she looked directly at Zoa who had turned towards the house.

"That was Sam," Jovita said.

"I know," Zoa said to herself. "Frederick Douglas Sunstrom...what have you done now?" She lit up with a hot red aura and flew straight towards the house. Jovita's jogging turned into a sprint as she tried her best to keep up. When they reached the mansion's front steps, Torrance was dropping out of the sky. Janesha and David were already there.

"What happened, Mom?" Janesha asked. "We heard Sam screaming. Is he okay?" Suddenly, the front doors flew open, and Sam stormed out of the house with Douglas following closely behind him.

"Damn it, Sam," Douglas said, obviously annoyed. "Wait. Let's talk this out."

Sam's scowl softened a bit. He started down the steps and looked at Jovita. "I'm done," he said. "Leave me alone, Dad. Vita, we're out."

Zoa grabbed her son's hand. "Sam, what's wrong?"

Sam turned and looked over his shoulder at Douglas. His voice shook with rage. "Why don't you ask Dad about the new superhero team he's been planning for his kids without telling anyone?"

Zoa aimed an angry, disappointed stare in Douglas' direction causing him to rest his hands on his hips and stare at the ground in frustration. And as Torrance, Janesha, and David turned their eyes on one another, Jovita apologized to Zoa. Without another word, Sam and Jovita made their way to the car.

CHAPTER 7

Antarctica was a harsh, dangerous wasteland of endless ice to most human beings who had ever been privileged enough to visit. But to people like Douglas and Zoa Sunstrom, it looked much different. Instead of focusing on the frozen desolation that stretched on for miles and miles, Douglas saw something of a vacation spot. Being here today, defying sub-zero temperatures reminded him of the time he and his android friend Alexandor raced one another to the top of Mt. Erebus just for bragging rights. For Zoa, this was one of the few places in the world someone like her could just stand with her eyes closed and be free if only for a few moments from the noises of the modern world. There were no villains to battle here, no one who needed her help. She could actually breathe out here in this inhospitable place on the underside of the world.

Nearly an hour ago, Douglas and Zoa landed in their red and silver family jet and met with Special Agent Marcus Covey and his five science officers. Covey and his people were wrapped up in padded thermal suits that closed under their noses. Furry hoods covered their faces and thick goggles shielded their eyes. Zoa's glowing red energy field kept her suitably warm, and Douglas wore a white, red trimmed insulated version of his uniform. They walked steadily through crunching snow and ice towards the tiny colony of rectangular shelters off in the near distance.

"Cold world, isn't it, Sunstrom?" Marcus joked in Douglas' earpiece.

"Temperatures don't affect me as much as they do you," Douglas answered.

"Course they don't. Been a long time, though, Sunstrom. You and Mrs. Zee haven't invited me to dinner in quite a while. I was beginning to think you'd gone Hollywood. Forgot about us little people. Thought at least I'd have a spot on the reality show."

Douglas looked at Marcus as the group reached the doorway of the nearest shelter. "Haven't changed a bit, Covey," he said.

But before Marcus could begin typing his access code into the keypad on the door, Zoa gently grabbed Douglas' arm. "Wait," she said, pointing into the drab sunlight. "Look. Something's coming this way."

A red jet descended from the gray sky and began its squealing landing procedure right in front of the shelter. Covey and his science team looked on while silvery steel claw-like structures extended from the bottom of the vessel and grabbed hold of the icy terrain, anchoring the jet securely in the ground. Zoa's powerful eyes scanned the two-person cockpit and instantly recognized its occupants. Sam and Jovita rested in their seats wearing all black artic wear emblazoned with the bold white Sapien Rex logo.

It had been nearly a week since Douglas had seen Sam, but their argument- the way Sam had yelled at him, yanked away from him- was fresh in his mind. His eyes found Zoa for a second as Sam and Jovita climbed out of the jet and started towards them.

Marcus put his hand on the pistol holstered at his waist. "This gonna be a problem, Sunstrom?" he asked.

"No, Marcus," Zoa said with a smile. "That is our son."

"And Dr. Jovita Vargas from Sapien Rex," Douglas added with relief in his voice. "How about that. They actually came."

"Huhn," Marcus grunted. "You know I hate surprises." He turned around and punched numbers into the keypad on the shelter's rusted door as Sam and Douglas shook hands and hugged tightly. Zoa and Jovita quietly greeted each other, satisfied that Sam and Douglas were speaking.

"I didn't like the way we left things," Sam admitted.

"Neither did I," Douglas said.

"When we get a moment..."

"Yeah. We'll figure things out."

The shelter's door opened, and Marcus ducked his head as he walked inside. His crew followed. Douglas slapped his hand down on Sam's shoulder like an old friend. "Come on in," he said. "Let's have a little fun."

An hour later, Sam and Jovita were standing behind Douglas and Zoa inside a dark room with a blue glow that radiated from the projector in the ceiling. The science team stood all around them, leaning on walls or sitting in folding chairs. Marcus was in front of the room where a wide white screen covered the wall next to him. On it was something that looked almost human, only it had four arms and bony razor sharp thorns protruding from its head and face. There were artful blue marking all over its pale, nude body.

"We're referring to them as Stygians. It's a word we picked up during our research. Probably not what they call themselves, though. But until I meet one alive face to face, that's what we're callin' em. Apparently, they've been coming here for decades."

"That's accurate," Douglas said. "Met one in 1992. And... he was very much alive."

"Of course," Marcus said with a hardened smile. "Forgot who I was talking to."

The projector above their heads clicked, and a large space vessel shaped like the head of a whale appeared on the screen. "This is the thing that crashed and buried itself just two point six miles from this site," Marcus said. He pointed at the topmost section of the ship's hull, which turned red when he touched it. "We will insert the science team right here. The superheroes will take care of the navigation and fuel centers as their bodies can most likely handle any radiation they may encounter better than ours."

Jovita cleared her throat. "What about the rest of us?' she asked.

Marcus licked his lips. "Oh, you two are on with my team," he said. "And we got the best job of 'em all, sweetie. We'll be looking for literature, databases, weapons, tools, even children's toys. Anything that would give us any insight as to the nature of their culture."

Jovita's eyes lit up, and she rubbed her hands together in anticipation. "Scavenger hunt on an alien spaceship," she said. "Can't wait."

The sun had set over an hour ago. It would be another few hours before the science team would be ready to begin the excavation. Sam trudged up an icy hill with his hands in his coat pockets. He stared at the frosted, dusky horizon and continued punching his boots through the ice until he saw his parents standing several feet in front with their backs to him. Zoa noticed him first, and before Sam could speak, her warm red aura enveloped her. She shot into the night sky without a sound. All Sam could do was watch her become one of the stars as he came shoulder to shoulder with his father.

Douglas turned slightly so that he could see if Sam was still wearing the Sapien Rex logo on his snowsuit. Of course, he was. Douglas smiled and then became serious. "I'm sorry, son," he said. "I shouldn't have pushed. Should have respected your position."

"You're good, Dad," Sam said. "I'm not proud of the way I acted. I just...you assumed that everything would be cool."

"I did. I tend to be a bit overzealous at times. Your mother and I have had more than a few intense conversations about that."

"I can imagine." Sam folded his arms and looked out at the cold white terrain stretched out in front of them. "Dad, I want to make this clear. When we get back to Amica Bay...if...when Sapien offers me a management position, I'm going to take it. I'm going to make a career of it. It's what I want. I love you and Mom. I appreciate all that you've taught me, and I even respect the work you've done in the world. It's just not what I choose for myself. And it never will be."

Douglas exhaled as if something had knocked some of the breath out of him. He rested his hands on his belt and reluctantly accepted his son's words. "I understand," he said. "You're a man now. And it's time for me to start treating you like one."

Sam made eye contact with Douglas and nudged him gently. "Thanks," Sam said.

"I'm only going to make one request," Douglas added.

"Which is?"

"That scar you carry. The thing you've refused to acknowledge since it happened. Son, promise me that you won't let what happened to you in Mali all those years ago define who you are."

There was a long silence as Sam turned his eyes to the night sky. "I'll try, Dad," Sam finally said. "I'll try."

CHAPTER 8

The excavation site was a lopsided ice plateau. But this was no naturally occurring geological structure. There was something massive and alien underneath the ice. Marcus, his science team, Douglas, Sam, and Jovita all stood back as Zoa hovered high in the air, lighting the area around them. She pointed her fist at the ground. A wide laser beam erupted from her that cut through several feet of ice and metal, forming a giant circular slab, which tumbled and vanished into the shadowy hole she'd made. The ground shook underneath their feet.

Soon, Marcus and his team of five were lowering themselves by cables into the unknown. Douglas, Sam, and Jovita followed, and as their boots landed solidly on firm silver floors, Zoa floated through the circular entrance with her cape fluttering behind her like angel wings. Her powers created their own red light, so in her presence everyone could see the long rounded corridors stretching in various directions as well as the pipes, wires, and tubing running along the deep purple walls. Marcus turned on his glow stick and held it above his head while everyone else did the same.

"Check your communicators," Marcus said. Everyone made sure that the green light on his or her silver wrist communicator was on. "You can thank the Sunstroms for those. Official superhero tech. Worth the price of admission."

"We meet back here in two hours unless there's a change in the schedule," Douglas said to Sam.

The team split into two groups with Sam and Jovita following Marcus' crew and Douglas and Zoa moving in the opposite direction. After walking for several minutes, Sam and Jovita were side- by- side scanning the foreign writings on the walls with cylindrical devices, and the rest of Marcus' team were spaced out all over the corridor kneeling, climbing, and looking for anything worth documenting.

"You do realize that you're setting the bar pretty high as far as vacations go," Jovita said to Sam without looking at him.

Sam smiled at her and kept scanning. "You are such a nerd."

Douglas and Zoa made turn after turn down one empty steel tunnel after another. Echoing water droplets and their clanking boots were the only sounds, and Zoa's red glow their only light source. The golden device in Douglas' palm beeped as he pointed it in front of him. They turned left.

"The steering chamber should be right up ahead," Douglas murmured. "No abnormal radiation as of yet."

Down the hallway, directly in font of them was a set of heavy metal doors covered in caked brown rust. Zoa landed and walked beside Douglas. There was a relaxed, worry-free smile on her face and a calmness in her walk. "You know, Sam and Jovita are good together," she said.

"The boy has good taste," Douglas said with a grin. "Just like his dad."

Zoa rolled her eyes and shook her head in disbelief at how genuinely corny her husband could be at times. As they moved closer to the doors, Douglas' device beeped loudly. "Wait," Douglas said. "Just got a spike. Give us a shield."

Zoa closed both her fists tightly, and a shimmering protective shield made of pure energy covered both of them. Douglas placed his palms against the doors and began running his hands across the coarse surface, searching for any kind of lock or pressure switch. Suddenly, the energy shield around him flickered on and off; the red light in the tunnel faded.

Douglas turned just in time to see Zoa drop to one knee and wince with her teeth clenched together. In one lightning quick move, Douglas went over and kneeled at her side, whispering softly into her ear as she took hard, rough breaths. "Zoa, listen to me," he said. "You're going to be fine. Do you need me to take you back up to the camp? We can stop right now. I'll come back later."

Zoa pushed his hand away and stood. "No," she said. The energy fields outlining their bodies flared into shining brilliance. "I'll take the medication and rest once we return to the shelters. Right now we have work to do."

Douglas knew better than to argue with Zoa, but his eyes communicated his concern before he turned back towards the metal slab doors standing behind him. "Would you like me to punch a hole in them, dear?" Zoa asked.

"No, just keep the shields up," Douglas answered as he pressed his fingers into the narrow crevice between the doors. Muscles bulging, warring against ancient alien alloys, Douglas pushed the doors apart just enough so that he could squeeze himself through them. But it wasn't enough for him. He groaned, and sweat formed on his brow while silver doors covered in corrosion squealed against iron floors.

With one last exertion, Douglas stopped. He popped his neck and led Zoa onto the ship's navigation deck. It was an enormous room with towering walls and dead computer panels. They were as lifeless as the five beings sitting upright in their blood encrusted steering chairs along the room's perimeter. "Drop the shields, Zoa," Douglas said almost unconsciously.

Her light dwindled gradually until it was completely gone, and all they were left with was the eerie blue glow coming from the thick glass tube stretching from the floor to the ceiling in the center of the room. Douglas and Zoa studied the corpses in silence.

One of them had been a four-armed bruiser with overdeveloped muscles and a face full of fangs. The blue-skinned, white haired creature slumped over in front of Zoa wore gigantic white wings surgically grafted to her back. Douglas' specimen would have been regarded as quite handsome by Earth standards had he not been sporting two holes in his skull. To his right, something humanoid sat with its head thrown back. Half its skeleton was showing and the remaining flesh was a charred mess. Across from him, his counterpart was a stone sculpture caught in a horrified scream. Zoa lightly touched its arm, and everything from the shoulder down turned to ashes. As Douglas pressed his fist to his mouth, he recognized the horns on their heads, the thorns jutting out of their faces. Each one of the five was different from the others, but they were all of the same origin.

"Rakken," Douglas said. His voice echoed more than he thought it would inside the tomb. "These people are of the same species as the being I met in '92. It means 'conqueror' in their language. The underworld has taken to calling them Stygians. But their proper classification... Rakken for sure."

"These people...they have been deceased...for years," Zoa said. "Decades. What happened here?"

Before she could turn around, a searing white-hot burst of wailing sun fire sliced though her back and burst through her ribcage. The bloody red mist spraying from the sizzling wound dissipated as she fell to the floor. Douglas dashed over to her, tears forming in his eyes, hands shaking. He dropped to both knees and examined her as he held her warm hand in his. Her eyes were wide with shock and terror. Blood trickled from her mouth. And when Douglas turned to look behind them, Isaiah Stone emerged from the shadows.

His polished black war suit soaked in the shadows, and the tattered red cape he'd been wearing since he began his criminal career dragged the floor behind his clunky metal steps. Cannons embedded in the black armored gauntlets covering his forearms crackled with orange smoke from the shots they'd just fired. "Hello, Douglas," he said, grinning from behind his stark white beard. "It's been quite a long time."

Douglas leaped at him, rage bubbling off him like boiling lava. "I'll kill you for this!" he screamed.

Stone raised his left arm cannon and blasted a hole through Douglas' chest, but he kept coming. With a burned, bloody hole in his sternum, Douglas punched Stone hard and knocked him into the wall behind them. His arms and legs weakening with each passing moment, he put his hands around Stone's throat and squeezed. But he didn't notice Stone closing his gloved right hand into a fist, which activated a sword made of golden light. The blade pierced Douglas' gut and came out his back.

As Douglas let go of him and fell to the floor, Stone walked away from him. He looked down at his two old enemies lying in pools of their own blood and then raised the blazing sword in front of his own eyes. "I'm sure you recognize this particular weapon, Douglas," he said. "Although I've made several modifications since you last saw it. You see Rakken science is on a far higher plane than ours. They've been murdering super people like you for centuries. Take these fission guns for example. Lovely pieces of machinery."

Douglas was up again, a wet crimson heap of flesh, standing hunched over and wobbling like a drunkard. Stone shot him in his chest again with another bolt of sun plasma from his armored suit. He spun around, hit the floor, rolled onto his back, and let out an agonized scream.

"The super carbon isotope that is the foundation of your amazing physiology, makes you so incredibly strong and impervious to the everyday damage and wear that us baseline humans must endure. Rakken weaponry rips someone like you apart at the subatomic level. You'd probably be more impressed if you were not bleeding all over yourself. I learned so much from my Stygian captors in the years they tortured me, kept me like a house pet. Godless bastards should've never let me escape. You know, each time I lost a battle to you, Douglas, I'd come back to this Harrower Ark and study my craft down here in the company of lifeless monsters. Oh, how perfectly symmetrical that the site of my rebirth would be the very place you draw your final breaths."

Stone placed two fingers against his right ear. "Marcus, you may begin."

Nearly a mile away in another section of the ship, Marcus walked up behind a member of his science crew. The man was crouching with his back to him, scanning the metal in the ventilation piping on the closest wall. Marcus had been to the man's home, met his wife and his three children. He had eaten at his table. With a deep breath and a cold glare, Marcus pulled out his pistol and shot the man in the head.

The silencer on the pistol made a sound like a wasp zipping down the hallway. The scientist fell to the floor and left his blood on the walls. The woman next to him screamed just before taking a bullet through her chest. Marcus' pistol flashed again as he pointed it at another of his team. Jovita looked up. "No!" she screamed. "Marcus, stop!"

The Chinese woman standing directly in Marcus' line of fire stopped still. Ignoring the thundering footsteps coming his way, he fired twice at her head. Sam covered the woman with his body, letting the red hot shells tear into his Sapien Rex jacket and impact against his flesh while white tufts of insulation flew into the air. Marcus squeezed the trigger three more times, aiming at Sam's skull. "There were only supposed to be two super humans," he yelled between rounds. "Not you. You're not supposed to be here!"

Sizzling bits of metal flattened against Sam's skull and fell to the floor. He turned away from the trembling woman he'd just saved and let her sink to the floor as he looked back at Marcus. The man had a detached, crazed look about him, pointing his weapon down the hall at the man who scurried away.

Before Sam could leap on him, Jovita had moved into position, kicked his gun away and punched him in the mouth. Marcus' head snapped back; Jovita kneed him in the gut. Marcus recovered quickly and smashed his own forehead into her face. Jovita fell backwards and looked up to see Marcus' pistol pointed at her. "Sorry, Dr. Vargas," he said under his breath. "Master Stone said all of you."

Sam's fist exploded into the side of Marcus' head. He felt the jaw bone crumble beneath his knuckles. Slumping to the floor and dropping the gun, Marcus closed his eyes. Jovita picked up the pistol and pointed it at him. "He's out," she said. "But still breathing."

Sam looked around at the two dead bodies and the surviving members of the team who cowered in the shadows. "It's alright," Sam said to them. Then, he looked back at Jovita. "What the hell is going on?"

His thumb pressed down on his wrist communicator, and he raised it to his mouth. "Mom, Dad," he said. "We've got a situation here. Marcus Covey has gone rogue. I've got two dead bodies here. Where are you now?"

Silence.

"Mom? Dad? Can you hear me?"

Dead silence.

Jovita held the gun on Marcus and glanced back at Sam. "Ask them who Master Stone is," she said.

"What?"

"Before you hit him. He said something about Master Stone."

Sam's arms dropped to his sides. "Oh no," he said softly.

"If you need to go, I've got this," Jovita said.

"You're sure."

"Go, Sam!"

With a solemn nod, Sam bolted down the corridor, leaping over debris until he was well out of sight. Marcus stirred and opened his eyes to see the barrel of his own gun pointed in his face. Jovita stood over him and snarled. "You move and I swear I'll say it was an accident," she said.

Zoa was on her feet again. Hunched over and wheezing, her legs shook, threatening to fail her. She spit blood defiantly as her right hand covered the seared hole in her side. Stone turned his head and swept his cape behind him while he growled at her like a predator cornering a fawn. "Go ahead, Zoa," he said. "Do it."

With a wild, desperate scream, Zoa threw up both hands and fired several furious bursts of plasma hot enough to pierce reinforced steel. But those blasts merely splashed against the glowing energy field surrounding Stone's armor. Tears dropped from Zoa's eyes as she fired again and again, watching him walk towards her until he grabbed her by the throat and lifted her off her feet.

"You always were so beautiful," Stone said to her looking deeply into her angry eyes. "So full of passion. And power." Lightning coursed through his black battle suit and snaked through Zoa's body. She grit her teeth and convulsed violently before dropping to the floor. Stone smiled; Zoa was still moving, still alive.

"Damsel begged me to let her come here with me today," Stone said. "And there are others – enemies of yours- that would give anything to witness this moment. But they have no vision, no understanding of what it means to kill a superhero. It is not something to be taken lightly. It is something to be done with great care and only when there is no other alternative. Honestly, I've had nothing but tremendous respect for the both of you. I've considered you more rivals than enemies over the years. But now I am on the verge of taking mankind well beyond its established limitations. And you two – in your misguided desire to coddle humanity instead of leading us - would only rise up to hinder my work as you always do. And that…is unacceptable."

Douglas lifted his head. His eyes were weak and half-opened. "Whatever it is you plan to do," Douglas said between labored coughs. "We…we will stop you, Stone."

Stone raised both of his gauntlets and pointed them at Douglas and Zoa. A high-pitched, hydraulic whine grew louder as the canons charged and prepared to fire. "No, Douglas," he said. "This time…old friend… you will not."

The darkness within the Rakken ship's bowels shook with each of Sam's heavy boot steps. After turning yet another sharp corner, he threw off his ripped jacket, revealing the plain black t-shirt underneath. As he let the coat drop off him like a used second skin, cold air filled his lungs. "Mom? Can you hear me?" he asked again into his wrist device. "Dad? Talk to me!"

There was no answer. "Damn it," he yelled.

He ran for long, dark minutes until he was standing in front of steel double doors that had been pried apart. Sam noticed the handprints pressed into the metal, and his heart pounded inside his chest. After activating a glow stick, he turned himself sideways and slid through the narrow opening. Acidic smoke burned his nostrils.

For a few moments, the dead Rakken surrounding him arrested his attention, but he continued searching the chamber. "Sam," Jovita said into his earpiece. "What's happening? You hear me?"

As soon as she'd spoken, Sam looked down at the floor. He dropped his glow stick. It cracked and went out, leaving him with only the faint blue light in the clear control cylinder behind him.

"Sam? Are you there? Do you see anything?"

It was too much. Spattered blood, burned flesh, red and gray adventure suits, torn and ruined. Blood everywhere. Sam fell on his knees with his parents' bodies on both sides of him. So much blood. He grabbed his head tightly with both hands and dropped to the floor between them. His left fist pounded and cracked the metal underneath him, sending a low ringing throughout the entire vessel. Faint sobs escaped his mouth as he lay in the blue tinged darkness with Jovita calling into his ears over and over again.

PART 2

"Following the events of the Second Lunar Adventure, it would be years before I encountered Isaiah Stone again. But when my old enemy resurfaced in the heart of Amica Bay, he was quite different. The way he talked, his mannerisms, his general disposition. He had seen something. Like Paul after Damascus only I'm sure the nature of his transformative experience was much more vile. I remember saying to Zoa several months ago that there are two kinds of villains: the criminals and the demons. Stone, I fear, has evolved into the latter. And there may come a day when I will have to deal with him definitively."

Taken from The Adventure Log Vol. 8
F. Douglas Sunstrom

CHAPTER 9

The days immediately following Sam's return home from Antarctica were especially difficult. First, he held a family meeting and explained as best he could to Torrance, Janesha, and David that their parents had been killed. It seemed nearly impossible to get the words out of his mouth, but he told them plainly in a calm, measured voice that was hoarse from hours of crying. Torrance glared at Sam with eyes full of bubbling anger before he stormed out of the house with red- hot energy waves swirling all around him. He flew away in silence and set the sky ablaze as he disappeared into the clouds.

Janesha ran upstairs, vomited all over the bathroom floor, and collapsed like a jumble of clothes beside the shower. Once Maddie was able to get her into bed, she sobbed uncontrollably all day and into the night until she finally dropped off to sleep.

David, on the other hand, could only stare, his eyes betraying the panic and loss taking root inside. He said nothing. For a few days, he barely even ate.

Next, came the reading of the will. The Sunstrom children sat quietly around the dining room table as the squat, balding lawyer described how the family's money, patents, and property would be divided between them. "What about Julian?" David asked. "We have to tell him what happened. No matter what he did in the past, it's only right."

Janesha's entire body went stiff. "Who's Julian?" Jovita probed. "Never heard you mention him before."

"Dad didn't like for us to talk about him too much," Torrance said. "But he's our brother. Janesha's twin actually. Mom and Dad put him away when he lost it."

"Lost it?"

"No," Sam said, shaking his head. "No one is to make contact with Julian Sunstrom. Under any circumstances." None of them mentioned it again. Janesha's breathing returned to normal.

And then there was the press conference from hell. On the Sunstrom Estate's front lawn, Sam stood in front of a handpicked group of news reporters to let America and the rest of the world know that two of their beloved heroes were indeed dead. He answered the intelligent questions, sidestepped the sensitive ones, and totally dismissed the stupid ones.

There was a quiet, festering storm in his voice when he stepped out in front of the cameras in his gray business suit and uttered the words, "Two days ago, Douglas and Zoa Sunstrom were murdered." Something bitter and violent burned in his brown eyes, writhed underneath his flesh, gnawed at his insides. Jovita could sense the change. She'd been at his side during the whole ordeal, holding his hand when he needed it, listening to him worry and reminisce in the night's lonely hours.

She was there when he chased several snooping reporters out of the estate's backyard early one morning. The fact that she was yelling for him to stop and distracted him was probably the only reason he missed when he picked their news van up over his head and hurled it at them. Needless to say they didn't return. But the newspapers, magazines, and blogs weren't very kind in the least after that.

Sunstrom Successor Loses His Mind!!

Sam Sunstrom: The World's Newest Super Thug?

Sunstrom Heir Pisses on Family Legacy

Sam barred all media from the funeral, and only close family and friends were invited. After attending the memorial service at Mercy Cathedral, Sam, his siblings, Maddie, and Jovita gathered at the Sunstrom family burial ground which was only a few miles from the mansion. This was when the superheroes showed up. Sam was well aware of this particular tradition, so it wasn't unexpected. Each hero had a discreetly kept a list of witnesses within the hero community whose job it was to verify that particular hero's death should he or she ever pass away. And there were also those who came just to pay their respects.

Lord Brash –a teenaged upstart hero who had received his support from the most successful internet crowd funding campaign in history – hung out underneath one of the large pine trees wearing a loose white dress shirt and dark slacks. The android wrapped in pseudo- flesh who called himself Alexandor stood a few yards behind the family respectfully wearing the emerald uniform and golden cape ensemble that Zoa had created for him years ago.

Insect Island's King Mansekt wore a black hooded cape that hid the antennae sprouting from underneath his blonde locks. He held his gold bladed staff firmly in front of him as buzzing insect men encased in polished, armored exoskeletons flanked him on both sides. Representing China's heroes, Jun Ren lowered his head and closed his eyes behind the red, gold- laced cowl that covered most of his face.

And there was the Protectorate – the superhero elite. Bronze-skinned Messian Spacefarer silently watched over them in the sky, his smooth blue and white ceremonial armor glittering like a jewel in the sunlight. The hero king's all white cape was a regal banner over the somber proceedings. His wife Jabril Novastarr was covered from head to toe in golden liquid metal and stood silently beside tall, broad Mirakles who represented in his own dark blue, red emblazoned uniform.

As Sam stood between Janesha and Torrance, he put his hand on David's shoulder and clenched his jaw as two burgundy, black-trimmed caskets dropped slowly into their plots in the ground. Behind him, Jovita placed her palm against his bald head while a tear dropped from behind her sunglasses.

Sam's mind travelled back to Mali for split seconds at a time. The images flashed in and out of his consciousness as he tried to forget them.

The laughter he and Douglas shared while they explored deep, mysterious caves. Zoa teaching him to fire a laser cutter. How his young, high-pitched voice pierced the darkness of the caves when he realized that he had been the one to uncover the ancient diagrams hidden behind the walls.

The minister read the appropriate verses and said his final words while Janesha looked down into David's eyes and quietly asked him if he was okay. David sniffled and wiped his eyes. "Yeah," he said. "I'm cool." Then he buried his face into her blouse and cried as Maddie kneeled, rubbed his back and whispered encouraging words to him.

Sam remembered the hot, dry Mali air and the dank, musty fumes within the caves. The insane babble coming from Isaiah Stone's mouth when he ambushed them. The numbness in his gut when Stone's atom splicing laser blade cut his belly to shreds. How Zoa covered his body with her own. Douglas viciously beating Stone nearly to death with his bare hands and Zoa pleading with him to stop until he finally dropped the supervillain and left him gasping and bleeding all over the cave floor .

Torrance moved up beside Sam and removed his own sunglasses. His eyes were as serious as his raw, anguished voice. "So," he said to Sam. "We planning on doing something about this?"

Sam snapped back to the present and took one last look at the caskets as they entered the ground. Then he looked his brother squarely in the eye. "Absolutely," he said.

CHAPTER 10

Isaiah Stone called his home the Orb. It was a perfectly rounded sphere hewn from metals and technology he'd discovered in a place far from our world. Tonight, the smooth silver war ship rested at the bottom of the ocean off the coast of Somalia, settled in a black undersea bed of broken earth. Stone's genetically engineered sea mutants crawled and swam around its circumference, devouring fish and searching for intruders with glowing eyes that pierced the darkness.

The Orb was levels upon levels of living quarters, science laboratories, and weaponry. The sharpened steel needle adorning its topmost section projected a distortion signal that rendered the hulking vessel virtually invisible to satellite detection.

Most nights, Stone would be in one of his labs, teaching himself new ways to bend and subvert the universe's laws. But on this night, he slept wrapped in his bedroom's tranquil darkness with Osiria nuzzled closely beside him. However, his restless mind wouldn't grant him any peace.

The same dream he had virtually every time he closed his eyes assaulted him once again. Thorn-faced Rakken stood over him in clear plastic surgical masks, using laser blades to slice him to the bone. Tiny tubes and pins injected burning medicines into him that quickened something deep in his being, causing his lacerations to heal right before his eyes. And once he had healed, the Rakken cut into him for the hundredth time.

The beautiful female with the flowing ivory mohawk. A doctor he guessed. Bellion. He never learned the husband's name. He could only remember his angry barking and arguing as he stood over him in his ominous black armored suit pointing scalpels at him. Stone closed his eyes as the cutting began again.

He opened them again in a lonely cell on a cold, rough floor dressed in a white healing suit. Underneath it, he could feel the burning, itching scars, the mending tissue. And just as he started to roll himself up into a whimpering ball, Bellion walked in covered in silken crimson and black, a red cape flapping behind her.

She kneeled beside him and caressed his shaven head, examining the scar tissue left by her husband's brain probe. "I'm sorry we must do this to you," she said.

"Bellion...please listen," Stone mumbled. "You have to let me go. Listen to me. My name... my name is Leonard. Leonard Isaiah McGurran. On Earth...I have lived my life...as a scientist...an explorer. But here... I...I...am nothing. Let me go. Please. I have a wife...a son...and..."

"Yes, yes. You say the same things to me each time I visit. I know who you are. Stone, the so-called super criminal. And do not worry about your mate and offspring," Bellion said with a smile. "We aren't savages, you know. We had the decency to put them down when we procured you. I made sure that they would not suffer."

Stone's forehead ground against the concrete floor as he sobbed like a small child. Bellion rubbed his face, soothing her new puppy. "My husband wants to have you destroyed," she said. "Says there is nothing of value in you. Nothing new to learn. You are but a shadow of us with none of our innate abilities...and yet you have survived here for many seasons. None of the other specimens lasted longer than a day. Oh, do not think that I haven't noticed how you lie there on the operating table, learning our language, observing our behavior even as we dissect you. There is something transcendent at your very core, Isaiah. Something as rich and treasured as the most precious gem."

Bellion grabbed his flaccid right hand and pressed it against her chest as her lips forced themselves against his. She tasted like bitter chocolate and oranges.

A dazzling white light flooded his eyes, and he was standing behind Bellion with a panel of Rakken scientists before them. A heavy collar closed around Stone's throat as he looked Bellion's husband in his distorted face.

"Bellion, for the love of Mellenius, please tell the council that you don't plan to take this thing, this... animal of yours into your home as some sort of pet," the Rakken scoffed. "In my expert opinion, you should have put it out of its misery years ago."

"I have reason to believe that there is a special although unseen quality inside this particular species," Bellion stated with her head high. "Whatever this is, it allows his kind to connect with one another, to experience multiple levels of emotion, display boundless creativity. And I have reason to believe that it continues to exist even after they die. I mean to study this individual until I can find it, cut it out, and reproduce it."

Stone and Bellion exited the room together, leaving the grumbling scientists behind, and suddenly, they were worlds and years away. Now, they stood in front of colossal spheres made of pure swirling light with what looked like burning suns at the heart of them. Each one larger than the last, Bellion and Stone were ants next to them.

"Astounding, are they not?" Bellion asked. "Each fuel cell contains the amount of energy equivalent to the molten core of a typical life producing planet."

"You're manufacturing your own geothermal energy," Stone observed. "Amazing. Now explain to me again how this powers the window technology you Rakken use to travel the universe."

"Universe?"

"The Unified Continuum as you Rakken call it."

Bellion kissed him on his bearded cheek and ran her fingers through his neatly combed hair. "You are quite the conundrum, Isaiah," she said. "You clearly possess an advanced intellect and yet you haven't stopped asking questions since I brought you home all those sequences ago. Tell me. What would you do if you were ever able to escape your collar?" Stone started to speak, but he was nauseous, out of breath, and he couldn't stop trembling. He finally gasped and stepped away from Bellion. She fell dead at his feet, soaked in blood, joining the dozens of dead Rakken on the floor all around him. No longer clothed in a simple medical suit, Stone found himself sealed inside her husband's black humming war armor. Every part of him from his face to his metallic boots was splashed with Rakken fluids.

And then he laughed. It was a sad, heartbroken laugh. One of relief, horror, and cruelty. He laughed and snickered until his stomach hurt, and then until he could no longer breathe. And he kept laughing until he finally awoke from the nightmare that refused to leave him alone.

Stone sat up straight in his canopy bed and immediately looked for the warm blood that was surely streaming from between his fingers. His breathing slowed as he eventually realized that he was indeed aboard his ship and not on some Stygian world fighting for his life. That particular chapter ended long ago, he reminded himself. Osiria rolled over and stroked his chest. "Is everything alright?" she asked. "It was the dream again. Wasn't it?"

Stone stared into the darkness until his eyes adjusted and focused on the stolen suit of armor standing against the far wall. "I…I saw more this time," he said. "I remembered her name. Bellion. Her name was Bellion. And I saw the fuel cells. Wondrous machines they were." He smiled to himself as he stood and wrapped a white robe around his body. "It's true what they say about confirmation through dreams. I've been given the green light… so to speak."

Osiria sat up in the bed and listened while he paced the floor. "Get up," Stone said. "Summon my Headhunters. You and I have a world to end."

When it came to killing superheroes, Damsel's favorite part was finding and invading their secret bases. She loved hunting down the hidden places these people hung their capes and kicking down their front doors when they least expected it.

Serebro Volk built his lair deep beneath Moscow in the late 1990's, waging a one-man war on organized crime from underneath the city itself for years. The 'Volka' as he called it was the apartment-sized nerve center where Volk spent hours monitoring criminal activity on his crudely cobbled system of computers, police radios, and motion detection software. It was also where he trained his wolves and young daughter to aid him in his mission.

With its thick steel walls, he thought his wolf's den undetectable, impenetrable. That was until Damsel punched her way into the Volka and put her fist through his sternum. With gray wolves lying dead around her boots, Damsel looked around at the cluttered room and turned up her nose. She actually felt a little sorry for the animals. She hadn't come to kill them, but they'd attacked her and paid the price for it.

Volk lay on the floor behind her, crumpled across the cables running along the hard, black floor. He was still wearing his charcoal uniform and cowl, and the hole in his chest where Damsel's fist had been bled like a fountain. She turned to admire her work once more.

"Easiest million I ever made," she sighed.

The whimpering in the corner distracted her, and she turned an annoyed stare on the frosty-haired six-year old girl bawling in the corner. Wearing a copy of her father's uniform, she held a white wolf pup in her arms and sank to the floor refusing to look at the woman who had just murdered her father.

Just then, a communicator vibrated against Damsel's belt. She detached the thin device and read the repeating symbols flashing on the tiny screen. The call for all Prime Headhunters to come in out of the field. Without pause, Damsel turned and began walking towards the deteriorating hole she'd just made in the wall. "Stop crying, Galina," she said. "I just gave you an origin story, you know. You've been left alive because the crime families only paid enough for your father's head. So grow up. Train. Be better than this weak man who left you a defenseless orphan. Use what I've done to you to become something unimaginable. And maybe we'll meet again someday. I'll look forward to it."

With that, she flew out of the Volka, leaving the little girl alone, buried at the bottom of the city with her father's corpse.

The Headhunters had assembled at the Orb, and Damsel was the last to arrive. She strode into Isaiah Stone's dimly lit meeting hall with a gladiator's confidence and sat down at a long curved table amongst a handful of the world's most fearsome assassins.

On her left was Dreadmettle. He sat quietly and deathly still beside her, clothed in sleek silver and black armor with a helmet that covered his head and most of his face. A large steel sphere with several glowing circular ports on its surface orbited the former Army sergeant and floated in the air directly behind his head.

To Damsel's right sat Malignus, the creature they called 'the walking cancer'. A fat, monstrous pile of tentacles, eyes, teeth, and limbs, he reclined in his specially made cushioned chair hovering a few feet off the floor. He crunched noisily on a snack that sounded like it was made of bone and licked his knife-edged teeth before burping up a chunk of undigested meat.

Further down the table was the Bull. He purposefully sat away from everyone else and meditated with his eyes closed, his fingers tapping gently on the table. Glossy black limb guards covered his arms from his shoulders to his wrists, but he wasn't into the costumes and capes that most super criminals wore. His only other dressings were his camouflage pants, military boots, and the tattoos of women, guns, and skulls that decorated his upper body.

The lights in the room brightened a bit, and in walked Stone and Osiria. Clothed in white linen and sandals, Stone made his way to the center of the room so that all of his assassins could see him. Osiria followed him, making sure to remain close to him at all times. Her white one-piece suit and boots hugged her curves and shimmered under the shining ceiling lights.

Damsel bristled at the very sight of her. Since Osiria had come into their lives, she'd watched as this young stray captivated Stone's gaze as well as his affections. She knew they were sleeping together and had been hearing rumors of their recent 'business trips'. Some expensive shopping trip in Dubai, a discreet murder spree in Tokyo. Osiria had taken Damsel's place in Stone's bedroom and apparently in his heart as well. And Damsel hated her for it.

Stone had even given Osiria a short crimson cape that hung off her right shoulder. The color and hem were the markings of the Rakken Science Lords, and Damsel remembered the night Stone had given her one just like it. He'd told her that at the end of the world there would only be the two of them. Now, it seemed that there would be three watching everything burn.

Osiria looked Damsel in the eye and then turned her head as if she hadn't noticed her at all. But there was no time for jealousy or pettiness. Her teacher was about to speak.

Stone folded his hands together. "By now I'm sure that all of you have heard the news," he said. "But I want you to hear it from me. The rumors are true. My most tenacious enemies – Douglas and Zoa Sunstrom – are indeed dead. I performed this action with my own hands."

The Headhunters at the table glanced at one another with genuine surprise and intrigue. Noticing their expressions, Stone smiled and clicked a remote in his hand, causing the screen on the wall behind him to come alive with a collage of black and white news photos focusing on Sam, Torrance, David, and Janesha.

"Now it's time to finish the job," he continued. "So. Let's talk about who we're going to kill next."

CHAPTER 11

Commander Lisa North slowed her black SUV to a stop in the Sunstroms' circular driveway. Dressed in jeans and a leather jacket, she stared at the mansion through the driver side window and wondered how she let the president talk her into this job that required her to deal with demi-gods and their messy affairs on a constant basis. She put the truck in park, but before she could get out, she noticed someone marching towards her from the front of the house.

It didn't take long for North to recognize this stern-looking person from the set of surveillance photographs she'd been studying over the past few days. It was Maddie. The Sunstroms' housekeeper and professional assistant, she noted. As the sturdily built woman in the pink jogging suit grew closer with each grouchy step, North realized that getting into the house was going to be a bit more difficult than she originally thought.

Carefully, she popped the truck's door open and set her brown leather boots out on the pavement. A set of three steel gray spheres instantly shot out of the lawn and began scanning her entire body with thin red laser beams. "Oh, you've got to be kidding me," she said as the mechanical globes swarmed around her. She put her arms up and shielded her face from one of the spinning robots that propelled itself right at her head and veered off at the last possible second. "Come on, you ridiculous machines. I'm not the enemy here. I promise."

She spun around just in time to meet Maddie nose to snarling nose. "Ma'am," Maddie said. "I'm only going to ask you once to leave."

"I'm here to speak to Samuel Sunstrom."

"He's grieving. Are you going to make me remove you from the grounds?"

"Aren't you the help?"

"Ok. Make sure you tell whatever cable news network you work for that I tried not to damage your face."

North took a breath and shoved her hands in her pockets. "I'm not a reporter, lady," she said. "Commander Lisa North. I work for a government agency, and I have sensitive intel regarding Marcus Covey."

Maddie's face softened; her shoulders relaxed. "I...I think you should come inside, Ms. North," she said.

"Thank you," said North as she followed Maddie into the mansion.

Leaning forward in his chair with his forearms crossed on the kitchen table, Sam glared at North with cold, dark eyes. His face was granite-like and expressionless. Torrance stood behind him with his arms folded, and Jovita leaned against the nearby sink. "You've got five minutes," Sam said.

North tried to look as relaxed and nonthreatening as possible. "I'm here because I knew Marcus Covey. The two of us headed up several classified missions together over the past decade. Some of it the president doesn't even know about. Anyway, we were selected for a special project involving magnipotents. And that's when everything changed."

"What do you mean?"

"Well, Covey. Started getting weird on me. Started collecting all these books and pamphlets. Downloading these underground science lectures from dark internet sites. All of them by Isaiah Stone and associates of his. At first I thought he was just doing research on a target, trying to figure out how the guy thinks. But he became obsessed with him. Tried to get me reading the stuff. I read one of his essays, you know, just to humor him. It was all about how he believes that cancer is the first step in humanity's transition into super humanity. Like it's not a disease at all. He was saying that our current forms can't handle the change because of missing DNA strands or something, so it has to be surgically removed or it will kill us. Interesting, but kinda strange if you ask me."

Sam leaned back in his chair and looked North up and down. "So you came all this way to tell me that the man who killed my parents was a madman," he said. "And he turned your partner into one too. Not very informative, Ms. North. Thank you for wasting our time."

"Wait." North reached into her right coat pocket, pulling out a key card and a folded piece of yellow paper. She slid them across the table to Sam. "Covey kept a safe house in Peru," she said. "Whenever he finished a mission, that was usually where he went. But there's been no activity out of there since we put him away. Here is the access and the location. If there are any clues as to Stone's whereabouts, you'll find them there. A black ops team will discover the place sooner or later. I'm giving you first crack at it. You deserve at least that much."

Sam turned the key card over in his hand and stared at the barcode on it before looking North in the face with grateful eyes. "Thank you, Commander," he said.

North got up from the table and moved towards the kitchen door where Maddie stood waiting to escort her off the premises. She looked back at Sam before she left. "The people I work for want you to know. Your parents were highly respected and admired. I'm sorry for your loss."

Sam nodded as she left the room.

"What's next?" Torrance asked.

"I'm leaving Janesha and David out of this," Sam answered quickly. "The three of us. We make this piece of garbage answer for what he's done. And we start in Peru."

Sam patiently rode the elevator up ten floors to the top of Sapien Rex's Corporate Affairs Building. The entire floor was one huge penthouse-style office space with several rooms that belonged to the company's CEO. Sam had met with important figures before – in fact he'd grown up around them – so it wasn't Garrison Vargas' position that intimidated him. It had more to do with the fact that he was Jovita's father.

The elevator doors opened, and Sam walked into Garrison's main office just as the executive dismissed his secretary from a meeting. The intern's black flats carried her rushing past him with a digital tablet in her hands. Garrison sat down behind a wide oak desk and gestured towards the cushioned guest chair.

The decorations surrounding them betrayed his rather eclectic taste. Broken stone tablets from the ancient world hung on the walls behind glass frames. At the center of each fragile tablet, a vertical column of spheres began as small etchings at the top and bottom until one large master circle planted itself firmly in the center. Sam noticed an identical symbol on a glass, rocket-shaped award sitting on his desk. And on each side of the long window that stretched across the back wall were prehistoric trees with beige trunks and violet leaves that Sapien's bio labs had given to their boss as a recent holiday gift.

Sam sat down across from him and watched the man pick him apart with his intense black eyes. Garrison was a handsome man with a physique that filled out his navy blue business suit the way a professional athlete's would. His meticulously trimmed mustache and beard were streaked with hints of gray and white, but he carried his age like a classic gentleman.

"Samuel Aleser Sunstrom," he said, considering each syllable as he said them. "Aleser. From the Arabic. Means lion. Very appropriate I might add."

"I was supposed to have a meeting with you a few days ago, but..."

"Don't apologize, Samuel. Considering what you've been through, the fact that you're here at all is admirable by any standard. Let me begin by saying how hurt I was to hear about your parents. I actually met Douglas once. Charming fellow. Unparalleled work ethic. The sharpest of minds. I trust you are taking care of yourself?"

"Yes, sir. I am."

"Good. Jovita speaks very highly of you. You should know it takes a great deal to impress her."

Sam smiled. "Yeah, I've kinda figured that out."

"So. Let's talk Launch Team business. As you've probably already been made aware, the team has performed well beyond expectations. And the board wants to expand. We are extremely interested in exploring and studying the natural resources of these extra dimensional environments you and Jovita have become so adept at finding. We'd also like to catalogue even more environments at a faster rate. And that brings me to the topic of your position here at Sapien."

Garrison opened a leather binder on his desk and laid a series of personnel files across the shiny wood finish. "We're going to expand the Launch program. More teams which means more Platforms and more missions. I want you to be in charge of it all. These are the candidates who have been interviewed and vetted so far. But there are more we'd like to talk to. You know, magnipotents like yourself who are just looking for an honest day's work and a way to use their abilities to actually help society instead of tear it apart."

"And my job would be...?"

"You'll recruit, train, and lead our personal supermen into the hidden pockets of the universe. I want a dozen or more special employees under your supervision who can do what you do. By the way, the pay raise will be...worth the time and effort. You stand to do very well financially if you accept. How does Special Projects Manager sound?"

Sam stood up and rubbed his head, unsure of what to say. "Mr. Vargas," he said, stalling. "I'm sorry. It's...it's a tempting offer, but...but I'm afraid I'm going to have to take a leave of absence. The last few days have been... a strain to say the least. I'll return to my duties here once I've cleaned up some family business, but I'm needed somewhere else right now."

Garrison sat back in his chair and looked up at Sam. "Ah, I see," he said. "I suppose your mind is made up about this."

"Yes, sir. It is."

"Well, I can see why Jovita is so fond of you. A man of resolve. And will my daughter be going with you on this excursion or whatever this thing is you'll be doing?"

"She insists, Mr. Vargas."

"Of course she does, Samuel. I suppose that's who I raised her to be.

I do want you to remember this: Jovita is my only child. Keep her out of harm's way. That's all I ask."

"Yes, sir. Thank you, sir."

Sam started to leave the room when Garrison's voice stopped him in his tracks. "Samuel," Garrison said. Sam turned around at the doorway. "Isaiah Stone is not a man to be trifled with...or underestimated. If you're planning to chase that particular dragon, you would be wise to remember that."

Surprised at Garrison's statement, Sam stared at him for several seconds. Garrison smiled, lowered his eyes and returned to signing documents as Sam walked out of the office with a paranoid chill running down his back.

The Sunstrom Sky Piercer was the first plane Sam learned to fly when he was eleven years old. The round, fat-bellied cargo plane with the needle nose, long, thin wings, and bright red paintjob sliced through the clouds over South America as Sam handled the controls and monitored the digital displays like an expert pilot. Jovita sat beside him in the co-pilot's chair wearing a small black headset that matched Sam's while Torrance sat in the seat behind them examining a leather briefcase sitting on his lap.

"You're sure about doing this with us?" Sam asked Jovita.

"Ok, I'm going to eject myself from this plane of yours if you ask me that one more time," Jovita replied. "How many different ways can you phrase the same damn question? I'm here because I want to be, Sam. Not because I feel I have to be or anything else. And stop being so afraid of my father. You've been shaky ever since you left Sapien."

"Sorry," Sam said. "But he is your dad."

"Never really thought of him that way. After Mom died, his idea of parenting was building a better physicist. To him, love and affection meant giving me a super tricked out lab and a job at his company so I can discover things for him. Hugs and sleepovers and birthday parties are pretty mundane compared to super science, I guess. But you don't need his permission for anything concerning me. And you certainly shouldn't be afraid of him."

Sam glanced over at her, trying to read her eyes. "Noted," he said, twisting his mouth. He punched a few more buttons until he heard something click behind him.

The leather case in Torrance's lap popped open, revealing a clunky gray pistol separated into two pieces. "What's this?" Torrance asked.

"Polymer gun," Jovita answered proudly. "I've been working on that thing for the past two years. Finally got it to work, so I decided to bring it along."

"Man," Torrance said. "Beauty, brains, and you can fight too? You sure you don't have any sisters my age? I know I probably asked you before. Actually I like older chicks too, so... the age thing's kind of a non-factor."

Sam smirked at Jovita. "Forgive him," he said to her while his brother continued talking. "Brain damage."

He turned around in his seat and shot Torrance a look that screamed 'shut up' as Jovita smiled and checked the monitor with the flashing red beacon. They'd arrived at their destination.

CHAPTER 12

The Sky Piercer sat conspicuously perched in front of a tiny, dilapidated shack in the middle of the South American desert. In his gray Sapien Rex gear, Sam was the last to hop out of the cockpit, and as the plane locked itself down, he joined Torrance and Jovita a few feet away from it. Dressed in a black long-sleeved under sheath and jeans, Jovita snapped together and holstered her handmade pistol while Torrance zipped his burgundy one-piece training suit up to his throat.

The three of them walked up to the small leaning house and stepped up on the dusty porch. Sam kicked the door in. While Jovita kneeled and studied the iron trap door in the wood floor, Torrance walked from room to room. All empty. Sam grabbed the trap door's handle and pulled it open. A set of steps led down below the floor into quiet darkness.

After navigating the cramped, rickety staircase, Sam made sure that Jovita and Torrance were standing near him when he flipped the light switch. Torrance immediately stepped back from the dead man lying on the floor beside him at the bottom of the stairs. "Oh, God," Jovita gasped. Another man sat slumped against the far wall with a hole in his head.

"Damn," Torrance said. "Looks like Covey got rid of all his loose ends before he left."

"Keep walking," Sam said.

The dim bulb swinging overhead didn't provide much light, but it was enough. So Sam led them down a short hallway that ended in a dead end at a metal security door with an electronic lock attached to it on the right wall. He reached into his front pocket, pulled out the key card and swiped it. Nothing. After rubbing the card on the front of his pants, he tried it again. Nothing. Not even a beep.

"Want me to try and hack it?" Jovita asked.

Sam smirked. "Not this time," he said. "Torrance. Give me some fire."

Torrance's eyes lit up with pure heat energy. Sam and Jovita stepped back as he fired a red hot plasma beam straight at the door and cut it into two symmetrical pieces. Sam charged the smoldering door like a bull and knocked both iron slabs down with his shoulder. They hit the floor with a heavy, echoing boom.

The three of them entered the next room. It was small, confined, and a complete mess. A bed big enough for only one person sat in the far corner with balled up wrinkled sheets strewn from one end to the other. There was an old wooden table covered in folders, papers, and a laptop. An unkempt bookcase leaned against the left wall, and there were maps and diagrams covering the one across from it.

Sam walked over to one of the maps, which showed all seven of Earth's continents joined together in one gigantic land mass. He looked it over while lightly running his hand across it. "This is Marcus Covey's place alright," he said.

"What makes you say that?" Jovita asked.

"Pangaea," Sam said. "Dad was always talking about it. Used to sit me down in his lab sometimes and tell me about all his theories and findings. This was the world before the First Cataclysm. Before the ice age. Most scientists call it prehistory. But there are records from the First Age. I've seen some of them. Dad used to say that Stone was the only other person in the world who knew as much about it as he did."

Jovita smiled as she dug through a file cabinet drawer, noticing the quiet excitement that possessed Sam whenever he talked about his father's work. She slid two thumb drives in her pocket as Torrance paced behind her, flipping through some crinkled, shoddily bound books with titles like *The Infinite Construct, Conversations With the Aelitar,* and *Undiscovered Mansions.*

"Yeah," Torrance said, unfolding a wrinkled sheet of paper. "We're definitely in the right place. Listen to this letter. Signed by Stone himself. 'Marcus, you must remember that in order for man to ascend, sacrifices must be made. Burn away your so-called morality, my friend, for once you make the great transition, you will regard all other humans as you would insects.' Ok. Dude's crazy."

Sam turned and looked all around the room at the scattered writings and hand drawn diagrams of strange machines that lay like mixed up pieces of an insane puzzle. "Jovita, Torrance," he said. "Let's start packing this up. We'll analyze it when we get home."

"We should start with the books," Torrance said to Jovita. "I'll get the collapsible crates from the jet and we'll..."

The entire room shook like an earthquake had hit it. Jovita lost her footing and fell against the table. Books spilled from their shelving. The laptop hit the floor, cracking its screen. Sam braced himself on the wall behind him as Torrance held onto the corroded sink next to the rattling bed.

Suddenly, the wall behind Sam ripped open, sending brick, wood, and insulation flying. Gray muscle-laden arms and slimy tentacles forced him to the floor, and Malignus roared as he focused his sixteen shiny black eyes on Sam's face. One of the monster's four arms raised itself, the gleaming claws on its hand poised to slice off Sam's head.

"Get off him!" Jovita screamed as she ran at Malignus. A new thick, wriggling tentacle sprouted from the malleable flesh on the thing's back and smashed her back to the floor. Sam got an arm free and punched Malignus in his mangled, tentacle-covered face. Another arm knocked his hand away and pinned Sam to the floor while saliva and fluid poured all over him.

Torrance clenched his fists and covered himself in a burning red aura. His eyes lit up with fire. "Alright," he said to Malignus. "Time for a little surgery." And as soon as he raised his hands to fire blazing crimson energy beams at the cancer beast, the ceiling exploded.

Damsel dropped into the room from the jagged hole above them. With lightning speed, she landed in a crouching position and stood into an uppercut that sent Torrance barreling through the roof and into the sky.

Then she turned her attention to Jovita who had just gotten back to her feet. With a sadistic grin, Damsel charged at her, fists lusting to punch a hole in her head. But Jovita pulled her pistol and fired repeatedly at the madwoman's trunk. Slick beige pellets splattered against Damsel's body, releasing a thick, sticky, sand colored substance that oozed and swelled all over her until she was fastened to the wall and floor with only half her face showing.

Across the room, Sam kicked Malignus off him and stood up. Before he could catch his breath, the monster was on him again, pressing him into the wall with an immovable grip. They traded crushing blows, each one shaking the entire house.

Jovita smiled at the furious she-brute pushing and pulling against the impossible adhesive trap she'd created. "That, my oafish friend, is a weaponized bonding agent," she said to Damsel. "It's been tested on freight trains, fighter jets, and tanks. So stop struggling you ugly..."

One of Damsel's fists punched free. "Crap," Jovita whispered. With gaping eyes, she watched Damsel pull, punch, kick, and snatch herself out of the polymer cocoon. Long strides carried her towards Jovita once more. She fired again. Damsel slapped the pellet away. It burst against a far wall as Jovita pulled the trigger again. Click. Nothing.

Damsel reached out, grabbed the gun and crushed it into pieces. "No powers, huh?" Damsel said to her. "You should watch the company you keep." Her left hand clamped shut around Jovita's throat, making her gasp for air as her shoulder blades hit the wall behind her. "Hmm," Damsel mused. "Kind of like drowning kittens."

Tumbling high above them, somewhere in the cloudless sky, Torrance regained consciousness, realized who'd hit him, and cursed angrily under his breath. Glowing red energy outlined his body as he zoomed back towards the house.

After two sets of Malignus' tentacles finished slinging him all over the room, Sam lay exhausted on the floor wrapped in tightening meaty appendages. While he pulled at the tendrils around his neck, he looked up at Jovita who was choking to death right before his eyes. "Vita," he struggled to say. "Hold on!"

And just as Malignus yanked Sam back to him, Torrance's energy bolt sliced through the house and torpedoed Damsel through the rock solid floor. Jovita dropped to her knees and gulped down all the air she could get. Torrance landed beside her and fired two more blasts from his fists that lopped off Malignus' tendrils. The man-cancer bellowed as he let go of Sam and backed away from Torrance.

Sam didn't waste a moment. As soon as he was free, he was on Malignus with fists and boots, breaking flesh and bone alike. The monster answered with a massive fist of his own to Sam's chest. Sam wheezed as a clawed hand palmed his face and closed over his head. "Vita!" he yelled. "Sky Piercer! Now!'

Torrance helped her up. "What?" she said as the room shook again. "No! I'm not leaving you here!"

Sam brought his elbow crashing down on Malignus' skull. "Just get in the air!" he barked.

She glanced over at Torrance, but his attention was focused on the hole he'd just created in the floor. And there was a rumbling under her boots. She turned and ran out of the room just as Damsel shot out of the pit. Torrance flared up and poured waves of burning energy at her. Damsel kept her head down and endured the onslaught, absorbing all of heat he threw at her. She laughed as her cape caught fire. "Ooooh, so warm," she said. "Look, Malignus. He's an energy manipulator just like dear old Mommy."

Torrance stopped. Malignus backhanded Sam and took another hard fist to his neck. Damsel tossed her cape away and started towards Torrance. Sam dropped to one knee and hung his head with blood streaming from his nose. "Torrance," he said between deep breaths. "Everything you've got. Right now."

Torrance fired a heated bolt at Damsel's knees that hammered her legs out from under her. "You're sure?" Torrance asked, watching her slowly get up.

Malignus slammed Sam's face into the floor. "Trust me. I'm sure," Sam said as Malignus hoisted him up by the throat. "I can handle it. Do it!"

With Damsel flying directly at him, Torrance let every bit of nuclear fire he felt inside him build to an unbearable crescendo. And then, swinging his arms out wide, he let it loose. The entire house exploded in a blinding column of fire and light.

Malignus' charred, smoking form rolled around in the debris, limbs blown off but steadily regenerating. The house was nothing but cinders, and the desert sun beamed down on the destruction. Stunned and barely conscious, Sam and Damsel stumbled around knee deep in rubble just a few yards from one another. Sam's head throbbed, his hearing was all but gone, and he strained to see through all the smoke.

But when the Sky Piercer swooped in overhead and landed beside him, he couldn't help but force a painful, sideways smile. The cockpit opened, and Jovita motioned for him to come aboard. Sam leaned limply against the plane and began to pull himself in when he saw panic on Jovita's face. "Sam, behind you!" she screamed.

Damsel grabbed Sam's shoulder with nothing but raging insanity coming out of her mouth as she crunched his flesh. Too spent to fight back, he ducked a clumsy punch that missed him and dented the plane. His knees buckled, and when he hit the ground, he rolled on his back. While Jovita yelled Sam's name, Damsel raised her leg, intending to bring her boot heel down on his face.

At that moment, Torrance skimmed the desert surface like a rocket and hurled three sun fire beams at her. They ripped up the ground and sent her bouncing across broken wood and stone. As Torrance zoomed back into the sky, Sam climbed into the jet and closed his eyes while Jovita flipped the buttons that closed the cockpit and detached the landing gear from the ground.

The Sky Piercer shot into the sky. Torrance flanked the plane on its left and flew close enough that he could see Jovita and Sam. He pressed his earpiece. "What the hell was that?" he asked.

Sam put a headset on and talked without opening his eyes. "Headhunters," he said in a raspy voice. "Contract hero killers. I...I thought they were only a rumor. But that was Damsel back there. Stone must've sent them."

"If he sent them after us, that means..."

"It means we better get home fast," Sam said.

On the ground, Damsel stood on her feet and watched the Sky Piercer soar away. With a menacing grumble, she leaped into the air, but waves of nausea and splitting headaches overcame her. She fell back to the ground and rested her head against the hot, scorched earth. Malignus lumbered over to her, picked her up in his remaining arms, and as his tentacles and secondary limbs reformed themselves, he uttered a thundering howl at the sky.

CHAPTER 13

It was lunchtime at the Sunstrom mansion, and for the kids that usually meant one thing: sandwiches by Maddie. Since the day they found out that their parents were dead, Maddie took it upon herself to make sure that the children kept up with their studies and maintained their basic routines in a deliberate effort to create a sense of normalcy for them. One of those routines was indulging in Maddie's sandwiches, which Douglas had often referred to as 'damn near perfect'.

Janesha and David sat on tall wooden stools at the black marble kitchen bar sipping their bottled fruit drinks as Maddie placed Janesha's steaming chicken Philly cheesesteak in front of her on a plate. With a hungry grin, Janesha picked up one half of the sandwich and let the creamy white cheese sauce drip onto her dish while she bit into the bread, chicken, and crunchy bacon. "Mmm," she hummed. "Thanks Mad."

David stared at the other half of her sandwich and swallowed. "Don't even think about it," Janesha warned with her mouth full.

"Be patient, David," Maddie said from over by the stovetop grill. "Your Panini is almost ready. Roast beef this time?"

David turned around on his stool and pouted a little. "Sure," he said, resting his face in his hands. Then, Janesha's juice bottle caught his attention, and he smiled. After finishing a bit of food, she reached for it. The bottle fizzled with red energy for a second, vanished, and reappeared on the opposite side of her plate.

Janesha rolled her eyes at him. "Don't do that again," she said just loud enough for him to hear.

"What?" he answered. "Didn't do anything."

Janesha went to grab her drink again, but it glowed again and instantly materialized on the other side of the bar. "I said stop," she demanded.

A mixture of both sigh and groan crossed Janesha's lips as she lifted her outstretched hand and commanded the bottle to zip back towards her. Before the drink could slap against her palm, her sandwich blinked out of existence and popped into David's hands with a bright red burst.

"David!" she yelled. The bottle dropped and shattered, spilling its orange liquid contents all over the bar and floor. David shut his eyes and placed Janesha's sandwich back on her plate. He could feel Maddie standing behind him, looking directly through him with that iron stare of hers.

"Turn around, young man," she instructed. David got off his stool and stood facing her. "We haven't raised a hooligan, have we?"

"No, Maddie," David said, lowering his eyes to the floor.

"Get a mop, a broom, and whatever else you need. But I want this mess cleaned up. Now."

"Yes, Maddie."

"And stop playing with your sister's food. If you want to practice with your powers, go outside or down to one of the basement levels."

"Yes, Maddie."

David crossed his eyes and stuck his tongue out at Janesha. She scowled back, balled up her fist, and mouthed silent threats at him. But as soon as Maddie plated David's Panini sandwich, the entire house went dark and blood red security lights flashed on. A serene female voice sounded all over the mansion. "Warning. Multiple potential threats located on the premises."

"Maddie?" David called, looking over at her.

She moved quickly over to the children and grabbed both of them by the hand. "Stay behind me," she said.

Suddenly, the ceiling above them splintered into thousands of pieces as a hot, golden flash ripped the roof apart. Dreadmettle's humming silver sphere dropped slowly through the gaping wound in the ceiling, carrying both Dreadmettle and the Bull behind it in a crackling yellow energy web. The sphere hissed whenever it turned or moved, pointing its largest oval shaped sensor like an eerily glowing eye in every direction.

Maddie glared at the three of them while standing in front of David and Janesha. "You're trespassing," she said. "Leave this house immediately or I will not be responsible for what happens to you."

The sphere turned its eye on Maddie and fired a zipping laser bolt at her that pierced her chest and came out her back. She slumped to the floor, and her eyes closed while David screamed.

With a desperate grunt, Janesha thrust both hands forward and pushed the sphere away from them using the telekinetic force welling up inside her. The sphere shot backwards, slapping Dreadmettle and the Bull to floor while obliterating an entire set of oak cabinets. She spread her fingers wider and picked David up into the air with a thought. For a second her scared eyes met with his, and she floated into the air before flying up the winding staircase with her little brother tethered behind her.

Dreadmettle stood and called his sphere to him, allowing the gleaming orb to circle him as he looked around the kitchen and peered into the next room from behind the silver helmet covering his face. "So this is the home of the fabled Sunstrom family," he said with a dark, mechanical voice. "I'm a little disappointed. I expected something a bit more...elaborate."

The Bull stepped over Maddie's still, lifeless body and walked past Dreadmettle to the stairs. He closed his fists, and long, sharpened blades erupted from his elbows with the sound of steel slicing against itself. "You're a dull, idiotic bastard, Dreadmettle," he said in a heavy Spanish accent. "Forget the damn house. Let's find these kids so we can gut'em and leave."

In Janesha's bedroom, she and David crouched down beside her bed and watched the closed, locked door, hoping that it wouldn't suddenly come crashing down.

David tugged on her arm. "They killed Maddie, Jan," he whispered with tears running down his cheeks.

Janesha grabbed both of his shoulders and looked him in the face, pretending to be calm and in control. "I know," she whispered back. "But I need you to concentrate so we can get out of here, ok? I need you to teleport us out."

David dropped his head. "I...I can't. I'm too...I'm too scared."

"Look. Yes you can. Just...just take a deep breath and you can take us to the heart of the city and we can call Sam somehow and..."

"I can't. I can't feel my powers. Can't even think. And I've never done more than one person before."

There was thump outside the bedroom door. Two of the half-painted automaton models she was always working on fell from one of her shelves and hit the carpet. And just as Janesha turned to tell David to hush, the Bull's boot caved the wooden door. He and Dreadmettle walked into the room as the robotic sphere hovered and shined its glowing eye down on the children.

Janesha stood up and positioned herself so that she was directly in front of David. She squared her shoulders and tightened her lips, giving the mercenaries the best show of courage and defiance she could muster. Dreadmettle gestured in Janesha's direction, and the sphere fired at her. "Get down!" Janesha yelled. David dropped to the floor as Janesha raised both hands, blocking the laser blast with ethereal telekinetic shielding. Her mind pulsed with radiant energy as the sphere spewed a continuous stream of laser fire at her. The mental energy surrounding her and David went from invisible to pink to fire red while the sphere's screaming attacks were deflected into the ceiling and walls, causing them to crumble away.

Janesha's shielding kept her and David safe from the piercing laser beams, but each time the sphere blasted at them, she felt the burning and cutting in the innermost parts of her mind. And Dreamettle's sphere was relentless, pouring more power, more malice into each new explosion. *God help me,* she thought, pushing her mind well past any limits she thought she had. She felt her shield's outer shell crack and fragment. A tear escaped her eye.

Downstairs in the kitchen, Maddie's eyes popped open and radiated with a dim red glow that grew brighter until her body sat up at a ninety-degree angle. "Rebooting security systems," she said with her head cocked to one side.

"Stop," Dreadmettle said, coldly. The sphere stopped firing and flew backwards until it was floating behind Dreadmettle's right shoulder. Janesha dropped to her knees, mentally and physically spent. Her arms fell so that her weakened fingers dragged the carpet, and blood trailed from her ears. David moved closer to her.

"Nice effort, princess," Bull said, brandishing the blades that protruded from his forearms. "But you're dealing with professionals. And we have heads to collect."

The Bull raised his blades and trained his eyes on Janesha's neck. Another laser blast sounded in the room, but this one ripped through the Bull's shoulder, sending him to the floor. He rolled on the floor, screaming while he held onto the seared hole in his arm.

Janesha and David gasped; Dreadmettle turned around and looked to the doorway to see Maddie standing there, her right arm reconfigured into a black, smoking canon with sleek flashing lights at the barrel. Wires hung from the wound in her chest, and a clear lubricant stained her clothes. "Ok, kids," she said, wincing. "I won't be able to do this alone."

Dreadmettle tackled Maddie to the hallway floor, shooting lasers at her from circular openings in his silver armored suit. He straddled her and began smashing her face with his fists over and over again. A thin hot laser ray sliced her cheek, revealing the glossy black metal underneath. Janesha flew at Dreadmettle, but just before she reached him, the sphere zipped into her path and blasted her out of the air. She felt her ribs crack when she hit the floor, but she was back on her feet as the sphere circled back around for the kill shot.

Janesha threw her fist and launched enough telekinetic energy to punch the sphere down the hallway and into Dreadmettle's head. The sphere bounced off his silvery helmet and smashed through the nearest wall. Dreadmettle shook his head, groggy from the unexpected blow.

Maddie pressed her cannon's barrel against his chasis and fired. The searing blast lit the hallway. Dreadmettle rolled and got up while his sphere rejoined him. He was trapped. Maddie on one side; Janesha on the other. "Come on then," he snarled.

In Janesha's bedroom, the Bull had David directly in his sights. "Janesha?" David called. "Maddie!"

The Bull chuckled as his blades reflected the ceiling lights. "No one to help you now, boy," he said. "Close your eyes. Makes it easier." He lunged at David with a rabid growl. David stepped back and threw both hands up to protect his face.

A red energy field appeared in front of the Bull, and he vanished inside it. The dazzling display folded in on itself and disappeared with a pop as David looked excitedly at his own hands. "I...I did it," he whispered.

David made it to the hallway just as Maddie's titanium alloy fist clanged against Dreadmettle's helmet. Standing in Janesha's bedroom doorway, he watched the gleaming sphere fire rapid laser bursts at his sister as she struggled to deflect them with the telekinetic shields she was throwing up as quickly as she could imagine them. For a second, her focus wavered, and one of the beams grazed her right side and scorched her flesh. Janesha clutched her hip and leaned against the hallway wall as she threw up her left hand and defected another blast.

Dreadmettle tightened his armored fists and formed a sickle blade of pure concentrated flame that chopped Maddie's mechanical right arm off underneath the shoulder. The metal limb thumped on the floor. Maddie front kicked Dreadmettle hard enough to send him backpedaling all the way to far end of the hall. As the sphere changed course and flew to Dreadmettle's aid, David ran over to Maddie and cringed watching her left arm shift, separate, and restructure itself into a smaller snub- nosed canon.

Limping and favoring her wounded side, Janesha backed away from Dreadmettle, joining Maddie and David as the cybernetic beast stood and readied himself. His sphere charged its own guns, hovering at Dreadmettle's shoulder like a flying, robotic attack dog. "If I fall," Maddie said quietly to the children, "promise me you'll take care of one another."

Janesha stopped her hands from shaking and forced them into solid fists. "Promise."

The house's security system sounded again. "Sunstrom Sky Piercer approaching," the voice said.

Maddie smiled. "Sam," she said to herself.

Without delay, the sphere turned its mechanical eye as if it had seen something. It barreled through the nearest wall and shot into the sky in a dusty explosion of pulverized brick. A moment was all it needed to scan the clouds for what it knew was coming. The Sky Piercer was headed straight for the Sunstrom Estate with Torrance flying at its side lit up like a human star. Torrance dropped out of the sky and blasted through a set of second story windows, burning through wall after wall until he was standing face to face with Dreadmettle.

Propelling itself at hundreds of miles an hour, the sphere zoomed to meet the jet and ripped through its left wing, sending the plane spiraling towards the house. Jovita's hands fumbled over the controls as jet spun uncontrollably and Sam's head bounced off the console. Finally, Jovita's thumb found and punched the correct button, and her entire seat ejected from the cockpit with her still in it.

Inside the mansion, Torrance attacked Dreadmettle without hesitation. Booming energy blasts leapt from his hands and impacted on Dreadmettle's steel hide with the force of several small bombs. Janesha flew past Torrance and into the air, pounding on Dreadmettle with heavy caliber mind blasts that cracked the floor underneath his silver boots. She gathered another swell of telekinetic energy and let it loose in waves. The section of floor beneath Dreadmettle gave way and disintegrated as he plummeted down into the lower parts of the house with a wild scream.

"Maddie," Sam said into Maddie's earpiece. "The plane's out of control. Get everyone as far underground as possible."

Maddie looked directly at David and forced him to focus on her eyes and voice. "I'm going to need you to get it together, David," she said to him. "The four of us have to get to the elevators. Right now."

Almost as soon as she'd said it, the Sky Piercer gutted the mansion's north -facing wing. Multiple fiery bursts swept through the entire structure, each one louder and larger than the last. The plane's cockpit detached from the wings that carved their way through the house like giant, spinning hatchets and planted itself upside down in one of the Sunstroms' garages, totally demolishing the vehicles as well as the room itself. The cockpit's clear shell popped open, and Sam fell out onto the stone floor. He moved slowly at first and spit blood from his mouth. But the fire raging all around him snapped him back to attention, and he realized that his parents' home was about to be destroyed.

Upstairs, Maddie led Torrance, David, and Janesha through a dark red hell of fire and smoke to the nearest set of elevators. As chunks of ceiling, walls, and floor erupted in flames and violent explosions, they protected one another as fervently as they would themselves. Maddie and Torrance blasted away at falling debris, and Janesha provided shielding from the inferno and any crumbling pieces they missed. She lifted giant wood beams with her mind and tossed them out of their path. Even David teleported flying metal plane fragments away as they moved.

Finally, they reached a set of elevator doors, but the keypad on the wall was completely melted. Maddie placed her one good hand on the elevator door and attempted to pry them open, but it wasn't necessary. "I've got it from here," Sam said from behind her. He dug his fingers in between the doors and forced them apart. "Inside, now," he said.

David got in first. Then, Torrance and Janesha followed. Sam and Maddie were the last to get in. "Helmsman Twelve," Sam said as he leaned against the wall. And when the doors shut, the elevator carrying what was left of the Sunstroms descended with a bullet's haste into plunging darkness as the world above them ruptured and ripped itself apart.

CHAPTER 14

The Bull fell out of a swirling red opening in the sky and dropped to the hard, cracked asphalt beneath him. An old, dingy tractor- trailer blared its horn and nearly careened off the road trying to miss him. A tire hit a pothole and splashed stinking, muddy rainwater in his face. He sheathed his blades and rolled off the road into tall weeds and grass, narrowly avoiding the dented up Japanese sedan that almost ran him down.

He walked uphill about a mile before he arrived at the closest town, and it was then that it started to rain. It was a hot, steaming rain that was just as bothersome as the intense, sickening sunlight flickering from in between the old stores and restaurants surrounding him. He hit his wrist communicator with his thumb and put it up to his mouth while wading through a crowd of Asian teenagers and reading the painted sign on the building next to him, which he could have sworn was written in Chomorro.

"Orb. This is the Bull," he said into his wrist device. "Requesting pick up, immediately. From…Guam, I think."

A decades old agreement between Douglas Sunstrom and Amica Bay stated that he and his wife would keep the city safe from super criminals, monsters, and mad science all the while providing it with clean, renewable energy and access to certain bits of Sunstrom technology. It was a deal that turned a small experimental city in Washington into one of the world's true scientific wonders. In exchange, Amica Bay would never interfere in family affairs. So, when the Sunstrom mansion blew up and lit the afternoon sky with twinkling orange embers, no one came to help.

Gray hulled security robots of all shapes and sizes swarmed over the estate spraying foam and water. It took over an hour to do, but they'd extinguished every trace of fire just as Douglas had programmed them. It was too late. The house had been reduced to a fragile, blackened skeleton, and only crispy, mangled supports stood as a reminder of the Sunstrom home.

Dreadmettle's sphere found its master lying unconscious in what used to be a dining room. It hovered over his soot covered armored body and projected an energy field which lifted it out of the brittle, ashen garbage. Dreadmettle's arms and legs hung as the sphere towed him into the sky and disappeared into the sun's glare.

On the lawn behind the smoking remains, Jovita groggily pushed herself off her belly and untangled herself from the opened parachute that was wrapped around her. She let the tears flow as she surveyed the destruction before her and covered her mouth with both hands. "Oh my God," she whispered. "They're all dead. Sam."

She sat on the grass with her knees pulled into her chest, thinking frantically of what to do next. Who should she call? Her father? The police? More heroes? Surely the Protectorate would send out a few operatives to help the Sunstroms. Just then, a metallic fist-sized ball swerved in front of her face and hovered just a hair from her forehead. Jovita's eyebrow lifted with curiosity. It scanned her with tiny red lasers, and when the lasers stopped she heard a familiar voice emanating from it. "It's definitely her," it said.

Jovita scrunched her nose. "David?" she said half smiling. "Is that you?"

"Ok. Make sure you've got a clear visual and bring her in," said another voice. "And remember. Breathe and take your time."

"Sam?" Jovita asked. At that moment, the air around her buzzed with red static, and before she could say anything else, she faded from reality.

Her eyes were cloudy, her hands and feet tingled, and she tasted fire-grilled ribs and strawberry candy in her mouth as she rematerialized in front of Sam and David. She checked and made sure all her limbs and fingers were in tact before taking a look at the base's massive interior. Sam walked up and hugged her, his Sapien Rex gear burned and nearly falling apart. David sat on a stool beside Janesha who had just changed into a gray halter top and tights.

Across the high ceilinged chamber, in the robotics shop, Maddie hung from a set of metallic supports. Her legs were missing and black wiring ran from her open chest cavity and abdomen all the way down to the polished floor. Torrance plugged a set of cables into a connector in her scalp and smiled at her as she accepted new data into her processing core.

"What is this place?" Jovita asked.

"We're miles underneath the house," Sam said. "Or what's left of it. Dad built this. For me. For us. He wanted us to be a team. Wanted me to lead."

Jovita walked away from Sam, crossed the floor panels imprinted with ancient cave paintings of the Sunstroms' ancestors, and looked around at the base's science labs, libraries, and shining new vehicles. "Wow," she said. "Always kept one eye on the future, didn't he?" She looked over at Maddie. "When were you planning to tell me she was an android? I mean… 'synthetic entity'. I'm so sorry."

"Android?" Maddie scoffed from across the room. "I'm the world's first Mechanical Assault and Defense Downloadable Intelligence Entity, my dear Vita."

"Dad built her," Sam said. "Harnessed an artificial intelligence he and Mom discovered and combined it with his automated security system. Gave her a prime directive to protect his children. I only found out the day we got home from Antartica. Even they didn't know until today."

He and Jovita walked across the gigantic Sunstrom 'S' symbol engraved in the floor. As he walked past Janesha and David, he slapped David playfully in the middle of his chest. "Heard you two held your own today," he said. "Good job." David tried to act as if his chest wasn't stinging and smiled up at him. "You gonna be alright, Nesha?" Sam asked, stopping to look at her.

"Ready for another round," Janesha said, knocking David's hand away from her bandages.

Torrance walked up to Sam and Jovita. "Glad to see you're okay, Jovita," he said. "Sam, I started the uploads on Maddie. She ought to be ready to begin self-repair in a day or so. Sorry. It's a lot of data."

Sam lightly pounded his brother's shoulder with his knuckles and walked over to Maddie. "I hate that you have to see me like this," she said. "I feel so...useless. I should be out there... with you. It's what I was created to do."

Sam checked the digital readouts surrounding the robotics lab. "You've done more than anyone could expect, Mad," he said. "I have to shut you down for repairs now. We're going to need you as soon as you get on your feet."

Maddie's eyes narrowed. "You know," she said, "if I was a malevolent synthetic intelligence, this would be the part where I refuse to be shut down and start taking over the world."

Sam blinked and gave Maddie a worried glance. Jovita put her hand on his shoulder. "She's only joking, Sam," she said.

Sam allowed a questioning smile to come through. "Yeah?"

"I'm joking, Sam Sunstrom. Your father would have laughed out loud at that one. Before you put me into sleep mode, care to let me in on your next move?"

Sam looked straight ahead, eyes full of resolve. "My next move?" he asked. "Something Dad once made me promise never to do. I'm meeting with Julian in the morning."

As the color faded from Maddie's eyes, he walked away from her and endured his siblings' confused stares on his way to the door with the engraved nameplate that read *S. Sunstrom*. The door split down the middle and slid away, allowing Sam access to his personal quarters. And while Jovita and the rest of the Sunstroms slowly returned to familiarizing themselves with their new home, Janesha's world had just been stripped and peeled away. She stood still in the middle of the floor, haunted by the name Sam had just spoken. Julian.

CHAPTER 15

Amica Bay to Seattle was a three-hour drive, so Sam got up before dawn, charged one of the vehicles his dad left for him in one of the new base's hangars, and made the trip in less than two. The Agatha Bell Center for Specialized Medicine was a huge white four-story facility with rich green lawns, parks and tediously groomed nature trails for walking. As a light, misting rain drizzled from the morning sky, Sam got out of his smoothly contoured SUV wearing a burgundy polo shirt and jeans and walked through the main building's sliding double doors with a clear umbrella in one hand and a cluster of folders in the other.

He could feel the eyes of the doctors, nurses, and custodial staff on him as he moved briskly to the welcome station, navigating the scurrying employees who all wore some variation of Agatha Bell's white and gray uniform. Even those staff members who pretended not to notice the celebrity in their midst were conspicuous in their attempts to appear oblivious. When Sam arrived at the circular service desk, the slim, round-faced office assistant sitting behind it gave him a broad smile and handed him a clipboard so he could sign in.

"How may I help you today, sir?" she inquired in a practiced, chipper tone.

"Morning," said Sam. "I'm Sam Sunstrom. I scheduled an appointment with Dr. Weisz last night. I'm sure she's notified you. I'm visiting a patient. Julian Sunstrom?"

The intern typed dutifully for several seconds on her white keyboard and then swiped her fingers across the flat touchscreen monitor in front of her. "Ok," she chirped. "Samuel Sunstrom. I'll need to see some ID."

"Oh, that won't be necessary," said a friendly, grizzled voice just as Sam reached for his wallet. Dr. Margaret Weisz walked up behind Sam and gently placed her weathered, manicured hand on his back. The stocky, red-haired fifty-six year old smiled at Sam and rubbed his arm like a mother would. "You don't ask one of Douglas Sunstrom's boys for ID," she said. "She's new. You're the oldest, aren't you?"

"Yes, ma'am," Sam answered.

"Here to see Julian?"

"Yes. I need to speak with him. It's...urgent."

Weisz leaned closer to him and whispered in his ear. "It's been all over the news, Sam," she said. "Your parents. The house. All of it. I knew Douglas and Zoa well. Is there anything we can do to help your family?"

Sam noticed the muted television on the wall behind the counter. The news broadcast was airing video of the Sunstrom Mansion explosion for the third time this morning, and a so-called expert on superhuman psychology was nearly a minute into his talking points. "No. Just let me see my brother," he said.

"Well. Follow me. He's been doing surprisingly well if you weren't aware."

Sam walked with Weisz down quiet white hallways, across enclosed glass bridges, and into colorless offices where star- struck doctors eagerly shook his hand and welcomed him to Agatha Bell. All the while, Weisz talked incessantly, seeking to impress Sam with her extensive knowledge of the superhero world. He nodded or feigned interest whenever she used words like 'speedster' or "healing factor" or brought up one of his parents' old exploits.

Eventually, Sam found himself seated at a round table in an empty cafeteria that smelled like lemon scented cleaning fluid. He thumped his fingers in a rhythmic pattern on the folders he'd brought as he waited in silence surrounded by plain white soulless walls. And just when he thought he'd have to wait forever, he heard Weisz's clunky, leaden wedge heels echoing on the freshly buffed floor tiles.

Sam looked up from his folders and watched Julian – tall, lanky, and very much a young man – walk past Weisz and over to his table dressed in a white short- sleeved medical tunic, matching pants and generic gray sneakers. Weisz put her hands on Julian's shoulders as he sat in front of Sam. "I'll leave you two alone," she said. "Just give us a call if you need anything."

Sam nodded in her direction, and the doctor marched out of the cafeteria. Julian leaned back in the chair and studied the older brother he hadn't seen in years. "Well," he said with the sweet smile Sam remembered. "If it isn't the great and powerful Sam Sunstrom."

"We've missed you, Julian."

"Oh, I think you guys have gotten along just fine without me. But I've missed all of you as well."

"I think I should start by telling you…"

"About Mom? And Dad? I know all about it. It's all they talk about in here. This is a mental institution for magnipotents, you know. That sort of thing gets everyone's attention in a place like this."

A tear dropped from Julian's eye as he looked at the table. "I refused to believe it at first," he half whispered. "I suppose when you're a child…you think your parents are invincible. You have this…fantasy in your head. As if the universe's rules don't apply to them. You're the first person I've talked to about it, though. Wouldn't know what to say to anyone else."

"Julian," Sam said. "I have to say…I tried to get Dad to come see about you. But…he was adamant… he wouldn't even let us…"

Julian let a smile through his tears. "Dad came to see me once a week, Sam."

"What? He never said anything."

"You have to understand. What I did that day terrified him. He didn't want to risk any of you being…infected with my madness. Especially Nesha. How is she?"

"She's well. Considering her parents were just murdered and she's been targeted by super assassins. What about you? Are you..."

"Say, it, Sam. Am I well? As a matter of fact, I am. The rounds of medication and subsequent surgery went better than expected." Julian pointed to his forehead. "The psionic organ in my frontal lobe has been dormant for years. The doctors believe my powers actually caused the psychotic episodes. I haven't had one since that day. No powers, no crazy. Now I know you didn't come all the way here to ask for a progress report, Sam. What do you want from me?"

Sam opened the folders and spread a series of diagrams and photos all over the table. "Honestly," he said. "I need some information."

Julian picked up page after page, arranged them in a suitable order, and flipped through them. Sam watched him and could tell by looking at his eyes that he recognized what he was seeing. And after minutes of shuffling through the papers, Julian looked up at Sam with concern written all over his face. "I must say, big brother," he said, "you are in a universe of trouble."

He laid the penciled diagrams down end to end until they formed a picture of a single machine. Its design was as simple as it was perfect. A massive circle of braided metal planted on top of a wide pyramid shaped base. Monstrous coils plunged deep into the ground. There were notes scribbled in ink on each page.

"This is Dad's stuff," Julian said.

"How do you know that?"

"After Mali, you lost interest in the work, and Dad lost his successor-in-training. He realized that I had a mind for science and started teaching me to do your job. Even after my ... last episode, he would come here and keep me abreast of what he was doing. Get my feedback on it. This is one of the blueprints he discovered. He called it a Window."

"This is related to Pangaea isn't it?"

"Isn't everything when it comes to him? Dad believed the Pangeans were using these things to travel beyond Earth. He wanted to build one to help Mom visit her home world. But the energy problem stopped him. He told me that he'd decided to scrap it before he even started building it."

"Energy problem."

"The energy required to take one trip through the Window made it too dangerous."

'Dangerous to who? Dad?'

"Oh, no. If someone were to utilize this kind of technology in its current configuration, it would allow an individual or small group access to other worlds with minimal danger to the traveller. But the energy overflow would decimate most life on Earth."

"Bastard."

"Excuse me?"

"Isaiah Stone. He's planning to use something very much like this. And he wants us all dead so that we can't stop him."

"Sound reasoning. Together, Mom and Dad were his biggest threat, right? So he got to them first. Probably did it himself."

"How much do you really know about this Window tech, Julian?"

"Everything."

"If I could get you to it, do you think you could shut a machine like this down? Dismantle it?"

Julian's eyes came alive. "Sam Sunstrom," he said, "are you asking me to go on an adventure with you?"

"I'm asking you to help me take down the man who killed our parents. And maybe save the planet while you're at it."

"You do realize that would mean getting me released from this place, don't you?"

Sam leaned back in his chair. "Let me worry about that part," he said.

"No," said Dr. Okeke in his clipped Nigerian accent. "In light of that family's recent tragedies, Julian Sunstrom is better off here with us. I do not see how it would benefit anyone to release him into such a chaotic environment."

An aging dark-skinned man, Okeke clasped his hands together at the head of the large, rectangular meeting table, his salt and pepper twists trailing down the back of his neck. Weisz and Sam sat beside one another directly across from him. Stirring her coffee with a thin white straw, Dr. Costa sat on Okeke's right side, and the bleached blonde, perfectly tanned Drs. Marcus and Vanessa Stuart sat together on his left.

Sam stood up and pressed his fingertips on the table. "But according to your own documentation, and I quote, 'the subject's destructive alternate personality has vanished along with his psionic abilities'. He hasn't had an episode since the procedures."

Dr. Costa smiled in an attempt to ease the tension. "It's true your brother's mental condition has stabilized," she said with a Spanish inflection. "But I must agree with my colleague. Julian is not ready for the world outside these walls. Especially taking into consideration the added stress of your family's current situation."

"This is pretty ridiculous," Weisz said. "We have no reason to hold this young man any longer. All this...this fear I'm hearing is totally unfounded."

Marcus Stuart leaned forward. "Dr. Weisz, answer this," he said. "Do you remember what he did the last time this 'alternate personality' of his surfaced? The only reason he's here and not in a prison facility is because he has famous parents. Plain and simple. Can we ever be one hundred percent sure that it will never happen again?"

"He'll be my responsibility," Sam said. "I'll take care of him."

"Here's the thing," Weisz said. "Everyone here in this room is senior staff, and according to the Agatha Bell Charter, the five of us can put this to a vote. So I say let's settle this here and now and be done with it. Once and for all."

The room went silent. Sam sat back in his chair, eyeing the doctors seated around him.

Okeke stood up and looked directly at Sam. "Alright, I'll start," he said. "I say hell no. Julian Sunstrom stays here."

Julian's room was always the neatest of all the patients. There wasn't a thing out of place or a speck of dust anywhere in the relatively small living space. He sat on his immaculately made bed in front of a wooden dresser with his shoulders hunched over, holding an old family photo in his hands. He looked at the smiles on everyone's faces and let his tears hit the photograph as he remembered the closeness he once shared with his parents, brothers, and his sister.

But there were other memories. He could still feel the wind on his face as he stood on the roof of his dad's new skyscraper in downtown Amica Bay. The psychic energy twisting and rippling throughout his mind and body that day was dizzying. Maddening. It felt as if he could split the world in half with a mere snap of his fingers. He could still hear his own ten-year old voice crackling in his ears like electricity, threatening to bring the building down, killing everyone inside. What happened next had always been an incoherent blur of screams, fists, and explosions, but he would never forget his dad locking the white, hard plastic dampening helmet in place over his head and face, allowing men in Agatha Bell jackets to take him away from his home in the middle of the night while his mother fell apart.

"Forgive me, Mom," Julian whispered, still staring at the photo. "Dad. If I ever disappointed you."

His room door slid open and Sam walked inside. Julian looked up and wiped the tears from his eyes. "It was good to see you today, Sam," Julian said. "If there's anything else I can do to assist..."

"Pack your clothes," Sam said. "You're going home."

"What?"

Weisz walked through the door with a smirk on her face. "It was a close vote," she said. "But you, my dear Julian, are free to leave." Julian stood up and zoned out, looking wide eyed at the both of them.

It took a few hours to pack all of his clothes and other belongings, but after saying goodbye to a few friends he'd made over the years, Julian headed out to the parking lot with Sam. It was still raining, but instead of ducking his head and following Sam, Julian stopped still and turned his face towards the sky, letting the rainwater sprinkle all over his face.

Sam pointed to his SUV. "The truck's over here," he said. Julian didn't answer; Sam turned around and walked back over to him. He'd dropped his bags and stood breathing in the air, enjoying the rain.

"Is everything alright, Julian?" Sam asked. As soon as he'd said it, Julian wrapped his arms around him and hugged him close.

"Thank you, Sam," he said into his big brother's ear, voice quivering. "Thank you so much."

CHAPTER 16

David had been wide-awake since Sam left for Seattle. While the others slept in their rooms, he was teleporting all over the base, playing with the computers, and exploring the vehicles. A half hour behind the wheel of a crimson sports car, revving the engine. A couple more hours in the bright red family plane that sat on the landing platform. But he spent the most time sitting with Maddie, staring up at her closed eyes, talking to her lifeless face, wishing she'd say something. Periodically, he'd look past the cables spilling out of her separated steel torso and watch the flat screen diagnostic monitor mounted beside her. *Consciousness Upgrade 12%. 243 Hours Remaining.*

And just when he slumped his shoulders and sighed, the main doors slid open and in walked Sam and Julian. It took less than a minute for David to recognize Julian's face, and when he did, he zipped over to him in a red flash and hugged him, laughing and yelling all the while. Soon, Jovita, Torrance, and Janesha came out of their rooms to see what all the noise was about. The siblings exchanged tight, heartfelt embraces as they reunited for the first time in nearly a decade; there were even a few joyful tears. Jovita introduced herself and shook Julian's hand. Sam stood back and watched, smiling with his arms folded. But as he looked on, he noticed Janesha gradually moving away from the group, holding her arms as if she'd felt a cold draft.

Julian noticed it too. "Nesha," he said, reaching out for her. "What's the matter?"

She forced a cautious smile onto her face as she turned away from him. "It's nothing," she said, walking back towards her room. "It's...good to see you Julian. I'm glad you're home."

As her room door shut behind her, Sam put his arm around Julian and spoke so only he could hear. "She's just a little shaken up," Sam said. "You guys have a special bond that I admit I never really understood. Don't think Mom and Dad did either. When you get a chance, talk to her. Find out how she's feeling. I think she'll open up."

"I...I didn't mean to cause a problem," Julian mumbled.

"You didn't," Torrance assured him with a pat on the back. "It's just that she thought she'd never see you again. And here you are. Give her some time, man."

Julian looked solemnly at his twin's closed room door and then shot a childish grin in Torrance's direction. "So tell me about the model and this pop singer I keep hearing about. The same time? Really?"

Sam walked past David and over to Jovita, handing her a black thumb drive. "He wishes that were true," he said.

"Never mind Sam," Torrance said. "Keep hatin' on little bro. Jules, I'll introduce you to Princess Mirage the next time she invites me up to her studio."

"Oh, God," Jovita groaned from in front of a computer monitor. "Can we get to work please?"

David snickered and teleported into a rolling swivel chair.

"Go ahead and pull up the files," Sam answered. "Overlay them and project in the observation chamber."

Julian followed Sam into a small, dark room shaped like an octagon. The entrance way closed itself off with a hushed swishing sound, and the floor's perimeter lit up with tiny circles. Then, the area hummed to life as the ambient light in the room swirled around them until it formed a fully immersive map of stars, moons, and planets. Sam and Julian now stood in the center of a virtual universe observing the infinite number of worlds made of solid light particles. "It's been so long since I've seen this," Julian laughed.

"It's a three-dimensional interpretation of Stone's drawings," Sam said.

"The Unified Continuum. Dad created a digital model just like it years ago."

"Continuum."

"Yeah. For a long time – since the nineteen sixties - most astrophysicists believed in what they called the parallel realities. You know, a system of alternate universes and parallel worlds. Unlimited Earths. Infinite possibilities. You're probably the world's greatest underwater jazz pianist on Earth number three hundred and twenty-nine. Or maybe we're all fictional characters in a book on that particular world."

Sam chuckled. "So how is this Unified Continuum different?"

"Infinite Construct theory combines all realities into one master system. Earth three hundred whatever exists but not in another reality. It's in this one. Theoretically, we wouldn't even need to invent time travel to see the future of our world. We just need a means to get there." Julian pointed to a planet all the way across the room.

"Hmm," Sam pondered. "If you travel far enough within the construct itself, you eventually encounter the past, the future, alternate versions of yourself. Humans just lack the means to eliminate the distance."

"Or at least we did," Julian said. "Jovita, can you dump all the Pangaea stuff in here please?"

The Continuum disappeared from the room, and in its place was a giant digitized land mass. Sam recognized the interlocking continents with their rivers and mountain ranges that stretched halfway across the world. He'd been studying this map with his dad since he was a toddler. "Dad's great white whale," he said under his breath.

"Yes, he did love his Pangaea," Julian said. "But you have to understand why to appreciate it." He reached out and touched a glowing circular blip floating in front of him, and a hologram depicting fragments of an ancient stone tablet appeared. Julian pulled his fingers together and watched the pieces join into the perfectly carved image of a Window Machine.

"Just like Covey's blueprints," Sam said.

"Dad was convinced that the prehistoric humans who lived here were these super demigods and builders and scientists," Julian said. "The first superheroes. The original adventurers."

"You should read his Adventure Logs in the library," Sam said. "A lot of the missions in there involve looking for lost artifacts and technology from that first age. Or trying to stop Stone from getting to them first. So… I'm guessing you're going to tell me that the Pangaeans built the first Windows."

"Bingo. Where we struggle to get past the moon, these people came into contact with worlds and beings we can't even imagine." Julian pointed to the machine's giant round opening hovering over its pyramid base. "Just by walking through there. The tachyon membrane."

"Liquefied time particles. Stone must've built one of these things," Sam said. "Or he's in the process. You said that using it would destroy everything."

"One thing that the blueprints don't duplicate is the original energy source. Not even Dad figured how to recreate it. The only other option is to pull geothermal energy from Earth's core, which would destabilize the core itself. At that point, you're talking earthquakes, volcanic eruptions, poisonous gasses, the overall rupturing of the planet's mantle and crust. Do I need to continue?"

"No. Everyone dies if Stone uses the machine. Think I got that."

Sam stood silently for a moment and looked at the holographic tablet again. "You said you could stop it," he said.

Julian crouched down and thought to himself before looking up at Sam. "There's a kill switch," he said finally. "A cog about the size of a compact car that Dad would build into all of his big machines as a failsafe in case they fell into the wrong hands. He always built it first. Before the rest of the project was completed."

"But he decided not to build the Window at all," Sam interjected.

"After he'd built the kill switch and put it away."

"Where is it now?"

"Dad kept all his special projects in a secret base in the Atlas Mountains. Mom didn't even know about that place."

"Looks like we've got our next field trip."

Julian smiled. "It does, doesn't it?"

The ocean waves rolling up and splashing on Egremni Beach were the bluest and clearest Osiria had ever seen in person. With her white, strapless sundress blowing in the warm, gentle breeze, she held Stone's coarse hand as the two of them walked barefooted up the long stretch of soft, golden sand. Stone's stark white hair was in a long ponytail, and he wore an unbuttoned peach shirt and shorts. The Bull walked several yards behind them in a hat and swimming trunks, talking quietly on his cellphone but monitoring their surroundings at the same time.

Stone stopped and stared out at the water while Osiria turned her face to the sun and searched the clouds. "Never thought I'd ever come back to Greece," she mused. "You do realize that she's up there somewhere watching us don't you?"

"As were her instructions," Stone answered. "Security will always be of utmost importance until the very end. I like to have eyes everywhere. Damsel does as she's told. She's a good soldier. A long time ago, when I realized that my career was going to put me in direct and constant conflict with Douglas and his wife, I think part of me started looking for my own super companion."

"You wanted a Zoa Sunstrom of your own."

"Now that I look back on it, I probably did. I'm willing to admit that I fell into the 'supervillain' mentality and became obsessed with being my enemy's opposite number for a time. But during that period of my life, she was the best partner I could have asked for."

"If she's so valuable, she would have returned to you with Sam Sunstrom's head in her hands."

Stone smiled and pointed to his ear. "Careful, Osiria," he joked. "She has enhanced hearing you know."

"I hope that's not supposed to scare me."

"I wouldn't dare insinuate anything of the sort. You've proven yourself quite fearless over the last few weeks. Tell me. How is it that you remain so eager to see my plan through to fruition, knowing that I am preparing to kill every man, woman, and child on this planet?"

"I am a woman who understands necessity," Osiria said coldly. She and Stone began walking again.

"You ever hear of the London Makabrays?" she continued. "No, you probably haven't since I'm the last of us. When every member of your family possesses the ability to murder with a single touch, you tend to end up on all kinds of government watch lists. They used us and then wiped us out like a bunch of stray dogs. Hunted us down one by one. I was too young to fully understand what was happening, but I ran. Maybe they couldn't find me, maybe they thought I'd just die out there on my own. Can you imagine a five-year-old living alone in warehouses and condemned buildings? Making meals out of whatever vermin scurried across my path?"

"I'm... sorry you had to experience that, Osiria."

"I'm not. It taught me how to survive. Taught me how this world operates. It deceives you by appearing to be made up of all these unrelated systems, but there is only one. And it is designed for one purpose. To ensure that the privileged maintain their place in this unnatural, upside down hierarchy they've created."

"The so-called elite," Stone said. "They consume our souls after they've used and discarded our flesh. Warp our minds so that we freely offer it to them. That's how they survive. How they rule."

"And of course, they've got their 'superheroes' to make sure their corrupt, bloated governments don't crumble under their own weight."

"Precisely why I put together the Headhunter Association in the first place. The world needs balance. Sad thing is the average person is too brainwashed to understand the magnitude of what is happening right in front of their faces."

"Or she just refuses to acknowledge that underneath its colorful, sugar-coated shell, the sweet piece of candy she's spent her entire life coveting is really full of rotten garbage. It's time for a change, Isaiah. I've been everything from a thief and prostitute to the pampered wife of a premiere uber criminal. I've seen and heard it all. Sat mere breaths away from the most powerful men in the world. And I can't wait to watch this planet drown in smoke and magma."

Stone grabbed Osiria's hand and smiled at her as a flock of gulls scattered out of their path. With a wave of her thin fingers, Osiria sent out an invisible death wave and sent two of the birds spiraling back to the ground as she licked her lips like someone who'd just tasted something utterly delicious.

"You are an amazing woman," Stone said. "I would be honored to begin a new and better world with you."

"I was reading the journals you gave me last night. These...white chambers you write about. Real or metaphor?"

"The Pangaeans certainly believed they are real. Incredibly large white control rooms just on the other side of the tachyon membrane. The home of angelic beings who will allow us access to any world we choose."

Osiria pulled Stone close and kissed him tenderly on the lips. "We'll find an untouched, virgin world," she said. "We'll be gods there. Our children will be the Continuum's newest pantheon. And this failed, worthless place will be nothing but forgotten ashes crumbling on the backside of the cosmos."

Stone returned her kiss and ran his fingers through her dreadlocks while sunlight sparkled on the ocean surface like liquid diamonds.

CHAPTER 17

The air still smelled of smoke and ash at the Sunstrom Estate. Most of the debris from the fire had long since been removed from the grounds by Sam's robots, but now the mansion's absence was a constant reminder of the two people who couldn't be redesigned or reconstructed. Douglas and Zoa Sunstrom were never coming back.

That thought alone made Janesha want to scream into the heavens, use that overwhelming swell of telekinetic fury boiling over inside her to split the charred, fragmented basketball court in half or rip the ash laden pool out of the ground. But none of that would do any good, so she simply wiped her tears with the back of her hand and sat on the wet grass in her gold and black adventure suit. She crossed her ankles as she stared out at the burnt landscape that used to be her home.

Soft footsteps approached her from behind, but she didn't turn around. She flicked a tiny, scuttling bug off her shiny black boot and leaned back on her hands as Julian sat down beside her, wearing his own burgundy and gray uniform.

"Hi there," Julian said.

"Um...hi."

"This is a lot. Isn't it?"

"Too much. Look at us. Suited up as if we're anything like Mom and Dad. Assassins after us."

"Our nanny's been a robot. All this time. That's just...bizarre, isn't it? I know. This is beyond crazy. But I'm sure we'll come out of it alright. Sam will make certain that..."

"Sam doesn't even want to be here. He's gone once he's done with Stone. He never wanted to be here. We'll all have to just figure out what to do individually when it's over, I guess. If we don't get ourselves killed first. And I can handle that. I have to."

"I think you're wrong about Sam. He's going be a great leader for this family one day. Even if he doesn't see it just yet."

"I...I'm sorry about walking away from you earlier. Didn't really have...the words, you know?"

"Yes, I know exactly what you mean."

The two of them exhaled simultaneously, and Julian placed his hand on top of hers just as he would do when they were kids.

"I can still remember it, Julian," Janesha said after thinking about it. "Before the thing happened with you and Dad. Before they sent you away. We were playing over by that tree. And you told me to hold your hand."

"You never told me what you saw that day. You just ran in the house and refused to say anything."

"What did I see?" Janesha asked, shaking her head as once buried memories resurfaced. "Everything. I saw...heard...it was like every thought in the world was trying to crawl into my brain all at once. Like bugs."

"Well not every thought," Julian laughed. "But close enough."

"I'll never forget that. The people were...well so many of them...so ugly inside. It was...horrifying. And you. Your mind...it was...I've never felt that kind of hate before. That kind of fear. Is that what your power is like?"

"Honestly, I don't have a 'power' anymore."

"What?"

"They sort of...cut it out of me. To help me get better. But yes, I was once able to read minds, see others people's thoughts... ideas. I read more than a few medical journals at Agatha Bell, and there are actual documented cases of twin magnipotents who can actually share abilities. I think maybe you were able to access my telepathy by touching me."

"So...if you hadn't lost your powers... we might've been able to share our own little thought space. A psychic conference call." Janesha threw her head back and snickered with her hand over her mouth.

"What is it?"

"Can't you just see all the trouble we could've gotten into with that? Torrance would've absolutely hated us!"

"Yes. I can see him right now with that half-crazed look on his face. Smoke literally coming out his ears."

The two of them looked at one another and exchanged laughter as if they were seven years old again. Then, Julian stood up and reached down to help Janesha to her feet. "Sam tells me you've gotten stronger," he said. "Can I see?"

Janesha's smile darkened, and her demeanor became slightly roguish as she lifted her entire body into the air until Julian was looking up at her. Suddenly, far across the estate, what was left of the basketball court tore itself apart, sending a ripple of concrete slabs into the sky. "Oh yeah," she said. "You've missed a lot."

Julian applauded.

Each rounded, cushioned chair in the Sunstrom base's conference room had been embroidered across the back with a different child's name. Dressed in their adventure suits, Sam and Torrance sat in white chairs, facing one another so that the three green tinted holograms in the room's center could address each of them as well as one another. Jovita crossed her legs in an unmarked guest chair next to Sam.

It had been discussed before the three of them walked into the room for this meeting, but remaining loose and calm was a tall order especially when the President of the United States, the king of superheroes, and the family's media relations specialist were flickering in front of them, each one looking more displeased than the next. Still, Sam's words echoed in their minds as the meeting began. 'Act like you've done this before'.

Messian Spacefarer's grand image glimmered inside the sparkling emerald light beam cascading down from the projector embedded in the ceiling. He wore elegant blue and white armor sculpted to mimic his tall, muscular frame. A long white cape flowed down his back and disappeared somewhere within the moving digital picture.

President Michelle Bridgers was a wispy brown-haired woman who looked as if her second term had pushed her well into her sixties before her time. She sat behind her desk and folded her hands in front of a weary frown as Sam continued speaking.

"Madame President," he persisted. "We have everything under control here. I know it hasn't exactly seemed like it, but..."

"Under control?" Bridgers scoffed. "Young man. Sam is it?"

"Yes, ma'am."

"This is so far beyond 'under control'. Douglas and Zoa Sunstrom. Have. Been. Murdered. And not only that. I have a mansion full of superhumans exploding on all the cable news networks in the middle of the afternoon."

Whitney Priest's hologram stepped forward in her business suit and heels, holding her glasses in her right hand while the fingers on her left hand touched her blonde ponytail. "And that's why I'm here," she said. "We can fix this issue in two to three days if you let me get to work. Now. If we're going to repair the family image, you'll be open to doing the interviews I've been setting up for you all over the last few days. I've prepared several statements as well."

"The Sunstrom family will not be doing any interviews," Jovita said with a bit of animosity. "This is a highly sensitive situation, and we prefer that it remain a private one."

"Why is your girlfriend talking to me?" Whitney snapped at Sam. "I only agreed to this meeting because I thought I was going to be speaking with you."

Sam smirked. "Jovita Vargas has been officially authorized to make decisions regarding media relations, so continue speaking with her in regards to interviews and cameras and all other such nonsense," he said. "I could care less about any of it."

Priest crossed her arms and exhaled loudly. "So why the hell are we gathered here?" she asked.

Torrance slid forward in his chair. "To let everyone here know that the Sunstrom family will handle anything related to our parents' deaths and the destruction of this house," he said.

"I tire of this hero crap," Bridgers said. "I really do. If you people didn't save the planet every other Tuesday, I'd have you all locked away for the rest of unnatural lives."

"Go ahead," Jovita said. "Tell us how you feel. Don't hold anything back."

"Do not screw with me, child. And just so you all know, you are not to engage Isaiah Stone for any reason. The agreement Douglas and I had concerning his operations certainly doesn't extend to you. I will not tolerate some revenge-fueled superhuman war involving you petulant children happening on my watch. I have my own people. We'll find him."

"No, you won't," Sam said. "It's Isaiah Stone. He won't be found unless he wants to be. And when he wants to be, it'll be too late."

"Be that as it may. Just remember what I said, Sunstrom," Bridgers said as her image disappeared.

Torrance leaned back in his seat. "Looks like you just pissed off the President of the United States," he said.

Priest's hologram faded away while she cursed and mumbled something under her breath. And only Messian's hologram remained. He stared at Sam with intense gray eyes, virtually ignoring Jovita and Torrance.

"You do realize that you're going to get your family killed if you continue with this reckless course of action," he said.

"And what would you have me do instead of finding my parents' killer?" Sam asked.

"The Protectorate held your mother and father in high esteem, Sam. I have Jabril and Opticon on standby. They are ready to provide security for you and your siblings while you rebuild and plan your new lives. I am prepared to lead the search for Isaiah Stone and his surrogates myself."

Sam traded glances with both Torrance and Jovita before speaking again. "With all due respect, Messian," he said. "That won't be necessary. Family business."

"Don't delude yourself, boy. You are no hero."

"I'll pretend I didn't hear that as I am invoking Protectorate Law. Book Three. Red Appendix. 'A hero of the Protectorate shall not interfere in another hero's personal affairs or previously agreed upon jurisdiction unless such aid is formally requested.' I believe Messian Crestlord wrote that one during his one hundred year sabbatical. Sir."

"Your knowledge is impressive, Sam," Messian said with a light smile. "I hope it's not too late when you discover the unspeakably wide gulf that exists between knowledge and wisdom." Then, his face grew cold and serious. "As you wish, Sam. You are on your own." He turned his back and walked away while his image faded into nothingness.

"Did we really just do that?" Torrance whispered.

Jovita looked over at Sam who was hunched over and brooding.

"Yes, Torrance," Sam said. "We just told the only people who can help us to go to hell. But I refuse to have the government or Messian Spacefarer for that matter involving themselves in Sunstrom business. Spacefarer was right about one thing, though. We're not heroes."

"You speak for yourself, man," Torrance said, standing and looking over his white, gold-trimmed adventure suit. "Can't you see it? We're Sunstrom 2.0. Next generation adventurers!"

"You always were delusional," Sam said, rolling his eyes.

Torrance furrowed his brow, and his eyes glowed hot as he moved closer to Sam with his fists clenched. "And you've always been negative as hell. I'm sick of listening to it."

Jovita stepped between them. "Guys? This is a bit counterproductive don't you think?"

Sam looked past her and glared at his brother. "Look, if you want to be some costumed hero, fine," he said. "Join up with Messian and his Protectorate. Find a mentor. Be someone's understudy for a year or so. I'm sure it won't take you long to rise through the ranks. Me? I've got a career. And I plan to get back to it once I shut Stone down once and for all. It's the only loose end Mom and Dad left, and we owe it to them to get this done. But that's it. Stop living this fantasy you've created in your head."

The glow left Torrance's eyes, and he walked towards the door. "Always wondered why you left, why you wouldn't let Dad finish training you," he said. "But I understand now. You don't have the balls for it. You'd rather punch a clock, let a corporation use you up until you're too old to do anything else. You're hiding. Because you know Dad's world would chew you up and spit your punk ass out."

The door slammed shut behind Torrance as Sam flopped down in his seat. "Wow," he mused. "Gotta love it. I'm making everything worse, aren't I?"

Jovita kneeled beside him and kissed him on the cheek. "Growing pains, Sam," she said. "This is a brand new dynamic . Everyone's going to have to figure out where they fit. Including you. And as for whether or not you're making things worse around here, why don't you go ask the twins you just reunited?"

She stood up and exited the room, leaving Sam alone surrounded by hollow gray walls and empty chairs.

CHAPTER 18

Macaque Mountain peaked nearly fourteen thousand feet into the sky over eastern Algeria. The Atlas Mountains' surrounding plateaus allowed Sam, Torrance, Janesha, and Julian the necessary footing and space to search mountain walls and crevices while their cargo plane's anti-gravity landing gear held it in a vertical stand still above them in the clouds.

For hours, Sam climbed sheer cliffs; Torrance flew into canyons and over ice covered rocks while Janesha moved boulders and cleared away caves with her telekinesis. Julian, however, preferred to stay on his feet and scan the area for unusual energy readings and metal deposits using the silver electronic devices fastened to his hands, arms, and back. But no matter where any of them looked or scanned, there was no sign of Douglas Sunstrom's secret base.

Sam's super strong fingers dug into the stone and held him in place as he scaled the face of a tall gray rock that jutted up into the clouds. A thick orange zip line connected to his belt and fastened him to the topmost section of the mountain. His wrist communicator vibrated. "What's up, Julian?" he asked. "Find something?"

"No, I was just thinking," Julian said into his earpiece. "The jet we flew in. We need to start taking better care of our vehicles. You and Jovita are going to have to start doing some serious engineering if you keep crashing them."

Sam laughed. "Well there's this one and another one designed for leisure trips," he said into the wrist device. "But you're right though. Jovita's gonna be pissed if we wreck this one."

"I would think she is a bit perturbed with you anyway. You left her to babysit while we look for Dad's workroom. You know she would have loved to see this."

"I know. But David's too young for this kind of thing. And Maddie's down. Someone has to look after him while we're gone. I'll make it up to her somehow."

"Heavy is the head that wears the crown, hm?"

"I'm no king, Julian. But I get your meaning."

Sam's earpiece crackled again; this time it was Janesha's voice. "Sam, I think I've found something," she said.

"Julian, Torrance," Sam said into his communicator. "Zero in on Janesha's location and meet us there."

After nearly half an hour, Sam and Julian walked through a cave's dark entrance way, and it wasn't long before they saw Janesha standing in front of a wall made of sharp, uneven rocks. Torrance lit the cave with his glowing red aura as he walked in pointing his fist at the shadows, using it like a flashlight. "What do we got, people?" Torrance asked as he moved closer to them.

"Look down," Janesha said. Everyone lowered their eyes and noticed the shiny, circular steel paneling beneath their boots. "I was moving debris out of here and I discovered this. Dad's work, right?"

"Sure is," Sam said as he crouched and ran his gloved hand across the metal. He swept a few small rocks away and looked over at Julian who was locking his handheld devices onto his backpack. "Reminds me of the Launch tech we use at Sapien. It's for matter displacement. This is our way in."

The light surrounding Torrance grew brighter, illuminating every inch of the entire cave. "I don't see a keypad or any kind of lock," he said.

"Then we start looking," Janesha said, turning her eyes to the ceiling. Julian went to the nearest wall, feeling around for any crevice he could stick his hand into.

Sam stood still, watching the others and planting his boots firmly on the metal flooring. "Get close to me," he said. Everyone stopped and gave him quizzical looks. "Surround me. Now."

Julian and Janesha carefully walked over and flanked Sam on his left and right. Torrance went and stood behind him. "What is it?" Torrance asked.

"Quiet," Sam said. "Helmsman Twelve."

Those last two words seemed to echo throughout the cave as the metallic panels under their boots lit up and bathed them in warm, brilliant light rays. Janesha looked down and closed her hand over her mouth when she noticed her legs turning transparent. "Um, Sam?" she whispered.

"Be still," Sam said. "And be quiet."

"Cool," Torrance said as the entire team disappeared from the cave.

The very next second, Sam, Torrance, Janesha, and Julian were standing in a small claustrophobic room made of the same metal panels from the cave. A steel elliptical door loomed in front of them. "We're inside the mountain," Julian said. "Sam, you may want to hold..."

Before Julian could finish, Sam kicked the thick door off its hinges, sending the bent up iron slab sliding and clanging down a dark hallway. "Follow me," Sam said.

Everyone filed out of the room and started down the corridor behind Sam. Janesha levitated off the floor and floated while Torrance flew close to the low rounded ceiling. Julian lagged behind to study the smooth walls and the red lights around them that had just begun flashing. "Sam?" he called. "I believe it would be wise if we formulated more of a strategy before we just go barging into the place. Sam?"

A screaming laser blast hit Sam in the chest and threw him back down the corridor, denting the left wall with his body so that he flopped to the floor and rolled to a stop at Julian's feet. His chest sore and smoking, Sam looked up at Julian who stood over him, muffled a smile and merely said, "See?"

Torrance and Janesha landed beside Sam and helped him to his feet. "The hell was that?" Sam demanded.

"Let's ask him," Torrance said, pointing at the tall figure striding towards them in the shadows.

The figure stopped still as Torrance used the energy churning inside him to shine a spotlight on it. It had Douglas Sunstrom's face, his uniform, and even his posture. "Dad?" Torrance said.

Sam stepped in front of Janesha and Julian. "It can't be," Sam said.

The figure raised its palm at them, revealing a metal hand with a glossy finish. The oval-shaped opening in its palm pulsed with a quick light flash and fired another laser that narrowly missed Sam's head and ripped into the wall behind him. "You are not Douglas Sunstrom," the android said in a low monotone voice.

"Ok, that's not Dad," Torrance said with a hint of anger. He sent a searing laser beam of his own from his right fist and cut the robot's right arm off at the shoulder. The next blast went through its chest, sending it crashing face first to the cold floor.

"That...was crazy," Janesha said under her breath.

"No, that's crazy," Sam said pointing down the hallway where dozens more of the Douglas Sunstrom androids marched towards them. "Get ready to defend yourselves. Dad and his damn failsafes. Julian, you didn't mention this. I'm sure I would've remembered it."

Julian was bent over taking the damaged android's severed arm apart as he listened to the metal boots marching towards them just a few yards away. "I've never actually been here, Sam," he said. "I was only tangentially aware of its existence. There was bound to be some sort of security system, wouldn't you think? Come on. Where's the trigger on this thing?"

The leader of the android army stepped in front of the robotic group, raised its palm, and prepared to fire. "You are not Douglas Sunstrom," it said.

"Heard you the first time," Sam answered. He dove head first into a sea of androids, letting their searing lasers and energy bursts glance off his super dense skin as he dented their heads with his fists and kicked holes in their chests. Janesha watched her father's iron facsimiles swarm and cover

Sam's entire body like giant ants as another group of androids who were now lining the hallway on both sides turned and looked directly at her.

Just then, five more robots dropped from a circular hole in the ceiling and shook the floor behind her when they landed. Torrance opened up his hands and sent screaming solar plasma into their guts, slicing them apart. Julian pressed his back against Torrance's while he continued tinkering with the metallic arm in his hands. "Gonna need some room if we're gonna get to Sam," Torrance said.

"That's all you had to say," Janesha quipped. She violently pushed both fists downwards towards the ground. Several androids shot into the air and flattened themselves against the ceiling like used soda cans before crashing back to the floor. Then she walked a straight path through fifteen androids with red telekinetic energy spewing out of her, tossing some of them aside and totally dismantling others from the inside out.

"You should go help her pull Sam out," Julian said as Torrance blasted another android.

"No," Torrance said while turning two more metal men into piles of melted sludge. "I'm staying close to you. Since you don't...you know... have any powers."

Julian stepped away from Torrance, holding the robotic arm like a rifle. He stared down the pair of robots walking towards him. "You don't have to be uncomfortable, Torrance. I am content with who I am these days." He pulled on the plastic switch inside the wrist joint and fired two bright laser beams from its cold, stiff hand. The smoking robots fell at his feet as he moved towards another one. "Don't worry about me. I am fully capable of defending myself."

Torrance grinned and let loose an arcing blade of pure heat that cut several metallic torsos and limbs to pieces. Meanwhile, Janesha had found Sam although he wasn't that hard to spot at the center of the increasing metal mob. Each time he threw a punch, the hallway shook, and at least five more crushed androids flew into the air and hit against one of the walls. Janesha landed right behind him just as one of them climbed onto Sam's back and tightened its chokehold.

Janesha's eyes focused, and her mind willed the squirming robot to the floor where her thoughts commanded it to collapse into a pile of lifeless pieces. Sam backhanded another robot while another shot him in the back. "Damn, Janesha," he grunted. "Mom always said...if you ever get serious... Now. Put some shields around us."

Janesha wasn't listening. She found a steel door on her left and told it to come off its hinges, spin down the corridor like a helicopter blade, and decapitate every android in its path. Sam ducked the sharpened metal slab as it hummed by overhead. And then, he heard an electronic whine to his right. Another robot had raised its hand to fire. The hot, concussive burst hit Janesha in the chest, pushing her through the doorway and into the next room.

Stunned and seeing spots before her eyes, Janesha held her bruised ribs and rolled on the floor in a dark room that faintly smelled of fuel as the sounds of the androids' blasters, Torrance's energy bursts, and Sam's punches echoed from out in the hallway. She shook off the cobwebs and dragged herself over to towering structures in the shadows on the far wall. As she walked slowly into the blackness, the screeching laser fire from the hallway lit the room in erratic patterns, revealing long computer consoles and paneling in uneven flashes.

Janesha reached the nearest console and rested all of her weight on it while she caught her breath. Suddenly, a wide red light beam washed over her from the ceiling. She threw her arms up to cover her eyes while overwhelming brightness flooded the room. Tall, long computer monitors came on and instantly went to static as Janesha turned and studied the all but empty chamber and its seemingly never-ending floors and walls. "Some kind of storage unit," she said softly.

A Douglas Sunstrom android walked into the room from the hallway with its right hand raised in firing position. Janesha prepared a telekinetic blast deep in her brain's core, but she didn't need it. The red lights went dark within its eyes, and it crashed to the floor. She listened to the gears and electrical systems inside it shut down as a calming female voice sounded throughout the entire room. "Essential genetic elements recognized," it said. "Security protocols deactivated."

"Thank God," she sighed. "It's over. Sam! I'm in here!"

Only the eerie silence answered her. Then a familiar voice sounded behind her which made her back and shoulders straighten when she heard it. "Janesha," it said. "Over here." She turned around and gasped at the sight before her.

Sam walked through the door next with half a robot hanging around his waist. He ripped the metal man's hands off him and let it hit the floor. Torrance and Julian ran in after him. "What happened?" Torrance asked. "They just shut down."

"Are you hurt?" Julian asked Janesha. She said nothing.

"Nesha," Sam said. "Talk to us."

"I don't... know exactly what to say. But I think you need to see this."

She moved aside so that they could see Douglas Sunstrom's green hologram standing before them, looking at them as if he were actually there in the flesh. "Hello, my children," he said. "I hope life has been treating you well."

CHAPTER 19

"Dad?" Sam blurted. "What...what is this?"

Torrance and Julian stood with Sam and Janesha as the four of them watched a light-rendered model of their father pace back and forth in front of them while he spoke. "If you are watching this, then I know that the worst has happened. Zoa and I are no longer with you. That reminds me. Note to self: reprogram the androids to accept the kids with open arms as soon as possible. Wouldn't want you to be viciously attacked as soon as you stepped through the front door."

Sam and Torrance exchanged glances. Douglas continued. "I have to assume that you're here because you've learned about the Window technology I was working on. And you've come for the kill switch. Well, here it is."

The floor rumbled a bit as one of the larger panels slid away and a steel gray cylinder over ten feet tall and laced with golden reflective circuitry rose out of the dark hole. Sam walked over to it and placed his hand against the cog's cold metal. "But before you leave, there are some basic truths I must share with you," Douglas said, now sitting in a floating chair.

"Zoa...your mother... was ill. Terminally. As you know, we met when her space vessel crashed into our reality. What we never told you was that our physics...the way atoms and molecules and cells work here...were largely incompatible with her makeup. She was going to die in a number of years from molecular breakdown."

Quiet disbelief overtook them. Janesha took Julian's hand. "We tried everything," Douglas said with his fingers interlocked in front of his face. "Many of our adventures involved searching for a cure that just didn't exist. So I did what I always do. I figured out how to fix the problem."

Another gigantic panel on the other side of the room dropped out of the floor, and what rose out of the depths of the mountain was instantly recognizable. All four of them stared up at the twisting system of floating platforms surrounding the shining pyramid base that completely dwarfed them and covered them in its cool shadow like some terrible monument to forbidden science.

"He didn't just design it," Sam murmured.

"He actually built it," Julian replied.

"I...I constructed the horrible machine you see before you now," Douglas said covering his face. "It would have opened a doorway and allowed us access to Alpha's Precipice. Zoa's home world. But...Earth would have been destroyed in the process. I...I even went so far as to design several domed environments in order to keep enough humans safe so the species could possibly live on after my self-initiated apocalypse. But...nothing...nothing I could think of would justify my... my arrogance. My loss of perspective and... sanity. This destroyer I've built is an evil thing. I...I'm sorry, my children. But I couldn't bear the thought of losing her. I just couldn't."

"Dad...no," Sam said quietly with tears in his eyes.

Suddenly a broad yellow heat ray shot past them and obliterated one of the consoles. Smoke rose from the exploded equipment as Douglas Sunstrom's image blinked out of sight. His children spun around as Isaiah Stone strolled through the doorway followed by Damsel, Osiria, Malignus, Dreadmettle, and the Bull.

"The truth can be a painful thing, Sam," Stone said. "I apologize for the intrusion, but you didn't miss anything important. I'm sure he was about to say something heroic about preventing the Window Device from getting into the wrong hands. So let's just skip that part, and you can deliver unto me that magnificent piece of craftsmanship over there."

"You!" Sam yelled, rushing straight at Stone.

Visibly startled, Stone stumbled backwards and caught Sam's right fist directly in the center of his black armored chest plate. The metal cracked as he fell to the floor. Sam reached down to grab hold of Stone again. Osiria took a deep breath, stepping out in front of the Headhunters with two fingers covered in black writhing tendrils pointed at Sam's sternum. "Fall," she said.

Dark vein-like structures sprouted underneath Sam's skin, running up his arms, neck, and face. Putrid, inky rivers dripped from his eyes, nose, and mouth as he clutched his chest. Sam crumpled to the floor, twitching and clawing at Osiria's white boots.

Damsel stepped forward and stomped on Sam's chest, sending a vibrating boom all over the mountain. Sam stopped moving, and his fingers went limp. She grinned and raised her heavy boot again. "Hell no," Janesha said under her breath. Her mind lifted Damsel high into the air and smashed her into the ceiling, dropping sections of cracked concrete into the room. But Janesha wasn't done. She tightened her left fist and sent Damsel into the far left wall where she left a deep, crumbling imprint. Across the room, the Bull unsheathed the long blades housed inside his forearms. But before he could attack, Damsel came hurtling towards him like a giant flying bowling ball, slamming him to the floor.

Stone positioned himself behind his Headhunters and angrily pointed at the Sunstroms standing before them. "Eviscerate these...children," he commanded.

That's all Malignus needed to hear. The gray tentacled flesh monster roared and leaped in Torrance's direction with its claws spread wide and his many mouths running with saliva. Torrance's hot sunrays dug into Malignus and sliced tentacles from his body, but they only grew back and multiplied. And soon, they were all over Torrance, wrapping around his throat and pulling him down to the floor each time he tried to fly. "Gonna sssswallow you whole thissss time, boy," Malignus drooled.

On the chamber's opposite end, Dreadmettle and his robotic sphere closed in on Janesha and Julian. The shining sphere's glowing center eye blasted repeatedly at the twins while Janesha crossed her arms in front of her face and deflected the screaming incendiary bursts with telekinetic shields. Julian ducked behind his sister, allowing her shields to protect him as he recoiled from the heat swirling around them from the dispersed lasers.

Dreadmettle sneered at Janesha with his arms crossed. "You can't keep me out forever," he said. "Sooner or later. You crack."

Janesha grit her teeth and pushed both her fists together, hitting Dreadmettle with two mental bombs from both sides. His eyes rolling back in his head, Dreadmettle spun around and dropped to the floor. His helmet and armor were warped and fractured, and he crawled around on the floor in an attempt to regain his balance.

His sphere shot up towards the ceiling, watching its disoriented master trip and fall again. Then, it turned its malicious, glowing eye on Janesha. She hastily threw up another set of telekinetic shields, but they weren't enough. The sphere's mechanical rage built into an energy blast that shattered her shielding into a million light shards. Janesha and Julian flew backwards spilling all over the floor. The robotic arm Julian had used as a rifle spewed sparks as it slid on the floor inches from his fingers.

Dreadmettle was on his feet again. He lifted Janesha off the floor by her neck and smacked her hard with metallic knuckles and fingers across the face. As the cyborg squeezed her throat, she could see the Bull stepping on Julian's chest and preparing his blades for the kill through her watery, blurred vision. She couldn't focus nearly enough for another telekinetic burst. She simply braced herself.

Dreadmettle kicked her into the nearest wall and watched her flop at his feet. His android sphere orbited him as if it enjoyed watching the beating. Dreadmettle smiled down at her, nudging her face with his metal boot while he wiped blood from his mouth. "Told you, girl" he said. "Sooner or later."

Malignus had been beating on Torrance for minutes now, ripping at him with claws and teeth. But Torrance weathered the storm of tentacles and stinking, weighty flesh as he channeled all the heat he had inside him into his hands. The volley of blistering punches he launched at Malignus' body burned crispy, blackened holes in the beast that cooked him inside and out. He screamed and backed away from Torrance as the burnt flesh regenerated.

A few feet away from him, Damsel laughed with spiteful giddiness and kicked Sam across the floor. He rolled until he was lying at Stone's feet. Osiria stood beside him and continued forcing the black venomous streams into his body that slowed his heart to a crawl and threatened to stop it altogether. "He's extremely strong," Osiria said with her bottom lip between her teeth. "Never...had anyone fight me like this before. Think I like it."

"Yes," Stone answered while looking down at Sam. "These Sunstroms are quite resilient. But they can be killed just the same. Can't they Sam?"

Sam pushed himself up so that he was on all fours and glared at Osiria through cloudy, feverish eyes. As much as he wanted to grab her and rip her apart, he couldn't. He could barely breathe. With his hands clasped behind his back, Stone watched the life ooze out of Sam's body.

Several feet to his left, Malignus had Torrance wrapped up in four of his thick meaty arms. Torrance struggled to get his hands free as Malignus licked his teeth. "Sssstop moving sssso much," he said. "I like my meat ssssweet. Adrenaline makesss it all bitter."

Torrance snatched his left hand out, pressed his fist up against Malignus' face and let loose a surge of heat that split his head in half. Malignus dropped Torrance and unleashed a horrible, ragged scream with his several hands and tentacles covering his face. As the monster retreated to a far corner of the room dripping blood and all kinds of other liquids, Torrance rested on his knees, catching his breath. He happened to turn his eyes in Sam's direction and saw Stone standing over him. "Gotcha," he said to himself. Balanced and kneeling, he pointed his right fist at Stone and fired three hot energy bursts in his direction.

The first one missed him but disintegrated the hair just above his right ear. The other two hit him square in his armored chest, sending him sliding towards the doorway. Osiria ran and leaped on top of Stone to shield his body with her own.

"No one touches him!" Damsel howled in a super speed dash aimed at Torrance. His heart skipped a beat, and his body froze while his eyes fixed themselves on the human missile headed his way. Suddenly, Sam was standing hunched over and directly in her path. He pounced on her and slammed her to the floor, landing punch after thundering punch to her head and body. She caught one of his fists before it connected, but Sam brushed her hands aside and kept swinging.

Stone squinted his eyes a bit and turned his head as Damsel took the hardest blows she'd ever been given. Then his eyes shifted over to the bleeding Malignus. Over by the Window Device, Dreadmettle and his sphere had Janesha cornered, her telekinetic powers completely exhausted. But where was Julian?

Stone felt Osiria preparing to attack, but he held her hand and quietly instructed her to stay still. He'd found Julian at the other end of the room with the Bull's blades at his throat. "It's time to end this," Stone said. "Julian. You may handle your business, sir."

Julian looked the Bull in the eye. "Excuse me," he said. The Bull lowered his blades. Julian walked over to Janesha and placed his fingers on his temple. With Dreadmettle's loud, arrogant laughter in her ears, Janesha felt her power returning, stronger than ever. But she couldn't use it. She wasn't in control of it anymore. She rose high into the air swinging and kicking against her own telekinetic abilities. "What... what's happening?" she cried. "Who's doing this?"

"I am," Julian said. "Now be a good girl and shut your stupid little mouth."

Sam got up from Damsel who slowly rolled away, caressing her battered face. He looked over at Torrance and then at Julian. "Julian?" he said. "Explain yourself. Now. What is this?"

"Oh, you really are dull aren't you?" Julian laughed. "Did you truly believe that I would really let those idiot doctors near the psionic organs attached to my brain, let alone remove them? I certainly made them believe that they did. It's amazing what a little imagination and a psychic suggestion can do. I am ready Master Stone."

Sam clenched his fists. "Torrance," Sam said quietly. "We only get one shot at him."

Before either of them could move in Julian's direction, both of them doubled over in agony. Each grabbed his own head and screamed until he lay motionless on the floor. "Stop it, Julian!" Janesha yelled.

"Hush, Nesha," Julian answered. "I need your mind."

Julian pointed at the Window Device, and as Janesha's power surged inside her like a tsunami, the giant kill switch cog shuddered and disintegrated. Then, the pyramid base and its great ring separated into multiple planar sections that lifted into the air and rotated near the ceiling. "Very good, Julian," Stone said. "Welcome to the Headhunter Association."

His battle suit carried him into the air as Damsel took flight and joined him among the gigantic floating pieces of machinery. Dreadmettle's sphere generated a stream of light that enveloped its master, Osiria, and the Bull in a solid energy ball, levitating them to the same height as Stone and Damsel.

Julian looked up at Janesha who hung like a rag doll above his head. "Now," Julian said to her.

"Julian please," Janesha begged, staring at her brothers' motionless bodies. "Don't make me do this."

She watched her twin press his fingers against his right temple and lock eyes with her. "Bury this place," he said. His voice echoed inside her head, and her arms shot straight out involuntarily. Telekinetic energy erupted from her body in waves, splintering the walls, floor, and ceiling. Soon the mountain itself began to tremble. Dreadmettle's sphere shot another sparkling ray that covered Julian and pulled him into the air.

As the sphere used its lasers to cut an escape tunnel into the ceiling, Stone disappeared into the dark hole followed by Damsel and the rest of the Headhunters. Still wrapped in the sphere's anti-gravity cell, Julian was the last to leave. He mentally released his unconscious sister and let her drop to the floor like an empty, discarded shell casing. The floor split open underneath Sam, Torrance, and Janesha. The walls collapsed on themselves, and the ceiling ripped itself apart. The entire mountain was imploding. Sam stirred and glared angrily up at Julian. "I'll kill you for this," Sam said as a boulder crashed into the floor next to him.

Julian smiled at his brother's useless anger. "And I'm sure you believe that, Sam," he answered. "But if I'm reading this correctly, I'm the one actually killing you." And after one last wistful stare, Julian escaped into the tunnel.

High in the sky, Stone, Julian, and the rest of the Headhunters watched Macaque Mountain buckle and crumble until it finally collapsed on itself taking the Sunstrom's jet with it. Julian closed his eyes and contemplated what he had just done.

He remembered the night that one of Stone's surrogates, a psychic groupie – Pamela, he thought it was - used her telepathy to grant Stone access into his thoughts as he sat alone in his room at Agatha Bell. He and Stone walked around inside his mind and talked for hours about how to kill his parents and how to commandeer the Window Device. All Julian had asked for in exchange was a place among the Headhunters once he got himself released. Now his initiation was finished.

Stone placed his hand on Julian's shoulder as icy winds tossed his white hair. He looked around at the separate pieces of his machine like a child assessing all his gifts on Christmas morning. Dreadmettle and his sphere were carrying them to the Orb vessel using cables and platforms made of pure solid energy. "Remember this as the day humanity drew its last desperate gasps and something glorious and new took its place," he said into Julian's ear. "Let us burn this place and step proudly into the next age of man. And may the so-called protectors of this forsaken world die with it."

PART 3

"I've made many acquaintances in the superhuman community over the course of my career. But Zoa Xaquelina is without a doubt the best friend I've ever had. Every danger we've faced, every super powered maniac- whether it was Stone, The Abominoids, The Pharoah or even Black Gaze. None of them ever stood a chance as long as we were united. I love her. I trust her unreservedly. She is more important to me than my next breath. And because of that, I remain confident in even the darkest of ordeals.

Taken from The Adventure Log Vol. 9
F. Douglas Sunstrom

CHAPTER 20

Night fell, and the moon held a muted glow in the darkness over the Atlas Mountains. Macaque was completely leveled. Smoke and dust clouds rose quietly towards the stars. Deep within the bowels of the fallen mountain, Douglas Sunstrom's base had been utterly crushed and flattened, mangled beyond recognition by gargantuan earthen slabs that pressed together until they were indistinguishable one from another. Anything of interest or value would probably be excavated by fossil hunters a thousand years or so into the future. But tonight, there wasn't a trace of anything or anyone except in one impossibly tight crawl space within the mountain's inner depths.

That was the tight black hell where Sam Sunstrom wedged himself between tons of rubble and his family. Torrance and Janesha lay unconscious at his feet as Sam pushed against the sliding boulders above him, holding an entire mountain back with his bare hands. He could feel the cruel, insurmountable weight bearing down on him, gravity yanking it all towards him with constant, malicious inevitability. Salty streams trickled from Sam's brow. The broken mountain simply had to obey the laws of physics, settle completely, and he would be snapped in two like a pencil. Torrance and Janesha would die instantly.

The mountain buckled again. Something shifted underneath him, and Sam went down to one knee. Cartilage and tendons popped. He shut his eyes, concentrating on holding back the world.

He could hear his father's voice in mind, recalling that sunny day on the mansion's front steps as molten anger stirred inside his chest. He remembered pulling up the white t-shirt he was wearing that day and showing Douglas the fresh scar across his abdomen. "But look at how fast you got back on your feet, son," Douglas had argued. "I know it was a painful journey, but with the proper training, I'm sure..."

"Sure about what?" Sam had interrupted. "That if I get sliced to ribbons again, I'll grow back together just fine? Would you please stop trying to change my mind? I don't want this anymore! Just let me be normal!"

"Sam," Janesha said between coughs.

Sam cleared his mind and looked in Janesha's direction. He could barely see her with all the shadow and smoke between them. "Don't move," Sam said to her. "Not one muscle."

Janesha took a moment and looked around. "Julian dropped the mountain on us," she said.

"Yeah," Sam said with a grunt. They could hear rubble grinding and sliding out of place all around them. "He did."

"He used... me... to do it." She closed her eyes and forced her telekinesis against the slabs surrounding them. Sam felt the weight against his arms and back lessen, but the pressure was just as constant and unrelenting. "We won't be able to hold it forever," Janesha said.

"I know."

"We're going to die down here, aren't we?"

Sam shifted his own weight, swallowed another hot, dry breath. "No," he said. "I promise."

Torrance rolled over and turned his eyes towards the sharp rocks hanging just above his head. His fingers grabbed at his ribs, and his hands shook when he saw the jagged, bloody shrapnel planted firmly in his torso. An anguished scream rushed out of his mouth. "Sam?!" he yelled. "Janesha?!"

Sam grunted and pushed harder against the unsteady ceiling. Janesha reached out and grabbed Torrance's wrist. "Shhhh!" she said desperately. "I'm trying to concentrate." She closed her eyes and focused her mind on keeping the tiny pocket surrounding them from collapsing. "What are we doing, Sam?"

"You're going to put a telekinetic shield around the three of us," Sam wheezed. "The strongest one you've ever put together. Torrance. I need a laser. You're going to cut us out."

Torrance gathered the remaining bit of energy coursing through his cells. The faint yellow aura outlining his body pulsed in tandem with his slowing heartbeat. "Wait," he said. "What if the shields don't hold? What if I don't have enough power to cut through? How much of the mountain is on top of us?"

Janesha forced a smile as blood trickled from a scrape near her right ear. "I don't know, all of it?"

Sam stood up, grinding his back and shoulders against the low, crumbling ceiling. "We do it now," he said. "As quickly and as carefully as possible. I can think of some awesome ways to die, but being popped like three grapes underneath a damn mountain isn't one of them. Ready? One, two...wait..."

Something vibrated between his belt and lower back. And Sam chuckled. "Vita, you are one hard- headed ass woman," he said to himself.

High above the Atlas Mountains, inside the Sunstroms' last family plane, Jovita sat fastened in the pilot's chair and held the flat, triangular jet in hovering position over the Macaque ruins. As the moonlight reflected off its burgundy hull, she looked over in the co-pilot's chair at David who rubbed his hands together nervously.

"Ok, look at the monitor," Jovita said to David. She pointed at one of the wide digital readouts on the console. It displayed a mountain range with a red cursor flashing repeatedly within the base of the largest pixelated structure. "That blip is the tracer I put on Sam's belt," she said. "Reach down into the Earth until you feel them in your mind. Picture the inside of the mountain in your head. Can you do that?"

David closed his eyes. "I think so," he said. He pressed his hands together tightly, interlocking his fingers for several seconds. Suddenly, his eyes opened, and he looked at Jovita. "I found them. They're inside the ground. Deep. But there's only three of them. There's supposed to be four."

"Are you sure?"

"Yeah. Only three."

Jovita pinched her nose bridge and sighed as she imagined the worst. "Concentrate on them and that cargo hold behind us. Bring them in," she said.

"Ok," David said with his eyes shut again. "But I've only ever moved one person at a time. Never this many. What if I mess up? What if I hurt them by accident? What if I..."

"You won't. I believe in you, David." She thumped his chest with her index finger. "You've got everything you need right inside there. I know you do."

David wasn't listening anymore. "Um, no disrespect, Jovita. Kinda need you to be quiet now."

There had always been lightning bolts dancing in David's brain that fizzled and popped constantly like radio static. It was why his attention often hopped from one subject to the next like a television changing its own channel at random. It was also how he was able to transport matter instantaneously from one spot to another. As his face contorted, he coerced that energy field down into the mountains below, examining every rock and crevice until he found something familiar.

With a crimson glow crackling around her, Janesha smirked and relaxed her telekinetic hold on the mountain. "I don't believe it," she said. "David." The entire crawl space burned with David's energy, and onboard the family plane, David was hovering just a few inches out of his chair, saturated to the bone with the red plasma consuming his entire body.

Jovita turned and looked at David. This was too much. "David, stop," she said. "That's enough. We'll try something else."

David looked at her through eyes made of pure light. "Wait," he said.

Suddenly, a brilliant red flash lit the entire plane. Jovita shielded her eyes as David plopped down in his co-pilot's chair, utterly spent. Behind them in the cargo hold, Sam got up off his back, rolled over and checked Torrance's blood caked chest wounds while Janesha sat on the floor with her knees up to her chin and stared at the glass separating them from the cockpit. David's face beamed at her from the other side. She shook her head and gave him a weary, thankful smile before looking back at the floor.

The plane climbed higher into the clouds and circled over the mountain range several times. In the cargo bay, Sam bandaged Torrance as best he could, using the dressing he found in the medical kit. "You'll be fine until we get home," he said to Torrance. "Just try not to talk...or move too much."

Janesha held onto a rung mounted just over her head. A tear fell down her cheek as she watched the moon from the tiny round window next to her shoulder.

"Sam," Jovita said over the intercom. "There's no sign of Julian down there. Any idea what happened to him?"

"He's not down there," Sam answered, looking away from Torrance and Janesha.

"What do you mean?" Jovita asked.

"He means... the bastard betrayed us," Janesha spat. "And then tried to kill us using my powers. Using me."

Sam looked back at Janesha who was trembling violently and then lowered his eyes. How could he look at her directly when he'd nearly led her to her own death? "Yeah," Sam said quietly. "That's what happened. Let's get everybody home. We're done." The plane made one more sweep over the mountains and then rocketed away into the night.

CHAPTER 21

Stone's great silver Orb vessel hung over a string of islands in the Pacific Ocean reflecting the morning sun's intense glare. With a steady scream too high-pitched for the human ear, it produced an unseen wave that covered itself and the islands below, rendering them invisible to both radar and satellite imaging. On the largest of the black coral land masses, Stone and Osiria walked the island dressed in white linen and boots. Stone watched his pale sea mutants slither and crawl all over the towering Window Device he'd assembled there hours earlier. Dozens of the slimy, mindless creatures covered the island with their hulking bodies and lurked underneath crystal blue waves. Damsel flew by overhead as she patrolled the area around the Orb ship.

Underneath the tentacles and bulging flesh, the islands were laden with glistening circuitry that zig- zagged all over the surface like a metallic crossword puzzle. Silver cables the size of massive tree trunks ran from the machine and down into the surrounding ocean while conductors crawled into the Earth's depths, into the ocean floor, and invaded the planet's most intimate spaces on their way to the molten core. Tremors worked their way from the depths and escaped onto the surface.

As thunder sounded off in the distance, Stone walked past Osiria and up to the Window Device, placing his hand on its great base. He looked up at the giant thing and stared at it as if it were some kind of god. The iron ring near the top of it had begun to vibrate and hum. Soon, it would be glowing with heat from the center of the world. He pictured himself stepping onto one of those floating platforms above him and through the ring itself, into his destiny.

He felt Julian standing behind him. "Geologists consider these islands part of the Ring of Fire," he said without looking at him. "The geothermal energy coursing beneath this place will be more than enough to fuel our machine. Are you enjoying your new family, Julian?"

"Of course," Julian answered. "Although Damsel seems to be a bit... erratic. I have to wonder...are you prepared for the jealous tantrum she's going to point at your head when she finally gets enough of watching you fondle her replacement?"

Stone glanced far across the island where Osiria was sitting in a crouched position watching the tranquil ocean and enjoying the breeze. He laughed a bit. "You worry too much, son," he said. "A man in my position has certainly earned the right to indulge his sweet tooth a little. I'm sure with your amazing mental talents, you've had your fair share of wild nights with the fairer sex."

Julian hung his head. "No," he said ashamedly. "Not...not yet."

Stone smiled and put his arm around Julian. "Well, we'll have to do something about that. Let go of some of that anxiety, young man. You'll find that you'll have no need of it where we're going."

"I try. But...I've always felt...tense... uneasy. Like I don't belong anywhere."

"I know. Growing up can be a difficult thing. Especially when your purpose eludes you. I'm assuming your parents never shared with you some of the more... problematic... aspects of the Sunstrom legacy. I always thought Douglas could be arrogant at times, but I didn't expect that he would hide your true nature from you for as long as he did."

"What are you talking about?"

Stone placed his hand on Julian's shoulder and made eye contact with him. "With every new generation of your family, an individual is born possessing extraordinary intelligence coupled with a unique outlook on the world. Diametrically opposed to the established order. I suspect that you never believed all of that good versus evil, heroes and villains nonsense. No matter how much your parents preached it to you."

"No," Julian said after thinking about it. "I always thought it was a waste of time. Wanted to work on the important things. Create change."

"That, Julian Sunstrom, is because you are quite special," Stone said. "The Sunstrom genetic code ensures that every generation, a visionary rises within the family to challenge the status quo. It is how the genome evolves. How it strengthens itself for what's coming next."

"How do you know all of this?"

"I am a man who values preparedness, Julian. I've researched a wide array of subjects during the course my many adventures. Sometimes my own enemies. You, my friend, are the latest in a long line of anomalies who have been systematically eliminated by the heads of the Sunstrom family simply because they feared your power. But your father failed to get rid of you, didn't he?"

"Should have killed me," Julian answered with a demonic smile. "Instead, he locked me away. Tried to have me fixed."

"And what is it you're about to do now?"

Julian turned his eyes on the Window Device and nodded. "Create change. Like I was born to do."

"The Sunstrom legacy belongs to you alone now," Stone said. "As it always should have been."

Tucked away in the rear section of the base Douglas Sunstrom built for his children was the medical bay. But Sam hadn't paid it very much attention in the short time he'd been living there. He thought he'd never have any need for it. However, here he was, leaning against a rounded wall, arms folded watching Torrance sleep inside a clear glass capsule completely filled with translucent green liquid.

Bright ceiling lights beamed down on Jovita, David and Janesha who stood around the tube looking at the jagged shrapnel wounds on his bare chest and arms. David placed his hand against the cylinder's cool thick plastic casing and watched the tiny bubbles forming around the white breather attached to Torrance's face. "Is he going to be ok?" David asked.

Jovita watched the heart monitor at the tube's base. "He's lost a lot of blood, you guys," she said. "And there is minimal nerve damage. But this formula bath your dad created seems to be healing him very quickly. He should be fine."

Sam remembered how it felt to wake up inside one of those tubes. He'd never forgotten the stark panic, the disorientation and how his parents took turns sitting at his side until he was ready to be ejected from what his dad had named the 'healing cell'.

"Useless," he said to himself.

Jovita and the others looked over at Sam who was now standing by the door. He shook his head slowly before screaming and punching a hole in the nearest wall. Instantly ashamed of himself, he shot a quick glance at Jovita and back at Torrance who hadn't heard a thing. "It's useless," he said. "All of it. What have we accomplished besides making a complete mess?"

"Sam," Jovita said.

"No, it's time we stopped fantasizing and started living in our new reality. Dad set up extensive cash accounts for each of us. When Torrance is back on his feet, we'll secure living arrangements. Here in the city if you want. Figure out what you want to do with yourselves. Go to school, get a job, travel. But trust me. This? This isn't the life you want. I should have said that to you all from the beginning. And I'm sorry I didn't. Let someone else deal with this."

David didn't say a word. He leaned closer to Jovita and turned his blank eyes to floor's white tiles.

"Who?" Janesha said, stepping over to him. "Who else? This is our problem. Mom and Dad wouldn't want us to quit."

"No," Sam said directly. "Apparently, Dad wanted to blow up the planet as much as Stone does."

With that Sam stormed out of the medical bay, walking past the family jet and through several labs. He made it to the elevators without giving Maddie's drooping shell a second look, and when the doors opened, he stepped inside and headed to the surface.

CHAPTER 22

Sam kept the lights off in his apartment, but Jovita could tell he was home. He'd parked the burgundy SUV at the curb in front of the house, and when Jovita went to knock on the door, it creaked open because it hadn't been shut properly.

She walked through the living room where the scant sunlight squeezed in through closed drapes. Quietly, she walked past the silent widescreen television, the end tables, and the couches until she was standing in Sam's kitchen looking at his back. He was sitting in the dark with his hands folded and eyes closed. "You didn't have to come here," Sam said. "I'll be alright. Talked to your father a couple of hours ago. Told him I'd be back at work in a few days. We'll start designing the new Launch Teams in about a week."

"I didn't come here to talk about Sapien, Sam. I'm going to say this. You're going to listen to me say it, and then I'm going home. This...this fear of yours..."

"Fear?"

"Yes, fear. You're scared as hell. It's fine, but you're scared. And it has nothing to do with your parents or your family or even me."

Sam stood up and walked up on Jovita with angry tears in his eyes. "You don't understand this," he said. "You could never understand."

"Because I'm not superhuman? Because I can't lift that refrigerator over my head, I can't possibly fathom what you're feeling? You wanna know what this is about? Here."

Jovita grabbed Sam's shirt and yanked it up so that she could see the scar that stretched from his left rib cage to his right hip.

"Stop, damn it," Sam said.

"This is it!" she yelled. "This is your problem. The first time you stared evil...pure evil...in the face. It ripped your guts out and showed them to you. And it scared you to death."

"What if something happens to them? What if I can't protect them?"

"We're family. We...protect one another."

Sam turned away from her as more tears fell. "I can't believe Dad was going to destroy everything," he said.

"The only thing your father was guilty of was an insane idea. He didn't even execute it. And when he realized how terrible it was, he did the only thing he could do. He dismantled the practical application and hid it away. So no one else could use it."

"He...he was so obsessed," Sam mumbled to himself as he sat back down at the table. "I...can't let that happen to me."

Jovita sat next to him. "Douglas was a great man. With flaws. But you don't ever have to worry about his flaws taking you under," she said. "You've got an entire team. You've got me. And we'll follow you to Satan's front porch if you give the order. So, Samuel Alesser Sunstrom, what are your orders?"

Sam got up and walked over to the kitchen window. He pulled the drapes back and watched the neighbors unload grocery bags from their car. For a moment, his eyes darted over to gray van parked across the street from the apartment. "There are no orders, Vita," he said without looking at her. "I'll see you at work."

Jovita shook her head and walked out. "Might want to close those curtains," she said angrily. "That guy in the van across the street works

for Heroscoop dot com. Been trying to get your picture since I got here."
Sam heard the front door slam. He closed the drapes.

After several grueling hours, Torrance was on his feet again. He felt weak, sore all over, and full of pain medication, but his lacerations had healed enough that he'd already eaten and showered before sitting down with Janesha and David in the conference room.

He and Janesha had been passing Headhunter files back and forth for hours now, familiarizing themselves with the abilities and personality profiles of current and past members. At one end of the long table, David sat back in his chair grinning from ear to ear.

"Think we got ourselves a plan," Torrance said.

"So you pulled all this from Dad's database?" Janesha asked David.

"Yep," David said. "You guys won't let me do anything fun, so I just dig through the files all day. There's so many. Heroes too."

"I'll bet," Torrance said.

Jovita walked in carrying a duffle bag in each hand. "I just came by to get my things," she said. "I'll...I'll see you guys later. Give me a call if you need anything. And I mean anything."

"Matter of fact...we need you right now," Torrance said, his voice darkening. "You didn't think we were quitting on this, did you? Stone goes down whether Sam's here or not."

"Torrance, to be completely honest here, I wouldn't feel comfortable..."

"Team needs a science consultant," Janesha said. "And you've got a pretty good boxing game. Just look at what we've got. Five minutes."

Jovita grit her teeth, sighed, and placed her bags on the floor. She sat down at the conference table beside Torrance. "Five minutes," she said.

Janesha slid a manila folder over to Torrance who immediately opened it and pulled out a stack of papers and photographs. The digital black and white picture on top focused on a middle-aged black man in a zip up khaki suit surrounded by large black birds. One of the birds was perched on the man's outstretched forearm.

"Name's Laurence Volger," Torrance said. "The Fowler. According to Dad's writings and these files, he was one of Isaiah Stone's henchmen back in the day. Never did a stitch of prison time. The birds did all of the dirty work. There was some kind of falling out between them. Rumor is he hated the idea of the Headhunter Association and made sure he was vocal about it. He's retired now. Has a house on the California coast where he tends to his birds full time."

"So?" Jovita started.

Janesha leaned forward. "We show up at this guy's front door and ask him where his ex-buddies hang out in their spare time," she said. "We'll be polite about it, of course."

Jovita smirked. "No, you won't," she said. "Look, I can't be involved in this anymore, and if I'm being honest, I don't think you guys should either. Without Sam, I think..."

"Actually, it's a pretty good plan," Sam said from the conference room doorway. "Direct. Aggressive."

Surprised, Jovita turned sharply so she could see him. Torrance wouldn't look in his direction. "Sam, if you're here to tell us why none of us should be here doing this, save it. I'm real tired of hearing it, man."

Sam stepped further into the room, pulling off his t-shirt. It dropped to the floor while his scar was laid bare for everyone to see. "About six months after my twelfth birthday, Mom and Dad took me to Mali to explore a new system of caves they'd discovered," he said with a nostalgic smile. "We found so many old maps and diagrams and writings down there from what Dad called the First Age." The smile vanished. "Turns out, Stone was after those things as well. And he'd brought Damsel with him. There was a fight. Mom flew me to the armored drilling vehicle and told me to stay there. But I didn't. Maybe I thought that my strength would give us the advantage. The blade he was swinging that day. It was so hot. I didn't even feel it when he cut me open. I just went numb. I'd never seen that amount of blood."

Torrance looked down at the table. "They would never tell us what actually happened to you," he said. "I knew something was wrong. They just kept saying you were sick and you were getting better. And you never said anything."

"I couldn't deal with it. Wanted more than anything for that moment to just...not exist. I was in a healing cell for nearly two weeks straight until I was 'good as new' as Dad put it. And when I got out, I decided that

I would do everything I could to avoid ever being in that situation again. I've been running from my responsibility… from my inheritance, but I guess I've never really been that fast. So here I am. Mom and Dad passed their work on to us. And we're going to continue it even if it kills us. Suit up, everyone. Time to do some headhunting of our own."

Janesha, Torrance, David, and Jovita looked around the table at one another in silent astonishment as Sam left the conference room. "You too, David," Sam said loudly from another room. "You've done enough sitting around."

David smiled, repeatedly punching the air in front of him as hard as he could. Torrance pounded the table with his fist and laughed. "Well, hell yes," he said.

CHAPTER 23

Anyone who knew Laurence Volger could tell that retirement had been more than good to him. Gone was the violence and paranoia of his thirties and forties. There was no need for all of the scheming, hiding, and murder that had once consumed his life. His anxiety medication hadn't been refilled in years. Now that he was sixty-seven years old, he'd finally discovered serenity.

He spent most of his time with his birds these days – those specially bred, black, gray-streaked hawks he affectionately called his 'babies'. Tonight, he'd been feeding them and cleaning the vast domed aviary behind his six- acre home when he heard his wife shriek and call his name all the way from the main house. He ran to the nearest doorway and stopped in his tracks. There was a plane full of adventurers perched on his lawn, pouring floodlights into his home. He could feel his anxiety returning.

After a few soothing words to his babies, Laurence walked back to the house, his prosthetic forearm gleaming under the moonlight. He entered through the patio, prepared a glass of whiskey, and told his wife to get the front door.

Within minutes, he was standing next to the fireplace in his study – a large cozily lit room with wall- to- wall books, a large oak desk, and a few leather chairs. He kept his back to Sam and his team as he sipped the last of his liquor and handed the glass back to the shapely, dark-skinned twenty-three year old in the indigo mini dress and heels. "Thank you, Ibis," Laurence said. "Please see if my guests would like any refreshments."

"No, thank you," Sam said without allowing any cracks in the unfriendly expression on his face. Ibis looked at Torrance, Janesha, David, and Jovita. None of them paid her any attention. Every eye was focused on her husband. She took the glass and left the room. The door to the study closed. Laurence unbuttoned his white dress shirt until his throat could feel the cool air conditioning, and he thrust his hands inside the pockets of his gray cotton slacks. David watched the man's mechanical left arm as a frozen uneasiness rippled through him.

"I knew I'd be receiving visitors at some point," Laurence said still facing away from them. "I told Isaiah a long time ago that killing heroes was counterproductive to what he was trying to do. But he only listens to his own fractured thoughts these days."

"Really," Sam deadpanned.

"And Sam. You need to understand. As many times as I fought your parents, I…and others like me for that matter…we never intended for anything like this to happen. I've…I've been wanting to say that to you in person."

Then he turned around and faced Sam, suddenly feeling frail and powerless in the presence of the super family before him. "With that out of the way," he said humbly, "how may I help you this evening?"

"Long story short, we're after Stone," Sam said. "And I need to know where I can find the Headhunters."

Laurence's eyelids fluttered as he searched for the words. "Well… there are so many," he stammered. "All over the world. Some operating out of secret cells. Others individually. You couldn't possibly find them all."

Sam smirked. "Yeah, we could," he said. "But I don't want them all. Karla Lockwood's crew. That's who I want."

Laurence's eyes darted away from Sam and glanced across the rest of the grim faces in the room. "Damsel," he said, grabbing a hold of his false left arm with a nervous chuckle. "Stone's attack dog. She has a hell of a grip doesn't she?"

"He's stalling," Torrance said.

"You're stalling, Mr. Volger," said Sam.

"You do understand my hesitation," Laurence said. "Damsel can...she can be extremely cruel...brutal, even... when provoked."

The entire room lit up as Torrance charged his right fist with golden energy and pointed it straight at Laurence. "So can I," Torrance said with light and shadow dancing in tandem across his face.

Sam moved over to Laurence and put his hand firmly on the man's shoulder. "My brother is a bit of a loose cannon, Mr. Volger," he said. "And I'm not entirely sure what he's capable of from moment to moment. So, I'm going to need you to start talking, sir."

Laurence stared at the blazing fist pointed at him from across the room, seemingly entranced. "Yes...Mr. Sunstrom. Of course," he said. "What...what was it you needed again?"

Sam inched closer to him. "Where does Damsel hang that red cape of hers?"

Osiria's personal quarters aboard Isaiah Stone's Orb ship had become her favorite place since she'd become connected to her new mentor. It was a cozy bedroom and bath that also served as an observation deck from which she could see all that transpired beneath the ship.

Having just emerged from a steaming peppermint and lavender bath, she lay across a peach circular couch with sheer white material draped over her coffee skin. She sipped from a wine glass and stared out the rounded windows at the islands and ocean below just as a section of earth vomited its igneous guts and spewed lava high into the sky.

Osiria smiled. It had begun. The Window Tower's thick mechanical roots had plunged deep into the planet's core, using it as a battery. Soon there would be eruptions everywhere, in cities all over the globe. Unnatural weather patterns and earthquakes would rip entire continents apart. Then, the planet's ice and water would begin to move, swallowing hundreds of thousands at a time. Nations would fall, and wars would ignite. With her palm pressed firmly against the glass, she watched fiery lava flow into the ocean and along the ground as black smoke rose in plumes. The Tower's iron upper ring glowed bright red and sang aloud in low, creaking metallic tones. "At last," she cooed under her breath. "Let me see you burn."

CHAPTER 24

Years ago, when Damsel joined the Headhunter Association, she used her first millions to invest in real estate. One of her business deals allowed her to buy a skyscraper in the heart of Santiago. To most tourists and late night partyers with expensive tastes and money to burn, it was a nightclub, casino, and hotel known as Los Asesinos. Under the watch of the snowcapped mountains in the distance, it lit the night sky with blue strobes, and steady, bass heavy beats could be felt by anyone passing through the area.

But its true purpose- a hiding place for Damsel's Headhunter operatives- was known only to a half dozen individuals in the world. Nearly a mile beneath the main building, in an empty white storage level, the Bull stood in front of a wall-mounted mirror straightening his gray designer suit, smiling arrogantly at himself. He smelled of a musky cologne, and his head was freshly shaved.

Behind him, Dreadmettle sat at the only table in the room and typed anxiously on a laptop with his steel covered fingers. His spherical companion rested on the floor at his sculpted steel boots. "Stone's money still ain't hit my account yet," he said, his eyes flashing brightly from underneath his faceplate. "That crazy old man better not be tryin' to stiff us. Especially with all the work we put in for this plan of his. Hell, I built most of that damn ship he dreamed up."

Bull turned around with a scowl on his face. "Stop complaining and give him a few days, Mettle," he said. "Stone wouldn't dare cross us. He's insane, not stupid."

In the room's far corner, Malignus sat on the floor surrounded by several large, open food troughs. He surveyed the multiple chickens, sides of beef, and smoked hogs, drooling over them while his dozens of fingers and tentacles groped the air. "Yeah," he said between slurps. "If he sssstiffs us...we just kill him. And then eat him."

Bull screwed up is face and looked over at Malignus who inhaled another whole chicken. "You're disgusting, you know that?" he asked. "Me? I'm just glad Damsel got called away to do security at the Orb. Needed a break from all that crazy. I'm goin' upstairs for a few drinks. You should join me, Mettle. I know you're pretty much bonded to that suit of yours, but the girls I'm meeting tonight ain't got too many standards to speak of. Ain't got none at all, matter of fact."

Dreadmettle's silver hull reflected the ceiling lights, and he flashed his red cybernetic eyes at the Bull, glaring at him without saying a word. "Forget it," Bull said making his way to the set of double doors. "I'll see you sorry bastards later."

He reached out to open the doors as Dreadmettle stood up staring off into space. The sphere rose from the floor and hovered just behind his neck. "Hold on a second," Dreadmettle said. The Bull turned around. "Something's not right. We have an intruder."

Before the Bull could answer, a brilliant flash turned the room an intense red for a split second. And when the light was gone, David Sunstrom stood behind them. The Bull unsheathed the blades in his forearms, ripping the sleeves on his suit jacket. "It's the Sunstrom kid," he said, moving towards him.

Malignus got to his feet and knocked one of his food troughs over. "No," he growled. "It's dessssert."

David smiled and stood his ground. "You guys might actually want to be running," he said to them. Then, he spoke into his wrist communicator. "Any time, guys."

With that, an entire section of ceiling disintegrated above them, and Torrance dropped into the room inside a hot, swirling haze. An arcing red energy wave launched from his hands and struck Dreadmettle across his chest, knocking him across the desk. Janesha entered next from the hole in the ceiling, carrying Sam and Jovita inside her telekinetic bubble. When all of their boots touched the floor, Sam crossed his arms and watched Dreadmettle get to his feet.

"We're here for information concerning Isaiah Stone," Sam said. "You can be cooperative, or..."

Malignus rushed at them, saliva flying in every direction. Sam cursed and braced himself. He was able to get off one skull-splintering punch before the monster grabbed him, smashing his body through the white concrete wall. The two of them tumbled hard into the next room.

Dreadmettle's sphere spun angrily in Janesha's direction and opened fire at her with wailing heat rays, which she mentally deflected as she backed away from the silver globe-sized marble.

The sphere's master was a walking tank, punching craters in the tiled floor with his boots while the guns embedded in his steel hide blasted away at Torrance and David. Torrance flew around the room evading bullets, grenades, and lasers while David created a circular energy field in front of himself that allowed the gunfire to pass out of our reality without hitting him.

The Bull's fist crashed into Jovita and knocked her into the nearest wall. She narrowly ducked one of his curving blades but took a sharply aimed knee to the ribs. The Bull backed away from her, watched her spit blood in defiance, and threw off his jacket. "Had a pretty good night planned, honey," he said. "Guess you'll have to do."

Jovita tightened her body into a boxing stance and looked the Bull in the eye. "Alright then," she said to him. "Let's go."

On the other side of the broken wall, Sam shook the fuzziness out of his brain and got up. He looked around the shadowy gray room and the sets of steps surrounding him that led to the room's upper levels. As his eyes jumped from the hole he'd helped create in the far brick wall to the dozen or so masked human heads adorning the iron pikes, his breathing quickened. He recognized some of these decapitated men and women from his dad's files. He even remembered one or two of them coming to the mansion for dinner when he was younger. This was a trophy room for hero killers.

Malignus stood up behind him and roared, waiting for Sam to attack. For the first time since he'd faced the massive cancer beast, Sam was unmoved. The hair on his neck didn't straighten, his stomach wasn't in knots. What he saw all around him swept him clean of apprehension, and all that was left was the quiet, simmering rage that had been boiling in his soul since he left Antarctica.

Sam turned around to meet Malignus as his right hand unfastened the gold plated pistol holstered on his hip. As the creature stomped over to him, Sam pointed the rounded barrel at his chest and fired. The clunky, oblong shell exploded inside Malignus, doubling him over and bathing the room in a muted orange light. Sam holstered the gun while flesh bubbled and ran from the monster's body like melted tar.

Malignus howled in pain, dropping to his hands and knees as meaty sludge spilled off and pooled around him. "How's that taste?" Sam asked, looking down on him. "A little something I call ultimate radiation therapy, you miserable piece of garbage."

The radioactive light faded, and Malignus lay face down on the floor at Sam's feet, a frail, bald man revealed underneath the liquefying ooze. Sam looked back over at the gaping hole in the wall behind him. Suddenly, David appeared beside him. "We need you back over...ewww!" he said, noticing Malignus. "Nasty. Ready?"

One of the Bull's blades grazed Jovita's cheek. She ignored the stinging and punched him in the head and throat before sending a front roundhouse kick at his head. He gasped for air seconds before catching an elbow to the face. Blood seeped from between his lips and tears blurred his vision. Jovita bounced steadily on her toes, her relaxed fighting guard openly taunting him. With a crazed scream, he propelled himself at her blades first.

His vision was so muddy that he didn't see Sam appear in front of Jovita enveloped in one of David's red flashes. The blade housed in his left arm hit Sam's face first, sending sparks flying from his hardened skin. It happened too fast to tell for sure, but Jovita could've sworn she saw a smirk on Sam's face when he punched the Bull all the way to the opposite end of the room where he collapsed.

"I could've done that myself, you know," Jovita said, almost annoyed. David smiled at both Sam and Jovita while shrugging his shoulders.

"I'm sure," Sam said, watching Torrance and Dreadmettle throw energy bursts at one another.

"Oh, you don't believe me?" Jovita asked.

"It's not that. I just..."

"Watch me." Jovita hit a button attached to a glistening bracelet she had fastened to her wrist. Interlocking metal braces unraveled from the apparatus and wrapped tightly around her forearms and knuckles until fiery blue current coursed through every bit of the metal gauntlets.

Dreadmettle's armor had pushed well past its limits as it whined and groaned, blasting away at Torrance with white- hot laser beams. The energy crackling around Torrance's fists blocked those attacks and sent sizzling responses back at the gleaming cyborg.

Behind him, Janesha stretched both hands out in front of her and pulled them apart like she was playing with invisible yarn. Dreadmettle's sphere sputtered in front of her face and ripped itself in two. She watched the halves hit the floor, dumping all of the robot's nodes, wires, and processors. "Tired of playing with you," Janesha said.

Dreadmettle heard screeching metal, and for the first time since the Sunstroms arrived, he took his eyes off Torrance. "No!" he shouted, trembling as he watched his broken robotic friend's lights go out. Torrance forced a swell of fire into his palms and let it go right in Dreadmettle's face. The man-machine screamed and turned his smoking metal body directly into Jovita's fist. The humming blue energy field accompanying her punch exploded against Dreadmettle's chin and chest. The blow lifted him off his feet and cracked his armored suit in a hundred places. Completely dazed, he crawled at Jovita's boots, looking up at her with smoke and sparks spewing from the ruptured splits in his ruined suit.

Jovita looked over at Sam and flexed her fists as two blackened, exhausted cartridges ejected from the gear attached to her arms and hands. "Told you," she said with a predatory grin. "You can do so much with localized gravity."

"You're awesome," David said.

"Yeah, I know."

Sam ignored them, and walked over to Dreadmettle, lording over him with his fists clenched. "I didn't...sign up for this," Dreadmettle said, looking up at Sam from the floor.

"No, you thought you'd just kill my family and make a quick million or two, right?" Sam asked.

Dreadmettle looked away and hung his head in defeat. "Well?" Sam continued. "Where is he? Where is Isaiah Stone?"

"You expect me to turn him over just like that?" Dreadmettle sneered with blood in his teeth. "Why would I help Sunstrom trash like you? And besides, you'll never find him anyway. Heh. He's invisible."

"Never mind him, Sam," David said from across the room. "We don't need his help." Half of Dreadmettle's sphere was beeping sporadically in David's hands as he tinkered with wiring and toggle switches. "There," he said.

The sphere's eye port turned a bright red and sprayed several holographic diagrams of itself and Stone's Orb ship into the air around them. Dreadmettle lunged at David. "No!" he yelled. "Leave him alone!"

Torrance fired a laser bolt that burned a hole in the floor just in front of Dreadmettle, stopping him in his tracks. "Next one's gonna be a lot closer," Torrance warned. "Now sit still."

Jovita studied the holographic schematics surrounding her, turning from cross sectional views of the Orb ship to the twisted sphere's own blueprints. All the while the sphere beeped and whined like some wounded electronic hound. "Stone's ship is just a macro level application of this thing," she said pointing to the sphere. "And they're joined by some kind of digital tether. A signal. The original model should be able to home in on its larger baby brother and pinpoint its exact location whether it's cloaked or not. And I should be able to make it talk to the plane's onboard navigator. Never seen tech quite like this."

A map of the world, hidden among the holographic diagrams caught Jovita's eye. She swiped her fingers across it, commanding it to expand so that she could see each of the continents in detail. Two red overlapping circles at the North Pole flashed repeatedly. "Satellite monitoring," she said. "Sam, there's been two quakes in the Arctic. It's starting."

"Then, we need to move now," Sam said. "David bring that thing with you."

David gathered up all of the sphere's parts and followed the rest of the Sunstroms on their way out of the room. Dreadmettle stood up, his entire body in spasms from the jolts of electricity jarring him every few seconds. "I hope you do find him, Sam Sunstrom!" he yelled after them. "So he can slaughter you just like he did your parents!"

Janesha turned around with murder in her eyes. She was the only one of them who hadn't left yet. With the Bull lying unconscious on the floor beside her, she opened a pent up burst of mental fury that hit Dreadmettle with the power of a speeding tractor- trailer. Cinder blocks loosened from the walls as the telekinetic wave shattered Dreadmettle's suit and blasted him off his feet. His eyes rolled back in their sockets, and entire sections of the metal plating attached to his body disintegrated into twinkling black dust. Janesha released her fists and walked out of the room.

Michelle R. Bridgers – President of the United States
Lisa M. North – Battalion Commander
Messian Spacefarer – Protectorate King

Digital Audio Recording: **The President of the United States consulted Commander North and Messian Spacefarer following multiple, consecutive natural disasters.**

Classified meeting conducted at **(REDACTED)**
**This document may be incomplete and may require further editing.*

Bridgers – Okay. Saudi Arabia. Spain. France. Argentina. China. Japan. That doesn't even include the incidents here in the states. Point blank? I need solutions. It's happening everywhere. So where are we on this?

Spacefarer – I have several of my people working on it from various angles. Their collective assessment is that the planet is in fact destroying itself.

North – That's the consensus on my end as well.

Spacefarer – And at this juncture, there does not seem to be a point of origin for disasters we've experienced. But this will culminate in an extinction level event.

Bridgers – By the way, two more incidents this morning. Iowa and North Carolina. That's five of these disasters on U.S. soil so far. I'm not happy with this at all. I continued the relationship between the White House and the superhumans for this very reason. So that when (expletive) lava starts shooting out of the damn ground and blowing up American cities, you (expletive) people could figure it out and put a stop to it!

North – (inaudible) My team was in Wilmington, North Carolina twenty minutes after the (expletive) started. The Vanquisher prototypes got as many people to safety as possible. We're doing the best we can.

Spacefarer – But it's not enough is it, Commander? The Protectorate has heroes all over the world, performing search and rescue, providing food and medicine, shelters for the displaced. But if this continues, what does it matter? We'll all be destroyed in days.

Bridgers – Yesterday, I sat in a meeting with heads of state and emissaries from virtually everywhere. Everybody's trying to figure this thing out. But in the midst of all the handwringing? You could almost hear them sharpening their knives. Licking their (expletive) teeth. All it's going to take is for one nuclear cache to go off. For one military power to destabilize. And it's the next world war. On top of all this.

North – There has to be an origin. A place where all of this started.

Spacefarer – And it needs to be found before the end of the day. Make no mistake. There will come a point at which no matter what we do, the damage will be irreparable, the process irreversible.

Bridgers – (laughs) Douglas and Zoa sure picked a fine time to (expletive) die.

Spacefarer – Michelle, I've never pretended to understand your particular brand of humor. They were our friends. Certainly they deserve our respect.

Bridgers – Don't lecture me on my end-of-the-world etiquette, Messian. I have nothing but the utmost respect for them. I was just saying... (expletive)... I wish they were here to help with this. Douglas knew the inner workings of the planet better than anyone. He'd have a solution on my desk in a matter of – (inaudible)

North – They'd fix it, then call later and explain in very obtuse terms how they did it. (laughs) But the Sunstroms aren't with us anymore, are they?

Spacefarer – No. They're not.

End of Recording

CHAPTER 25

With the world underneath him burning a sparkling, liquid red, Julian Sunstrom sat on the floor in his cool personal chamber aboard the Orb, legs crossed, eyes closed. He breathed in slowly and exhaled peacefully. His mind wandered, travelling from the hovering Orb ship itself to the gray-skinned, amphibious mutants crawling and swimming miles below. As he quietly sifted their primitive thoughts, he merged with their single-minded loyalty to Isaiah Stone, their religious fear of the Window Device that stretched into the sky, gleaming under the sun.

Julian smiled. Stone had supplied him with a black and gray version of his father's adventure suit, and it fit perfectly. He stretched his fingers inside the new gloves while his mind combed the entire ship and bathed in Osiria's thoughts. He could feel her excitement, her longing to hold Stone's hand and rest her body against his as they entered a new reality. Damsel's tangled, convoluted imaginings were focused one moment, disgusting and murderous the next.

Julian steered clear of Stone's mind though. He was sure that his new mentor was somewhere overlooking one of the islands, basking in the world wide cataclysm he'd unleashed. But he dared not read his thoughts like he routinely did the others around him. The last time Julian tried that, Stone's mental defenses left him feeling as if he'd split his own skull open like a cantaloupe. He never said anything about it, but all he could surmise was that whatever the Rakken had done to Stone all those years ago had turned his mind into an endless black labyrinth, impervious to psionic meddling. Julian smiled, appreciating Stone's pragmatism. Only a man with that kind of psychic fortification would be comfortable keeping a telepath in his midst.

But just as Julian toyed with that idea, he sensed something else on the horizon. Determined, almost vengeful thought patterns. Familiar ones. Five of them. Julian's eyes popped open. "Oh, no," he said to himself. He jumped to his feet and ran to the circular viewport behind him. His entire body froze for a moment as his eyes followed the last Sunstrom jet streaking across the gray smoky sky. "You're supposed to be dead," he seethed.

Inside the plane's cockpit, Dreadmettle's halved sphere was plugged into the console, spitting out staccato beeps and chirps from its butchered robotic innards. Hot wiring spilled from within the metal casing onto the floor where the cables draped themselves across Sam's boots. He pointed to the digital monitor in front of Jovita. The pixelated image highlighted the islands that lay less than a mile directly below them. "There it is," Sam said. "The entire area's been cloaked, but Stone and that Window thing are down there somewhere."

"We just need to figure out where to land," Jovita said, scanning the image.

Behind them, David leaned out of his seat and pressed his hands against the glass as he looked down at the glistening ocean. Without warning, the perfect blue waves erupted in a burst of fire and lava. The shockwave jolted the plane and sent David's head into Janesha's shoulder.

"Stay in your seat," she said.

"Yeah, li'l man," Torrance said, watching the skies carefully. "Things are about to get real ugly. And fast."

The black speck Torrance had his eye on grew larger as it sliced through the clouds and approached the plane like a speeding missile. Janesha's heart stalled. Damsel. "Um, Sam," she said. "I think you might wanna-"

"I see her," Sam snapped, turning the controls so that the plane went into a sudden roll. Damsel missed entirely and tumbled through the sky. Jovita glanced over at Sam. He locked eyes with Damsel as she propelled herself fists first at the cockpit. "Really starting to dislike you," he said under his breath. "Vita, say hello."

Jovita's right hand jumped to the controls in front of her. Her thumb launched a spinning warhead that hit Damsel directly and exploded with red fire and thunder. Damsel emerged from the blast unharmed and catapulted herself at the plane again.

"Again," Sam said to Jovita. But before she could launch another missile, Damsel lowered her head, pressed her arms to her sides, and used her body to shear away the plane's entire left wing. Sam's head cracked the cockpit's glass into a spider web pattern as the plane fell into a spiraling free fall. He ripped off his seatbelts and pulled Jovita close to him. "Get yourselves to the ground," he yelled as the cockpit housings released and separated from the plane.

Sam leaped into the sky with Jovita's face buried in his chest. They held onto one another as Sam straightened himself into a nosedive pointed straight at the island below him. With debris zipping all around his head, David shut his eyes and vanished from the destroyed cockpit. Torrance and Janesha jumped from the plummeting wreckage, taking flight in separate directions as soon as they touched the sky.

Sam's boots cracked the island's surface when he landed with Jovita in his arms. The towering Window Device hummed and crackled a half-mile away across the island from them. "You okay?" Sam asked, looking into her eyes.

"Think so," Jovita answered once she caught her breath.

As the plane exploded in low altitude, a wet, sticky tentacle wrapped around Sam's leg from behind. He wound his hand up in the slimy appendage and threw the attached sea creature into two others who were approaching on his right side. Still cradled in Sam's arms, Jovita looked around at the dozens of amphibious monsters stalking them. "You might actually wanna put me down," she said.

Sam looked past the creature on his left and saw Damsel speeding across the ground like a human bullet. Her eyes locked directly on him. He let Jovita's boots hit the ground and closed his fists.

Stone stood in front of the Window Device, staring up at the glowing steel ring at the top of the grand structure. The lights on his armored suit flashed in a rhythmic pattern as it synched itself with the tower's inner components.

"Now," he said under his breath. "You will obey me, you beautiful abomination. Open your doors." He pressed a button on his black gauntlet, causing a sequence of tiny red flickering lights all over his armored suit's chest and shoulder guards. A crimson lightning storm began overhead as one of the floating circular platforms surrounding the tower swooped down and allowed Stone to step aboard. It carried him upward into the sky until Stone was face to face with the Device's massive ring.

Sparkling liquid rained down like a waterfall inside the ring until the liquid coalesced into a wet shimmering pool. The tachyon membrane was operational. Lava exploded from the ocean in wide fiery geysers that shot straight up into the air. Stone basked in the incredible, relentless heat, closed his eyes and smiled.

CHAPTER 26

Damsel kicked Sam to the other side of the island. He scraped the ground and bounced into the air several times before splashing into the ocean and sinking beneath the waves with tentacles wrapped tightly around his throat. Jovita's gravity gauntlets were fully charged with enough power for three punches each. She unloaded one in Damsel's lower spine, and the remaining five exploded against her head.

Damsel went down to her hands and knees. Blood dripped from her right ear. Her heart racing, Jovita reached for one of the batteries attached to her belt. She couldn't afford to let Damsel regain her footing. The battery snapped into place against the steel housings strapped to her right hand. Too late. Damsel grabbed Jovita's arms and squeezed until the gauntlets burst open and bones cracked. A sharp head butt sent Jovita reeling to the ground where she lay reeling. After blinking away the double vision, Damsel stood over her and removed her red cape. She pulled and stretched it out in front of herself, creating a makeshift rope out of the crimson fabric.

With monstrous glee swelling in her eyes, she grabbed Jovita up by her shirt and pulled the cape tight around her face and throat, feverishly choking the life from her. Jovita clawed at her neck and gagged as Damsel dragged her like a broken wagon across the ground. "Didn't Mommy ever tell you?" Damsel laughed. "You try and mingle with the gods, you're bound to get stepped on."

Jovita's eyes bulged, and her lungs burned. Chipped fingernails dug into the twisted material around her neck. But then, a familiar red light flashed silently beside them. Damsel turned her head just in time to see David Sunstrom reach out with both his palms facing her. "Point and click," he said with a sly grin.

Damsel started to lunge at him, but in a dazzling explosion of light, she and half her cape were gone. Jovita rolled on the ground, snatching the remaining material away from her throat as she coughed and gasped for air.

Another crimson flare lit up the ocean floor, and miles underneath the water's surface, Damsel appeared. Bubbles trailing from her nose and mouth, she looked upwards past the long, wide tendrils spawned from the Window Device's machinery, past Sam and the swarming sea monsters trying to kill him. Her powerful eyes pierced the dark, murky ocean water and found the sun. She pushed herself off the sea floor and flew towards it, screaming into the water. There was a child who needed killing.

Isaiah stood atop his levitating platform like a gleaming deity overseeing a new creation. He stared into the giant ring in front of him, hypnotized by the bright, shifting hues of the liquid tachyon membrane. He wondered how it would feel when his body made contact with the condensed temporal matter. Would it burn him alive? Would it tickle? A bright violet light flashed on his gauntlet. The tower was almost ready. He took a breath, gathered all of his confidence, and prepared to take his first step towards the ring.

But a hot laser bolt sliced through the air just in front of his face. He cut his eyes to his left and glared at Torrance who was flying right at him, melting the sky with the raw heat pouring out of him. Stone readied the cannons on his gauntlets. They were the same Stygian guns that had killed Torrance's parents. Surely they'd be enough to cut this young upstart down from the sky.

Stone raised his right fist and aimed carefully. But before he could fire, Torrance tumbled out of the air and hit the ground, screaming in pain as slender black rivers of pure death stretched out beneath his skin and began sucking the fire out of his atomic heart. Pressed against the ground by an irresistible, unseen force, his muscles twitched and cramped, his lungs struggled to take in air, his eyes bled. And although he couldn't move, he could see well enough to watch while Osiria straddled his chest and sat on him.

Her bottom lip hung, and she panted like a wild animal as her hands caressed his chest and his face. Her touch stung and numbed him at the same time, drawing the life out of every piece of him. "Death tastes so... good," she crooned. "Especially when it's done by someone as powerful as you. Come on, baby. Die for me."

A little more than a half- mile across the island from the Window Tower, Julian stood with his hands clasped behind his back, watching another lava-burst erupt from the ocean. He monitored his siblings' battle with his thoughts and laughed at the pain he sensed in them.

Janesha's boots touched the ground as softly as autumn leaves behind him. He didn't even turn around and acknowledge her. His chin tilted upwards a bit. His chest rose with puffed up arrogance. "So with all of this going on," he sneered. "With the planet at stake, you take the time to have a final confrontation with me. I'm flattered. But make no mistake. This will indeed be final if you choose to pursue it. So answer this: are you absolutely sure you want this?"

A tear formed in Janesha's right eye as she ground her teeth together.

"Out of respect for our relationship, I will allow you to leave this place untouched," Julian said. Then, he turned around and looked into her eyes. "But if you choose to attack me, I will turn your brains into pancake batter."

Janesha reached out with her thoughts until she could feel the very foundations of the island. The hurt, betrayal, and anger rolling off her drenched Julian's mind, and it amused him. He rubbed his head and smiled at her. "Oh dear," he chuckled. "It seems I've really bruised your feelings. It's ironic, you know. When we were younger, I thought I didn't have any powers. I spent so much time envying you all, hating the fact that Sam and the rest of you could do all of these extraordinary things and I couldn't. But then, my gifts bloomed virtually out of nowhere, didn't they? Now, I'm powerful enough to kill every one of you. Be smart. Save yourself. Walk away from all this. It's much too big for someone like you."

"Dad was right to shut you up inside that place," Janesha said.

Julian smiled again, this time baring his teeth. "Yes," he said. "Now that I look back upon it all. He was right. Because this is who I've always been."

Sam crawled back onto the island, scaling an uneven wall encrusted with sharpened coral. Several heavy sea monsters were attached, biting, and sucking at him, weighing him down, threatening to pull him back into the simmering ocean with their tentacles. But he tore through them and hurled the rippling flesh away from himself. Covered in blood and slime, he stood erect and looked up into the sky at Isaiah Stone who stood atop one of the many floating platforms above him. He watched Stone move nearer to the Window's giant ring and stick out his hand so he could feel the constant throbbing vibration coming from the swirling liquid inside.

Sam pressed his fingers to his right ear. "Vita," he said. "Stone's activated the membrane. There's no time. I'm going to..."

Damsel's fist smashed into Sam's face and knocked him on his back. She raised her boot intending to stomp a hole in his chest, but he rolled out of her way. Her foot splintered the ground, and Sam shattered her knee with a crushing kick of his own. Damsel muffled her scream behind tight lips and bloated jowls as she clutched her right knee with both hands and dropped to the ground. Sam's shin smacked against her skull. An earth-rumbling elbow dropped into her rib cage.

And after grabbing her by her soiled black uniform, Sam hurled Damsel a thousand yards across the island and watched her skip and scrape across the ground like a thrown rock. He activated his earpiece again and leaped straight up into the sky as he spoke. "Team," he said, boots landing on one of the floating platforms. "I'm going after Stone. Damsel will be back on her feet in the next few seconds." He leaped once more onto another platform. "Keep her contained. Take her down. Whatever you have to do." Several running jumps later he landed on the master platform just a few feet away from Stone who stood with his back to him. Sam sized him up, looking at every inch of the man's bulky armor and the blood red cape that blew in the hot, smoky breeze.

Stone turned suddenly and examined Sam from head to toe. "You know, I am beginning to believe I should have actually killed you all those years ago when I had the chance," he said. "You have become quite the pest."

"Thank you," Sam said with tight fists and a snarl.

Another explosion from beneath the Earth split the ground and rocked the platform.

"And so it comes down to the two of us," he yelled over the volcanic rage. "Poetic. To say the least."

"You know I have to stop you."

"I know you believe that, boy. But you cannot stop man's natural transcendence. We have been searching for this lost technology since the time of the ancient Akkadians. Socrates sent Alexander the Great after it. Hitler sought it. As well as a handful of America's more enlightened presidents. It is the key to who we are."

"You can save the crap, Stone. God knows I've read enough of it in the past few days. Your dreams of travelling the Continuum, seeding dead worlds, becoming the new Adam. Hate to break it to you, old man, but you're just another super-villain with a sick power fantasy. And like most of your kind... you're over-reaching."

Jovita and David looked up at the platforms, watching Sam and Stone as they faced one another. "We need to get up there and help him," David said.

"No," Jovita replied with her hands on his shoulders. "This is something Sam has to do alone. That fight is his." She activated her own headset and pressed her fingers against her right ear. "Torrance. We need to regroup. Torrance? What's your location?"

The ground shook behind them. Jovita and David turned around as Damsel ran at them with jet speed.

CHAPTER 27

On the Window Tower's far side, Torrance crawled along the ground on his and knees, his limbs completely sapped of their strength and nearly all sensation. His entire body felt like a snuffed out cinder pile. Osiria rode his back, grunting and moaning with her arms and legs wrapped tightly around him like a human spider. Torrance clawed the rocks underneath him and tried to drag himself another inch as his skin darkened and insides grew colder. His face dragged across the ground, and he lay there, staring blankly at the tower as Osiria dug her nails into his back and began draining the last bits of his life from him.

Across the island, Damsel slapped Jovita away from her. The blow split her lip and sent her twirling to the ground. Jovita's eyes rolled around their sockets. Damsel turned away from her and glared at David, who stood still, watching her like a deer lost in oncoming headlights. "You," Damsel bristled in his direction.

She launched a lightning fast punch at David but missed him as he vanished in a red blaze and appeared behind her. With a wild scream, she whipped back around with her fist swinging at David's head. The quick light burst blinded her, and she missed again. David materialized several feet to her left. "Jovita!" David screamed. "Help me!"

Damsel smiled when she cut her eyes right and glimpsed Jovita still lying confused in the dirt. She snapped back to attention, sucked air into her lungs and blew a gale force gust that knocked David flat on his back. With an animal's ferocity, she growled and moved faster than his eyes could send the images to his brain. Before David could blink twice, Damsel plunged out of the sky, her boots closing in on his face.

There was no time to teleport away, no time to cut himself out of this spot in reality and place himself in another. So in a fearful instant, he closed his eyes, grabbed hold of the nervous fire expanding inside his hands and chest, and let it go. The arcing red teleportation wave bounced from the ground and danced all over Damsel's body like electricity until it flashed brilliantly around her legs. A bloody mist sprayed into the air and across her face as she fell and screamed so loud that the ground broke apart like shattered glass.

There was nothing left below her knees. Those chiseled slabs of muscle and bone had been sliced away and shunted elsewhere as if there had never been anything there at all. Damsel's hoarse bellowing slowly turned into wide-eyed shock and whimpering as she clutched and stared at numb, mutilated appendages that used to be legs. Jovita rushed over to David, yanked him away from Damsel, and then pulled him close. "Are you alright?" she demanded. "What did you...what happened?"

"I...I didn't mean," David stammered, looking upon Damsel in pity. "I didn't want to hurt anyone."

Sailing high overhead on the master platform, Sam's knuckles pounded Stone's armored ribs and sent tremors through his entire body. Blood filled his mouth as another of Sam's punches slammed into his jaw and sent him to his hands and knees. He couldn't see it, but Stone knew there was another blow coming. Almost immediately, he pressed a tiny triangular panel on his suit's belt. A tiny light blue explosion erupted from his chest plate and reflected all of Sam's inertia back at him, sending him sliding on his back to the platform's edge with a stinging electrical charge.

"Your father was a fool," Stone said as he stood. "A sad, pitiful man hanging onto an antiquated moral compass."

Sam tried his best to sit up and shake the rattling out his skull. "He could have used this technology and journeyed to Alpha's Precipice years ago," Stone said, his words sounding like hellish static in Sam's ears. "Could have saved Zoa from her condition and returned to a crippled Earth as a king. A savior."

A blue energy field hummed to life around Stone's armored form, and he stepped on Sam's chest just before he could get up. Stone closed his fists, forcing the blue-white lightning through every cell of Sam's body. He screamed, but there was no sound except Isaiah Stone's musical baritone and the searing blue fire consuming him from the inside. And then the lightning stopped. Stone removed his boot from Sam's chest, and watched the smoke rise from his trembling body.

"Look at you," Stone said, peering down at him with emotionless eyes. "Ridiculous. Time and time again, you and your family fail to live up to your potential." The cannons on his gauntlets whined as they heated themselves and glowed white. "My captors began killing their heroes ages ago because they no longer had any use for them. I would say that day has finally come for us."

His gauntlets fired a blazing white fission beam through the right side of Sam's chest. The blast ripped through the underside of platform, splitting superhuman flesh and alien polymers alike. The ocean erupted in flames all around them spilling magma into the gray sky. Stone turned once again to the Window's circular opening and the swirling liquefied time particles warming the air around him.

He pressed a button on his left gauntlet, and a series of metallic constructs formed around his head and face to protect him during his passage through the membrane. "Beautiful, isn't it?" he asked Sam, who was struggling to breathe. "I suppose you would disagree with me. But as you lie there with your life oozing out of you by the pint, you must realize that your childish notions of right and wrong are no longer relevant."

Through weak, half opened eyes, Sam watched Stone move towards the Window. "It is time to inherit all of creation," Stone said. "You and yours will not be missed."

Slowly, Sam rolled himself over on his stomach and stared down at the ground through the clear blood stained platform. He gasped for air and fought to keep his eyes from closing. As high in the air as he was, he could barely recognize anyone below him, but the Sunstrom colors were impossible to miss. And directly in his line of sight was Janesha's gold, black-trimmed form. She was still fighting. Sam closed his right fist and pushed himself off his face.

On the ground, Janesha launched a wide telekinetic wave at Julian that threw him into the air and across the ground while carving a trench through stone and coral. Julian sat up as Janesha walked around him, circling him like a predator stalking a piece of meat. Julian squinted and wiped the blood from his forehead. "Tell me why I shouldn't shatter every bone in your body," she said. "Leave you a vegetable while this place crumbles around your head."

Julian looked her in the eye and smiled. "'Well...for one," he said. "You can't do anything to me unless I allow it."

Janesha's hands clasped hard onto both sides of her head. She bent over, screaming as she grit her teeth. The high-pitched squeal inside her head was like a drill boring a hole into her brain. And just as one knee hit the ground, she felt Julian reach into her core and grab hold of that private, secure place in her mind that housed her true power.

The noise inside her skull built to an unbearable crescendo. Julian pointed his fist at Janesha and hit her with invisible ideas made of something much harder and heavier than steel. The ground under her feet shredded like tissue paper, and Janesha flopped hard on her face and chest. She scraped her face against sand and rock as David appeared directly in front of her in a red flash. "Julian, please stop it," he said with his hands stretched out towards him.

"I gave our sister an opportunity to surrender," Julian said with white energy swirling in his eyes. "Should've taken it."

On the ground behind David, Janesha propped her weight on her right shoulder. "Get...get behind me," she muttered incoherently.

Julian smiled. "Might want to do as she says, baby boy," he said. "Or you can keep standing there, and I can pop your head off your shoulders right after hers."

David's eyes went completely red, and the sky above Julian's head split open. The giant, knife-edged boulder he'd just moved tumbled through the blazing opening, pointed directly at Julian. Janesha mentally commanded her body into the air just as Julian raised both fists and smashed the falling boulder into tiny pieces with a raging psychic bolt. Janesha landed in front of David, grabbed a fistful of his uniform, and forced him farther away her.

Somewhere high above them, Isaiah Stone released a mad stream of jumbled, chaotic rants as he ran across a cracked, floating platform towards the Window Tower's massive glowing ring. An unwavering zeal overpowered the fear building in him. A system of organic engines activated within his suit, and a jet propulsion system fired from his boots' steel-plated soles, launching Stone into the air. He flew towards the Window, his destination only few inches from his face. But someone had a tight, two-handed grip on the cape that trailed behind him. Underneath his helmet, Stone smirked. He didn't have to turn around or check his helmet's display screens to know that Sam Sunstrom had made one more desperate attempt to stop him. "Too late, young adventurer," he said to himself. And with a triumphant laugh rumbling in his belly, he dragged Sam across the sky and splashing into the tachyon membrane where both men disappeared within the swirling liquid pool coursing with electricity.

CHAPTER 28

Julian and Janesha set the air on fire with telekinetic energy while the water surrounding the island churned with lava and smoke. As the two of them hurled their thunderous emotions at one another, they ripped their rocky surroundings apart, sending stone bits and coral fragments flying. And when the heavy, dangerous looking pieces leapt into the sky, David erased them from reality and opened portals above Julian so the debris would fall directly on him.

With a derisive grin, Julian tightened his death hold on Janesha's mind and built a series of interwoven force fields around himself. The rocks and boulders crashed all around him, but nothing even came close to touching him. Janesha's thoughts were locked in a grueling tug-of-war with Julian's. Each time she used her power, she met a nearly impenetrable web of her twin's hate, jealousy, and depression. Anxiety and fear drowned her. But she forced her face above the putrid psychic muck just long enough to take a short breath. And then she was submerged again, pulling her forearms together in front of her face to block another psychic onslaught.

A large misshapen boulder narrowly missed Julian and crashed to the ground on his right, and razor sharp coral sliced his forehead just above his eyebrow. He glanced at David and sent the boulder spinning in his direction. "How dare you!" he yelled. David teleported out of the way at the last second.

Janesha took advantage of the distraction and freed herself from Julian's mind if only for a few seconds. She threw herself at Julian wrapped in a furious telekinetic storm. Blood ran from Julian's brow, and his mind reached deep inside Janesha again, finding an overflowing psychic wellspring to launch back at her. The explosion opened the ground up from underneath the surface and launched both of them into the sky, tossing them like dead leaves in the wind.

Julian hit the ground first. Janesha landed a few feet away, rolling until she slammed into Torrance. The impact ripped Osiria's nails from Torrance's back and knocked her onto the ground. Torrance turned over onto his side and breathed heavily as the black tendrils underneath his skin faded. Julian got to his hands and knees and looked over at Osiria, who had a wild, glazed-over look in her eyes. "What are you waiting for, you godforsaken succubus?" Julian spat in her direction. "Do your job and murder one of these idiots!"

David reappeared next to Torrance and kneeled beside him. "Come on, man," he said. "Shake it off. We need you."

Torrance looked at David with dim eyes and rested his head on the ground. "So...weak," he whispered dryly. "Just keep... keep her...away from me."

But the feeding frenzy had a firm hold on Osiria. She'd tasted superhuman, and the need for more set the marrow inside her bones on fire. She screamed as she lunged for David's back. Too spent to teleport away, David braced himself. But a black baseball-sized rock struck Osiria's temple, sending her back to the ground. A tiny crimson droplet stung her left eye as she turned and glared at Jovita who held another jagged rock in her right hand. "Biggest mistake of your life, girl," Osiria said with her entire face trembling.

Jovita could feel the death emanating from Osiria from a distance. It made her cold and nauseous, but she dropped the rock and shifted her weight from side to side with her fists up in a tight boxing guard. "Come on then, princess," she said. "Let's see what you've got."

As Osiria took a wild swing at Jovita, Julian finally stood up. He gazed down at Torrance and watched his fingers twitch. David looked up at Julian, and the two of them locked eyes for a moment. And out of nowhere, Janesha pounced on Julian from behind. Her hands grabbed his head tightly on both sides. Their shared telekinetic burst ruptured the ground. They twisted and spun together as Julian fought her like a fish with a hook in its mouth. But Janesha wouldn't release him. Her telekinesis held her hands firmly against his scalp as if they'd been fused to it. "Get off me!" Julian screamed. "Get...get away!"

"I've always been too scared to think about it," Janesha said. "Too scared to try and understand what you and I really are. But Dad knew. It's why he wanted you away from me. So you couldn't contaminate me. Turn me into something like you. It was true even the first time we shared thought space. Every time you walk around inside my head...I find myself standing in yours."

"No...No!" Julian screamed.

"If you have access to my power...then, guess what?"

In the depths of Julian's being, a thin, wailing tone built upon itself until it sounded like a thousand voices singing in unison. And suddenly, there was a loud, sucking pop. Janesha let go of Julian and let him drop to the dirt as she levitated just inches off the ground.

Jovita's right uppercut smashed into Osiria's chin, and her elbow ground itself into her nose. But each time one of Jovita's blows connected, she felt weaker and dizzier. Her joints ached, and she shuddered with the chills. An aggressive roundhouse kick missed, and Osiria grabbed hold of Jovita's arms with both hands, forcing her down to her knees. Death sprouted throughout Jovita's arms, chest, and neck like black vines. Osiria smiled. There was a particular euphoria that consumed her just before every one of her kills, and this time was no different. She liked to savor that last moment before death for as long as possible. Only when she'd reached a point of unbearable yearning would she grab the totality of her victim's essence and snatch it away for her own.

She'd toyed with Jovita's life long enough. And she would have inhaled her life like a glass of fine liquor if not for the strange presence walking around in her mind. Osiria panicked, let go of Jovita, and turned around to meet Janesha face to face. Janesha stared into her eyes, and at that moment, Osiria realized her intent. "No...don't," Osiria pleaded. "Don't take it from me."

Janesha pressed two fingertips against Osiria's forehead like a gun barrel. "You're cured," she said. White light flooded Osiria's mind as Janesha grabbed hold of it, delved deeply into its intimate, hidden places, and turned her power off. Osiria's eyes blinked repeatedly, and for the first time since she was a toddler, she was cut off from the warm, radiant lives pulsating all around her. She breathed deeply as a tear dropped from her face.

"I...I'm free," she said.

"One more thing," Jovita added, grabbing Osiria's arm from behind. A hard punch to the gut knocked all the wind out of Osiria's lungs and doubled her over. And with a harsh grunt, Jovita smashed her left knee into her face, knocking her out cold on the ground. She gave Janesha a weary smile as lava exploded into the air miles away from them. "Nice," she said. Janesha nodded back at her as she caught her breath and gathered her thoughts. And while she levitated over to David and Torrance, Julian groaned and climbed once again to a standing position.

Torrance was on his hands and knees, his strength slowly returning with each beat of the six-chambered organic machine laboring inside his chest. He looked up at Janesha and pointed at the man standing several yards behind her with his head cocked to one side.

"That was a very gallant thing you did for poor Osiria," Julain said. "But it is only a temporary fix. You aren't skilled or ruthless enough to provide her with the telepathic lobotomy she would require in order to stop those infernal cravings forever."

Janesha turned around and made eye contact with her twin. Jovita moved out of their way. "Now get out of my head, and give me my powers back, you stupid little girl!" Julian screamed. He ran at her while pulling a sharp curved blade from his belt. He held it firmly between his thumb and forefinger. Janesha didn't move. She simply watched him dash towards her with all of his rage, insecurity, and madness filling her head as much as his. She made up her mind in that moment that she would kill him if she found an opening. But behind her, David noticed the steam and smoke rising out of the ground just a few feet in front of Julian's next steps.

"Julian, stop!" David cried. "Look out!" His next words disappeared in the red-orange eruption that catapulted Julian high into the sky. Janesha caught her brother's limp form in mid-air with a telekinetic bubble and lowered him slowly. But he was already lacerated and burned, his face twisted and uniform shredded. Janesha gently placed him on the ground and forced her eyes away from her ruined brother.

CHAPTER 29

Sam had never experienced such speeds. Feeling like a rubber band stretched to its limits, he'd long since let go of Stone's cape and zoomed along with his arms at his side and legs straightened. He shut his eyes as the blazing lights and ever-shifting colors passing him by on both sides, overhead, and underneath became too much for even his enhanced senses. The tachyon membrane's slick, wet gel covered him in a perfectly sealed, gelatinous cocoon, protecting him from the void space that was an inferno one moment and freezing liquid the next.

As lightning flashed silently all around him in colorless nothingness, Sam struggled to stay awake. He forced his eyes open just in time to see giant icy shards tumbling weightlessly in front of him. And then, the gel that had seeped into his pours, nose, and mouth lulled him to sleep.

He awoke lying on his stomach, surrounded by sheer blackness and numbing cold. Barely conscious, he pushed his hand through a wall of moist material and began pulling himself through a canal that smelled like antiseptic wash. He was finally able to rest on his back once he reached the circular room covered in gleaming white triangular panels from the pristine floor to its walls and ceiling. As the tachyon gel crystalized and fell from his body like glittering sand, Sam breathed in the perfectly manufactured oxygen in the room and looked around at the two large swivel chairs moored to the floor and the computer consoles with their humming monitors made of pure light.

"White Chamber," Sam said to himself as he stood. The laser blast in his chest was steadily closing, but still it burned and ached. He jogged across the enormous ivory room and stopped at the sterilized console with golden alien symbols engraved on the buttons. Knobs and levers were mounted all over the place, and the holographic monitor remained silent with nothing but fizzling static and zig zagging lines displayed on the screen. Sam recognized a handful of the glyphs from his dad's journals, and he figured out a few more as he clicked several of the buttons in succession. Time. Space. Doorway. Select. World. After typing several different combinations, the monitor in front of him came to life with even more symbols and images of Earth.

White doors slid open at the far end of the room, and Sam quickly spun around. Blue-skinned, covered in white robes and golden armored plating, two winged figures entered and moved towards Sam, stopping in the middle of the room only to stare at him with inquisitive, transparent eyes. Light seemed to shine brightly from somewhere deep inside them. "Aelitar," Sam thought aloud.

"You know of us, human?" asked the female with a voice that resonated all over the room. "How is that possible? Humanity hasn't been aware of us since..."

"The real question," said the male. "The real question is 'how'? How are you here? There are no pathways on Earth that lead to the Observatories. How have you done this? You are trespassing. Human."

Sam straightened his back and looked directly at the beings who questioned him. "I am Sam Sunstrom. My world...Earth...is being destroyed," he said. "A very evil man...he has stolen a Window...and he's using the planet's core as a power source. I have to stop him...before he kills everyone on my world."

The female's expression softened, and she moved closer to Sam as her wings rustled against one another behind her back. "And who is this 'evil' man?" she asked.

Fission cannons screamed throughout the chamber, and wide laser bursts cut through the two Aelitar . Their blood sprayed the white walls and floor as they fell, sprawled across one another with their wings twitching. Two more blasts punched holes in Sam's upper back sending him into the computer display. He slumped to the floor as Isaiah Stone slowly materialized behind him. Smoke rose from Stone's black armor. The invisibility generators housed near his shoulder blades had worked themselves to their limits, and a smoking disc- shaped power cell ejected from his armor plated back, clanging against the floor.

Stone laughed to himself as he examined the room. Then he looked down at Sam who lay squirming in a pool of his own blood. "Damn it, boy," he said to him. "How many times to I have to kill you?"

Torrance felt as if he were being ripped apart. Like he was dying. He pulled together every ounce of heat energy he could find inside his body, and he pushed it into the sky from both fists, focusing it into a searing laser beam that carved a hole in the Orb ship floating above the smoky gray clouds. Fire and sparks trailed across the sky from the ship's underbelly. Torrance could barely stand up in the first place, and this last effort took all his remaining strength. He flopped to his knees, briefly taking note of Julian and Osiria lying face down on the rumbling island.

Beside him, Jovita typed frantically on a computer display she'd found built into the Doorway Tower's base. The monitor flashing in front of her face showed a simple digital diagram of the tower. "Based on Dreadmettle's design, that opening should lead right to the Orb's fuel cells," she said to herself. Then she looked over at Torrance who was generating more power each time his weakened heart managed to beat. "You okay, Torrance?" she asked. "Gonna need you in a second once we disconnect this thing."

Torrance nodded his head. "Yeah," he said, flexing his fists until they glowed again. "But what about Sam? He's still inside."

Jovita was silent for a moment while she got rid of the lump in her throat. Her right hand found her earpiece and pressed it. "Sam will make it back," she said. "As horrible as this thing looks, it's nothing but glorified Launch tech. And Sam does that in his sleep. Janesha. You're up next."

High in the sky, Janesha stepped through the broad, ragged hole that Torrance had just cut in the Orb ship. As soon as her boots touched the scorched metal floor, she searched the huge engine room until she found the purring cylindrical fuel cells that reached all the way up to the ceiling on both sides of her.

The walls and floor buckled as Janesha grabbed hold of the towering structures with her mind. Raw telekinetic power surged within her, and it was more than she'd ever felt before. Julian's psychic tinkering had opened up a geyser inside her brain, and she bit down on her bottom lip until it bled. The fuel cells cracked, spilling blue liquid onto the floor. Then, the tiny explosions started near the ceiling. Fire burst forth from the giant silver cylinder across from Janesha. She could feel the heat on her body as two more explosions vibrated under her boots. It was time to leave.

Surrounded by psionic shielding, Janesha lifted herself into the air and flew out the same hole she'd entered. And as she sent herself hurtling back towards the ocean like a dart, the Orb ship above her was obliterated inside the hot fiery blast that lit the dull, gray sky like a miniature star.

She straightened her body into a perfect arrow, knowing that her mind's force fields would protect her from the impact when she hit the water below. Jovita's voice sounded in her earpiece. "Congratulations," she said. "You just blew up Isaiah Stone's house. And more than likely killed whatever was cloaking these islands from detection. By the way, I'm sending some company in your direction."

Janesha sliced through the waves like a knife and plunged deep as her telekinesis drove her far beneath the surface. As long as she held her concentration, she would be able to breathe inside the psychic shell she'd created. Pride swelled in her chest. If only Mom and Dad could see her now. Jovita's voice spoke into her ear again. "Look for the roots," she said. "Living metal. Should be woven into the coral. Into the earth itself. You're going to have to find a main artery. And cut it."

Janesha slowed her decent into the rough, cold water and turned her head as she peered into the dark, murkiness all around her. "I don't see anything," she said.

And suddenly, the blue-green depths were alive with shimmering light. A school of small fish scattered. Janesha turned and smiled when she saw Torrance floating in a standing position behind her, the glow from his heart beaming from inside his chest and outward for miles underwater. He smiled in that mischievous way of his and silently let Janesha know he was okay. But then, his eyes widened, and he pointed at what he saw behind her.

Janesha turned around. As the water sparkled with Torrance's luminescence, she spotted giant, tentacle shaped monstrosities that groaned and creaked as they pulled raw power from the heart of the Earth. The low, crooning sounds pounded their ears and rattled their bones. And there were so many of them – hundreds at first glance, stretching down into the blackness on their way to the ocean floor.

Torrance turned his eyes from the tower's massive roots and scanned the shadows below. Something was coming at them from the bottom like a speeding underwater cloud. As the frenzied churning in the water closed in on them, Janesha and Torrance could finally see them. Isaiah Stone's blood thirsty sea mutants. An entire swarm of them.

For half his life, Isaiah Stone had dedicated himself to studying ancient writings, tombs, and corpses - subjecting himself to virtually every type of danger – all in a quest to stand exactly where he found himself at this precise moment. He'd long believed the White Chambers were real. And he'd even travelled the globe, teaching about them to anyone who would listen. But that was his faith talking. Today, however, Stone stood in one of those perfect observatories with the red-stained bodies of the Aelitar lying face down at his boots. Satisfaction in the fruit his life's work had produced swelled and poured out of him.

Joyful tears filled his eyes as he looked up at the countless holographic planetary models being projected on every side of him. The three-dimensional images of pure light were like pieces of candy waiting to be plucked out of the air and crunched between his teeth. All he had to do was give the command, and the chamber would give him access to the worlds of his choice. Innocent, untouched habitats and living beings would meet their new god – Earth's last son. They would worship him, obey him, bear his children, remake their worlds in his image. The scriptures his Pentecostal grandmother made him memorize as a boy came rushing back to him all at once. "In my Father's house are many mansions," he recited softly.

One of the Aelitar stirred and rolled over onto her winged back. She looked up at Stone as she wheezed and choked. "You...your kind... is forbidden here," she said. "It was...decreed."

Stone turned his attention away from the holograms and pointed his wrist mounted plasma cannons down at her face. "Things have changed considerably, my dear," he said. "The humans have returned to take their rightful place." A piercing whine emanated from his guns as they prepared to fire. The Aelitar shielded her eyes from the lights beaming down at her from Stone's armor and braced herself.

At that precise moment, Sam's cry shook the chamber walls and yanked Stone's attention away from his prey. Stone looked up to see him sailing across the room at him, blood trailing from his wounds in ribbons. He turned his cannons on Sam and fired. One blast drilled through Sam's chest while the others glanced off his shoulders and thigh. Stone gnashed his teeth and prepared to fire again. But before he could activate the triggers inside his gloves, Sam's fist smashed into face and knocked him senseless.

Grunting and leaking blood like water from a faucet, Sam dug his fingers into Stone's armored suit and ripped his chest plate into pieces, sending the black metal plating sliding across the floor. Sparks and smoke spewed from exposed mechanical joints and wiring as Stone fell to the floor. Suddenly, without the control mechanisms and batteries in the chest plate, the remaining sections of armor attached to his body felt like tons of cumbersome garbage hanging onto his limbs.

Sam stood over Stone like a giant looming over a shrinking child. "I know what I was born to do now," he said to him. "All these worlds. All these living, thinking beings at stake. I'm going to protect them all. From you."

Stone clicked a button woven into the fabric covering his left shoulder, and the rest of his armor began splitting into sections before falling away from him in clunky fragments. After a few seconds, the only thing covering his body was a white sheath. "Mr. Sunstrom," Stone said with a light cough. "If your siblings destroy my tower, we'll be trapped here. You'll never see home again."

"That works," Sam said, cracking his knuckles. "Long as you're here with me, you can't hurt anyone or anything else. You're done, Stone. This is our prison. We both die here. Together."

CHAPTER 30

The ride from the White House down to the President's underground bunker lasted exactly forty-three seconds. Commander Lisa North clutched a manila folder at her side and tapped her fingers against the elevator wall behind her as the emergency lights in front of her flashed silently. At thirty-eight seconds, the elevator car slowed to a complete stop. North could hear steel housings locking into place all around her. Then, the doors split apart, and she walked into a lonely, well-lit corridor.

After twenty-six steps, North pressed her thumb against the digital scanner on the titanium reinforced door separating her from the President. A painless scanning laser array read her genetics, and the door slid open. North walked into President Bridgers' office and found the leader of the free world seated behind her red oak desk, watching the flat screen monitors embedded in the walls around her. Secret Service agents dressed in all black filled the room. Bridgers heard North's footsteps closing in from behind. But her eyes never left the screens where city after city destroyed themselves with earthquakes, fire and magma.

A tall, broad brown-haired man in a black suit and tie stood in the corner behind the desk with his eyes closed as if he were concentrating intensely on something far away. North recognized Special Agent Marlowe instantly. She'd had a hand in recruiting him several years ago. And she knew that the stoic expression on his face meant that he was using his force field generating ability to shield this secret office space from any number of possible threats.

North walked in front of one of the flat screens and slapped her folder down on Bridgers' desk. The President finally looked up at North. "What is this?" she asked.

North leaned over the desk and smiled. "We've found the origin site," she answered. Bridgers opened the folder and spread the digital black and white photos all over her desk. Fuzzy satellite pictures of flying superhumans. Boiling oceans and dead sea life. Fire erupting from water in steaming columns. An impossibly gigantic tower.

Bridgers fumed as she removed her glasses and rubbed her tired eyes. "Where is this?" she said, almost hissing.

"A ring of islands in the Pacific. First there was nothing there. Then there was. Isaiah Stone must have been projecting a cloaking field."

"Stone is there. Right now."

"Sat imaging picked him up at least twice."

Bridgers put her index finger on the photo directly under her nose. "Is that a Sunstrom uniform I'm looking at?" she asked, closing her eyes and rubbing her forehead.

"Yes, it is."

Bridgers quieted herself for a moment, looked down at the pictures, and then back up at North. "Deploy every asset in your department if you have to," she said. "It doesn't matter if the world literally cracks in half and we're looking at the damn apocalypse tomorrow morning. My first act will be locking every man, woman, and child standing on those islands away forever."

North saluted her commander-in-chief.

By now, Janesha and Torrance were at least a half- mile below the ocean's surface, and they plunged even deeper as Stone's sea mutants swam fiercely at them. The nearest one lunged at Janesha with an open mouth full of sharpened needles. She raised her right palm and sent the pale monster barreling into its kin, scattering them in all directions.

Torrance pointed his fist and burned a boiling, glowing arc through the water that separated heads and limbs from bodies. Red bloody clouds puffed into the water all around them as body parts floated down into the depths. Janesha looked over at Torrance who was burning through another group of mutants that had thrown themselves at him. She'd always known about his superhuman heart and how it generated everything he needed to survive. But to actually see him fully submerged underneath the ocean without any kind of breathing apparatus – to know that he'd willfully shut down his own lungs and was relying solely on the energy generated by the organic sun inside his chest for sustenance- made him seem absolutely amazing.

The pressure around her increased steadily, pressing against her telekinetic shielding. But as long as she focused her mind, the red-orange glow outlining her form protected her from crushing liquid tons and extracted the oxygen from the water, transforming it into a breathable form.

She pressed her earpiece after willing another sea mutant to split itself in half. "We've got a ways to go," she said. Torrance looked at her and pointed at the silver appendage behind her that looked like several gigantic mechanical tree trunks braided together. "Right," she said. "Let's see where it goes."

They propelled themselves downward into the bottomless darkness. Torrance led the way, letting his natural glow light the cold, black expanse. They followed the iron clad roots, launching themselves for countless minutes like human torpedoes. The gray mutants crawled along the humming root system like aquatic vermin and attacked them with tentacles and shining teeth. As steam and smoke rose from the fissures in the earth, Janesha cut loose with mental outbursts that exploded like bombs, maiming and ripping the monsters apart.

Torrance zoomed further into the deep, forcing the energy inside him to burn hotter and brighter. The mutants circling him covered their eyes and fell away from him, their skin crisping and blistering. Then, he saw it, and the sight of it stopped all his forward movement. Torrance floated, watching with glowing eyes the lava-filled split in the ocean floor and the giant bundle of metal tendrils growing out of it.

And wrapped around it all, bonded to the throbbing, scathing metal, shapeless, branching masses of meat and eyes and gills and teeth. More of Stone's mutants pulled themselves across the behemoth's skin with their tentacles while the flesh beast pushed more of them out of its flabby orifices. Janesha floated at Torrance's right as a dead creature's carcass drifted past them and into the molten abyss. A long, shrill scream sliced through the water and tunneled its way into their heads. "Jovita," Janesha said while pressing her earpiece. "I think we found the main artery."

"Good. You're going to need to sever it," Jovita shot back.

"And there's something else down here too. It looks like…like…"

Torrance watched as the giant meaty horror below them birthed several more of the tentacled horrors into the water.

"It's the queen," Janesha said to herself.

CHAPTER 31

Sam's blood pooled underneath his own boots as he grabbed Stone by the throat and lifted the man high into the air. Choking and grabbing at Sam's arms, Stone spit red specks into his dirty white beard. It would have been so easy to crush every bone in his neck with one squeeze, but he didn't. He couldn't. That wasn't the man Douglas and Zoa had raised.

Sam looked his enemy in his tired eyes. "You lose, Isaiah Stone," he said. And as soon as the words left his mouth, an explosion shook the White Chamber, and warm, natural sunlight radiated against Sam's broad back. He dropped Stone to the floor, turned and looked past the dead Aelitar on the floor, past the consoles and monitors, and focused on the far section of the chamber that had just separated into flat, planar sections revealing a miniature circular pool just large enough for one person. As he stared into its swirling tachyon membrane, he recognized the open skies. It was Earth. Home.

"Go... Sam Sunstrom," said the female Aelitar from across the room. Her voice was strained, and her bloody, trembling hands propped her up on a console at the back of the room, barely keeping her from falling back to the floor. "This is...this will be your only chance to...to escape. And Sam? If you love your planet. Your people. Forget you ever saw this place."

Sam nodded and limped towards the doorway as the Aelitar dropped slowly to her hands and knees. "No!" Stone screamed. Running like a mad dog, he intercepted Sam on his way to the doorway and tackled him to the floor. The skin tight sheathe covering Stone's body held a slight glow as emergency power sizzled through woven circuitry. He held Sam's head against the floor and spat into his ear while he talked.

"You were wrong earlier," Stone whispered. "When you said you knew what you were born to do. You're not here to save people. Your father. Your mother. They created a miracle. Look at you. Your immense strength. Invulnerability. Self-repair. Endurance. Your body was meant to survive the journey between worlds, young man. You were specifically designed to travel the Unified Continuum with me. Born to change humanity's course."

Burning sand and wind hit Osiria in the face as she stared at the lonely ring atop the Doorway Tower. She scanned the area for Stone, and when she couldn't find him, she knew in her heart exactly where he'd gone. Both eyes blurred with tears. She dropped to her knees under the sky's red haze. "Isaiah, no," she sobbed. "Don't leave me here. Please." Her fists shook, and her knuckles bled against the ground. "You lying sack of garbage! Don't leave me!"

With her chin tucked against her chest and tears falling freely, she didn't see the legless, disfigured form crawling towards her from behind. Osiria heard Damsel's right hand crunch the rock beside her boot. She gasped, turned to see, but it was too late. Damsel dove onto Osiria and locked her inside an unbreakable chokehold.

"Isaiah will never take me back now," she said with a deranged snarl. "I'm ruined."

Osiria struggled to speak.

"Now...he won't want you either," Damsel said into her ear. "Should have done this the moment I met you. No one wants...a dead girl."

Osiria's eyes bucked wide open with desperation, and she grabbed hold of Damsel's wrists, clawing at her arms and hands. Damsel's grip loosened and adjusted itself for just a moment. But it tightened again just before she screamed and snapped Osiria's neck. Damsel pushed Osiria's corpse away from her and lay on her back, bleeding, crippled and staring up at the sky.

Torrance gathered as much heat as he could summon within himself and focused it into a wide solar energy beam that cooked the queen mutant's massive back. Its piercing roar shook the ocean, but it wouldn't let go of Janesha. A long, thick appendage covered in thorns and barnacles protruded from the thing's underbelly and had wrapped itself several times around Janesha's body from her legs to her throat. She could feel its pulse beating furiously through her fading telekinetic shell. As Torrance fired searing laser beams at the giant mutant queen in rapid succession, it dragged Janesha across the black lava encrusted ocean floor.

Torrance looked into the dark, slick eyes embedded in the hulking piece of meat and then focused on the crusty, armored tentacle that held his sister and threatened to squeeze the life from her. If Janesha lost consciousness or control of her power for even a second, her shielding would instantly vanish. She'd be simultaneously crushed and drowned. So, he carefully aimed his right fist at the slithering tentacle and prepared to slice it off. But suddenly, the creature yanked and retracted the colossal appendage back into itself. The tentacle and Janesha disappeared inside the monster.

Torrance screamed silently into the watery void as more lava jumped from the rocks below him and another dozen sea mutants swam at him. He burned through two of them while the others moved closer.

A mucous opening sealed itself behind Janesha. She sat up, surrounded by slime and wet, shining flesh. Hot, foul air burned her eyes and nostrils. Gagging, she looked through the sweltering fog and her chest seized as she noticed the sharp thorny structures protruding from the scarred, fatty walls. "Janesha!" Jovita's voice screamed into her earpiece. "Can you hear me? What's happening down there?"

"I think...I think I'm being digested," Janesha said. Jovita's voice sounded for just a second and then it was cut short with loud, blaring static. Janesha took a long breath, balled up her fists, and forced all of the oxygen inside the alien stomach sac to concentrate itself on her form.

Telekinetic shielding trapped the oxygenated air and outlined her body with a renewed brightness. Janesha stood and pressed her thoughts against the quaking flesh surrounding her and instructed all of it to move.

Another of Torrance's laser beams eliminated more sea mutants, and as the amphibious corpses sank away, he felt a rumbling in the water. Turning his golden, luminous eyes on the expanse of mutant queen flesh below him, he watched a muscle-laden section buckle and explode, spewing crimson fluid and heavy chunks of exoskeleton upwards. Janesha rose out of the wound while the queen's tentacles detached from the Window Tower's mechanical supports. The queen released a siren of a wailing scream as she fell into the lava-filled trench below. And a horde of sea mutants dropped off the hanging, protruding roots, following their mother into a burning tomb.

The light from Torrance's eyes cut through the water like a pair of headlights. His heart drummed and head pounded. The golden wave he unleashed lit the ocean depths as if the sun itself had risen underwater, and the laser beam sliced through iron and rock alike. The metallic veins woven into earth regurgitated liquid fire like giant, robotic dragon-serpents when they exploded, spraying the ocean bottom with lava and black poisonous fumes.

Janesha expanded her shimmering, thought-powered protective shell so that it covered Torrance as the two of them shot up towards daylight. Explosive bursts popped along the tower's conductors. The sea mutants unfortunate enough to remain in their vicinity were instantly incinerated while others scrambled into the red-hot, seething gloom. Finally, Torrance and Janesha broke through the ocean surface and climbed high into the sky, propelled by both Janesha's telekinesis and Torrance's heart-engine.

A final volcanic eruption sent shining lava after them into the sky. Janesha closed her eyes, and with a sigh, she relaxed her mind, allowing herself to drop back to the water where she floated limply on her back like a dead woman. "Oh my God," she murmured. "We did it."

Torrance's body scraped hard against rock, sand, and gravel when he hit the nearest island. He pushed himself off his face and forced his lungs to inhale for the first time in countless minutes. The rumbling beneath the ocean rattled the ground underneath his ribcage, and Torrance looked up in time to see fire erupt from inside the great Window Tower itself.

The entire structure shook while fire and lightning consumed its base. Jovita and David ran as far as they could before another explosion knocked them both to the ground. Janesha landed softly beside them and helped them to their feet. They looked a few yards away and found Torrance still on his knees, quietly watching the tower go up in smoke. Melting, bending iron supports sounded like out of tune brass instruments as colossal, blackened pieces of metal crashed to the ground.

"Sam," Torrance said to Jovita. "Did he...?"

Jovita lowered her eyes and put her arm around Janesha as the tower's massive ring slowly began to unravel. "No," she said. "He's still out there somewhere. He's not coming back."

CHAPTER 32

Stone pinned Sam to the White Chamber's cold floor and his elbow locked in place across his windpipe. The electrical current racing through Stone's second skin set every nerve in Sam's body on fire. "Leave Douglas Sunstrom's tired, sad legacy behind," Stone said. "Start a new path. The one you were meant to follow. We can be the first modern humans to unlock the secrets of the continuum. I'll even act as your teacher, my son. The father you always needed."

Sam defiantly turned his head and looked at the churning pool of fluid space-time. The emergency hatch and the accompanying image of the sky above his home world was fading. In mere seconds, Earth would be a distant memory for him, and this white observation deck would serve as his permanent cell and eventually his tomb.

He grabbed Stone's arms and crushed them in his fists. Stone howled as his suit sizzled and went dark. Sam's forehead broke Stone's nose, and his knee splintered his ribs, driving all the air out him. As Stone bent over and coughed, Sam rolled across the floor until he'd splashed into the tachyon pool. He closed his eyes and allowed himself to sink into the electrified substance. "Sam, no!" Stone yelled in outrage. With sharp bone fragments stabbing his lungs each time he took a breath, Stone stumbled to the Window's rim overlooking the humming liquid swirl.

He looked into the spinning whirlpool, straining his eyes for any hint of Sam's body. But there was nothing until suddenly, Sam's sizzling outstretched hand breached the liquid surface, grabbed hold of Stone's suit and pulled him in.

He screamed but there was no sound as the liquefied time particles burned him from the inside out. Most of his body vanished inside the shining watery cauldron. Only his head and one of his arms stayed above the waves as he wailed and thrashed wildly. And suddenly, the entire pool went crystalline in a flash of light. The solid, sparkling tachyon particles cracked and split into thousands of glassy shards. Isaiah Stone's severed head rolled across the floor for several feet and finally stopped. The Aelitar who had opened the emergency Window had just closed it. She collapsed back onto the floor and stared into Stone's empty eyes as she died.

"Sam, I'm so sorry," Jovita whispered into the smoky wind. The ring above the Window Tower was a blackened husk and looked as if it would disintegrate at any moment. The fire had finally gone out. All of the explosions had stopped. No more eruptions. They had saved the planet even it had cost her best friend. The rest of the Sunstrom family stood around her and gave the crumbling tower a final look.

But there was one last explosion left. It rumbled from somewhere within the tower as the wide ring above it lit itself one more time and spewed a river of tachyon liquid into the air. Two bodies fell from the sky, and the tower caved in on itself, leaving a black ashen mountain of rubble. "Janesha! Torrance!" Jovita ordered.

Before she could say anything else, Torrance zoomed into the air to meet and grab one of the bodies while Janesha used her telekinesis to slowly lower the other to the ground. The one that gingerly landed at Janesha's feet was incinerated, headless, and missing an arm. Jovita backed away from it and pulled David away while Janesha turned her head in disgust. Torrance landed with a warm, golden glow surrounding him, cradling Sam's smoking form in his arms. He laid his still brother down carefully as Jovita rushed to his side, kneeled and brushed her lips against his bruised face. Warm tears fell from her face while her trembling hands hovered over the crisp holes in his chest.

Sam's eyes slowly opened and focused on each member of his family. Then, they settled on Jovita. "Time," he said, his voice dry and raspy. "Time...to go home...don't you think? I mean...since it looks like we've worn out our welcome and all."

Jovita's forehead dropped onto his chest as she laughed aloud. "Pretending to die and scaring me to death never gets old to you, does it?" she asked with a smile.

"No," Sam said, smiling back at her with his eyes shut. "Can't say that it does."

A device resembling a cellphone chirped and vibrated on her belt as Torrance, Janesha, and David helped Sam start the painful, laborious process of standing. Jovita backed away and checked the device on her belt. She whipped it open so that the screen was visible, and several blue holographic screens floated in the air above her palm, projecting live news reports and headlines from all over the world.

A dozen or more reporters spoke at length in various languages about the fire, mass destruction, and deaths affecting their cities. Their stories and experiences were all different. Infernos from underneath the earth. Crushed, fallen buildings. Broken cities. Friends and family members lost. But there was one common thread that connected all of their stories, one that resounded all over the world. It had stopped. Suddenly, the nightmare was over.

"Is the jet in any shape to fly out of here?" Sam asked with his right arm draped across Torrance's shoulders.

Jovita gave Sam a disappointed glance and shook her head. "There's got to be pieces of that thing all across the Pacific," she said. "Janesha..."

Janesha cut her off in mid- sentence. "I'm barely able to lift a few rocks right now," she said. "I...I don't even think I could get us all off the ground. Maybe after a few hours or so..."

Jovita looked up into the dirty sky. "We don't even have a few minutes," she said. Everyone else turned their eyes upward at the military jets and helicopters soaring overhead. Sleek black choppers and harrier planes began setting down in the distance on neighboring islands as much larger camouflaged cargo planes hovered above the Sunstrom family.

David looked up and a thin smile grew across his lips. "Well, there is one way out," he said to Sam.

Sam instantly knew what David meant. He cut his eyes at Janesha, Torrance, and Jovita, glancing across each of their faces. "Can you move everyone safely?" he asked.

"Course I can," David answered with his chest out. "You just make sure you're ready to fly."

"Sam?" Jovita called out anxiously as the airships descended.

"Do it," Sam said. "But that means all of us." He looked over at Julian who lay unconscious several feet away from them. "Even him."

Janesha started to argue, but Sam's eyes stopped her. "He's still one of us," he said. "Regardless of what he's done."

The first gray-hulled harrier jet set down just as David's power surged and lit half the island with a red energy flare. Lisa North's boots hit the ground two seconds before her co-pilot's. Her drawn pistol gleamed in the faded sunlight as the soldier at her back signaled to the helicopters surrounding them.

Commander North had taken the reins of the Battalion Division from Marcus Covey. It was America's covert military response to superhuman threats. They were counted among the most well trained soldiers in the world. Everyone knew their roles and executed with precision. So, as disciplined as her people were, why were five of hers standing in the center of the island, shaken and disoriented?

"What is this, Franks?" she said, walking up to the largest of them.

Franks instantly stood at attention. "My...plane," he said looking around at the other military vehicles. "First we were...we were up there." He pointed his thumb repeatedly into the air. "And then we...we weren't."

North looked up into the sky and spotted the missing black jet just before it shot away into the charcoal sky. "Damn you, Sunstrom," she grumbled under her breath. And with that, she swallowed her frustration and ordered her Battalion team to sweep the island.

CHAPTER 33

It had been three weeks since the world nearly ended. During that time, Sam made sure to visit the cemetery for about an hour every day. He'd pace, sit at his parents' gravesites, or simply stand there, facing the headstones and talking into the chilled winter air, conversing with old friends. There were days when Janesha, David or Torrance would join him, but they knew to leave him alone. They could see what was happening in him, the weight lifting from his shoulders, the peace settling in his eyes moment by moment.

But on this particular Monday morning per Jovita's advice, Sam decided to hold a press conference. He couldn't stand the idea of the Sunstrom estate crawling with media personalities sniffing around for some ratings-boosting scandal to report. So he only invited his parents' closest friends.

Dressed in white, burgundy-trimmed adventure suits, Sam, Jovita, Torrance, Janesha, and David stood behind a podium with a dozen reporters seated in front of them. The rebuilt Sunstrom Mansion remained incomplete behind them with exposed beams and metallic support structures visible from the outside. There wasn't even any true roofing yet, but as the small, shining construction robots buzzed through the air like bees, the message was clear. The Sunstrom legacy was alive and well.

"...and as stated before in recent correspondence, there will be a packet released to each of you before you leave which will include a fully rendered explanation of the horrific events of the past months," Sam continued into the microphone. "Now. The reason you're all here. I'd like to present to the world the all new Sunstrom Scientific Research and Exploration Team."

"Mr. Sunstrom?" called Susan McKenna from the front row.

"Susan," Sam replied with a smile.

"Yes. You seem to be highlighting the science aspect of your new team. But all of you possess special abilities, and your parents never shied away from the word hero. So...well...I'll just ask. Will the new look Sunstroms be engaging in what has been termed 'superheroic activity'?"

Sam smiled at McKenna as if there was something he wanted to say but decided to hold between his teeth instead. "We'll just have to see about that, won't we?" he asked. Sam walked away from the podium with Jovita at his side. Torrance gladly took over and answered more questions while the two of them walked across the lawn holding hands, fingers interlocked.

As the newly rebuilt and upgraded Maddie walked towards them from the front of the house with a digital tablet in hand, Sam listened to questions being thrown at Torrance one after another.

How would you describe Sam's leadership style?

What is Jovita Vargas' relationship to the family?

Is there a partnership between the Sunstroms and Sapien Rex?

Torrance, is it true that you don't eat?

Sam shook his head while Maddie glanced over at Torrance and his captive audience with a smirk. "I'll let him handle them for now," Sam said.

"You know he loves the attention," Maddie said.

"Always has. So, Maddie. Vita. I've been examining your work on the house. Future forward enhancements. Security's impenetrable. You two have actually improved on Dad's original designs. Looks good."

Jovita took a step back and gave Sam a grouchy stare. "Good?" she said mockingly. "We turn this place from a literal hole in the ground into…into this, and all you can say is 'looks good'?"

Maddie folded her mechanical arms. Sam smiled and grabbed Jovita's hand. "It's phenomenal," he said. "Much like yourself. Thank you. For everything."

Jovita smiled back as she put her arms around him. "Now that's more like it, Sam Sunstrom." And they softly pressed their lips against one another's, letting the world and all its cares melt away if only for a few heart beats.

"Ok, you two," Maddie interrupted. "We've got major sit down interviews coming in the next few days. We need to get a roof on this place, Jovita, if we want to make a great first impression."

Jovita stopped kissing Sam, licked her lips and glanced mischievously at Maddie. "You enjoyed being deactivated, didn't you?"

"Ah. I understand your point, Ms. Vargas," Maddie said. "Feel free to continue."

Sam chuckled and kissed Jovita again before loosening his embrace and looking into her eyes. "Vita, I…I just want you know…if there was ever any question…"

"Sam," Maddie interrupted again. "Not to be a nuisance, but…"

Sam looked away from Jovita and across the lawn at the young woman in the black jacket and jeans standing under the trees. "It's North," Sam said softly.

"Well," Jovita said. "Let's see what our new best friend wants, shall we?"

Lisa North's eyes calmly took in the projectors, tables, and empty chairs decorating the Suntroms' underground conference room before focusing on Sam and Jovita who sat comfortably across a wide glass table from her. "The President wants you gone," North started. "You know that don't you? All of you. Even David. She wants each of you locked away inside your own little tailor made prison cells and buried. Deep. Miles beneath a remote artic wasteland. And she has everything she needs to make that happen."

"So why haven't Battalion operatives stormed the big, evil Sunstrom castle yet?" Sam asked.

"Because that would mean yet another destructive wrestling match involving magnipotents and explosions and property damage that we have to explain to the American people. Hell, we're still trying to convince everyone that they didn't just experience an aborted apocalypse. And... because I happen to believe that we're all a lot better off with you and your family out here doing whatever the hell it is that you do. I happen to think that you are very much your father's son."

"Thank you. But you don't know me at all."

"I know that you and your family just saved the entire planet. I know that four days ago, you walked into Sapien Rex and turned in your resignation. Jovita Vargas here just did the same thing. With Daddy's blessing I hope. But see...I don't think you give up that kind of career unless you're committed."

"So the President decides not to come after us because what...you have a hunch about us?" Jovita asked.

"The President brings me into situations like this because I've been dealing with magnipotents for most of my career. She trusts my judgment. If I thought you were a threat, I'd have all the special projects I'm currently working on aimed at your living room right now."

"Sounds exciting."

"You have no idea."

"What do you want from us?" Sam asked.

"Something's happening out there," North continued. "Isaiah Stone was crazy...but he wasn't stupid. The planet's on the verge of some kind of exponential leap forward. I don't know what that entails, but...it's happening. Everything I've read about your parents suggests that they knew it too. There are individuals sprinkled all over the world...working their way through underground circles...calling it the next age. And the chatter is getting louder. The other heroes are out there taking down the aliens and super criminals and the monsters. Someone has to be there for humanity. For whatever's coming next."

Sam leaned forward. "Let me tell you something, Commander. I once swore that I'd never follow in my Dad's footsteps. But here I am. Head of the family. With one hell of a support team around me. Now, I walked out there today and introduced the world to a research group. But make no mistake, what I'm building here is nothing short of a state-of-the-art, cutting edge super problem-solving unit. When the world needs us to work, we'll be ready. And by the way, you ever come to my home with ill-intent, it'll be the worst day of your life. We eat special projects for breakfast around here."

North leaned back in her chair and smirked. "Fair enough."

"Any other concerns?" Jovita asked.

"Oh, yes. I want my damn plane back, Mr. Sunstrom."

Sam and Jovita smiled at one another.

The press conference had been over for thirty-seven and a half hours before Sam received his first emergency call. It was from a private number. One of Douglas Sunstrom's old associates. A dead subterranean city in Greenland. And zombies.

For a few moments, Sam paced across the floor of the newly rebuilt hangar with his hands clasped behind his back. Maddie's robotic architects had definitely been working overtime, salvaging and constructing new functional vehicles from the wreckage left behind by the Headhunters' attack. His boots standing firmly on the golden Sunstrom 'S' engraved in the polished floor, he looked around at the empty spaces on the hangar floor where one day the new racers, tanks, and jets he was designing would eventually sit. But for now, the massive, blade-shaped family plane, which was perched on the circular landing platform in front of him would do. After all, it was conceived by merging his parents' vehicular concepts with his own. So, in that respect, it was perfect.

Jovita walked past him and boarded the new Sky Piercer. As she strapped herself into the co-pilot's chair, Janesha, Torrance, and David entered the hangar. Janesha and David got onto the plane while Jovita swiped her fingers across a broad touchscreen, causing the engines to come alive with purring menace. Torrance stood beside Sam and placed his hand on his shoulder. "Meet you up there," Torrance said, directing his eyes towards the ceiling.

The sound of a low bass drum emanated from inside Torrance's chest and vibrated within the floor. His eyes glowed and crackled while he rose into the air. A hexagonal section of ceiling slid away. Sam watched his brother fly into the opening and head into the secret tunnels that would lead Torrance to the sky.

Sam walked up the loading ramp and plopped down in the swivel pilot's chair. The landing platform disconnected from the floor and pushed the plane towards the ceiling as Sam secured himself and put on his headset. He glanced behind himself at David and Janesha. They nodded silently, confidently in his direction. Jovita pressed as series of symbols on the touchscreen, and the entire ceiling split apart into two halves, allowing the plane to lift into the air and rocket away into the clear, boundless blue.

Torrance joined the family plane at thirty thousand feet, a glowing light field outlining his entire body. He flew just a few yards away from the right wing, catching Jovita's eye from her cockpit window when he barrel rolled to his left. She shook her head at him, mumbling, "show off" under her breath.

Sam put the plane on autopilot and daydreamed into the sunlit horizon. His right hand found Jovita's and gripped it snugly as he smiled. He couldn't help it. He hadn't been this excited since he was twelve years old.

EPILOGUE

When Sam returned to the Sunstrom Estate from the Window Disaster – as he now referred to it- the first thing he designed wasn't a new home or equipment. No, that first day, he met with Maddie and Jovita about constructing a prison. Buried deep beneath the lowest level of the mansion was a containment cell with only one purpose: the imprisonment and neutralization of Julian Sunstrom.

Still drowsy from weeks of pain medication and sedatives, Julian sat in a black holding chamber just around the corner from his cell. Scar tissue covered the left side of his face and body like thin, encrusted carvings. Dressed in all white, he could barely move his left arm, so he let it hang at his side as he sat, strapped firmly into his wheel chair. The weighty, cumbersome helmet that was locked into place over most of his head and face forced a buzzing electrical signal into his brain that kept him from accessing any of his psychic abilities.

A pale, freckled woman in a peach button up blouse and glasses sat across from him, using a black pen to check boxes on her clipboard while keeping a close eye on his behavior in between pen strokes. Julian cringed and twitched every few seconds, and there was a faint constantly grinding hum coming from his throat. She scribbled down more notes as he listened to the spherical, robotic sentries hovering in the air all around him, waiting to cut him down with weaponized lasers if he acted the least bit hostile.

"Julian," she continued. "You didn't answer the question."

He finally stopped humming and straightened up a bit, tilting his head to one side so that his neck was more comfortable. "I'm sorry, Dr. Noelle," Julian said, his voice strained and raspy. "Got distracted... for a moment. Yes, you could say that I had made a few friends before ending up in here. Two of them died. And the other...the other...the soldiers zipped her up in a black bag. But she was still breathing. Still alive from what I could surmise. Even with both her legs blown off. We tried to end the world, you know? Didn't exactly work out. But yes, I'd consider them friends of mine. Or the closest thing. Don't you find that a bit sad?"

"It's not my job to express my own personal opinions here, Mr. Sunstrom," said the psychologist.

"That's right. You're only here as a favor from Agatha Bell to my brother. I remember you. Our early morning conversations when Mom and Dad first put me in there. Thin, kind of scratchy voice of yours used to make me forget how unhappy I was. You were the one who brought me those reindeer cookies that one Christmas. I'm guessing...you're here to make sure the helmet is working? Or to find out exactly how crazy I am."

"No one called you crazy, Mr. Sunstrom. We'd like to prep you for skin grafts in the next few days. There are bones that need resetting. Sam has a special team of doctors lined up for you. If you'd like, we could..."

"Told you already. I don't want any surgery. I don't want a damn thing from Sam Sunstrom."

Dr. Noelle quietly wrote something else on the clipboard and took a deliberate, uneasy breath before she spoke again. "Are you... are you still interested in harming your siblings?" she asked with care.

Julian leaned back in the wheelchair and smiled as if lost in a fantasy. "Eventually," he said. "But not yet. See, they have no clue what they've done to the world. Can't even fathom what's coming. But I want Sam to see it happen. To realize that there's nothing he can do to stop it. And when he thoroughly understands what a horrible mistake he's made... then, yes, Christmas Cookies. I will murder them all one at a time."

END OF VOLUME 1

ABOUT THE AUTHOR

Writer and artist Gene Willoughby, II is a graduate of East Carolina University with a BA in English and Writing. He also earned an MFA in Creative Writing at Full Sail University where he was valedictorian of his class and recipient of a Course Director's Award. Presently, he enjoys teaching Literature and Composition to middle school students in Goldsboro, North Carolina.

He loves superheroes, science-fiction, and animation as well as classic 90's hip hop. When he isn't mining the secret worlds in his head for new stories, Gene can be found with his beautiful wife Tameshia and their two awesome, inspirational children Alaysia and Jalen.